HOW I MAGICALLY MESSED UP MY LIFE IN FOUR FREAKIN' DAYS

THE TALE OF BRYANT ADAMS, BOOK ONE

MEGAN O'RUSSELL

Ink Worlds Press

DEDICATION

To the "Greatest City in the World" and my friends who live there

HOW I MAGICALLY MESSED UP MY LIFE IN FOUR FREAKIN' DAYS

1

Monsters poured out the windows that surrounded Times Square. Dark angels with glistening black wings stretched their shadows across the afternoon sky. A ruby red-scaled dragon climbed onto the perch reserved for the New Year's Eve ball drop. Women and children fled as flames licked the sidewalk. There was no help to be seen, no savior to conquer the savage beasts destroying the best tourist trap man had ever created. But as the horde with their gleaming black armor and talons that dragged along the ground, dripping with sizzling ooze, streamed out of the hotel lobby, one boy among the throng was brave enough to stand up and fight. One boy to—

"Ouch!" I choked as something caught me hard around the neck, yanking me backwards.

"Sweetie"—an older black woman had me by the back of the hoodie and was dragging me back onto the sidewalk—"I don't know what you're daydreaming about, but you're about to get yourself killed. And no one wants to see a scrawny little white boy smeared on the street. You better watch out." Shaking her head, she walked away, shopping bag in tow.

"Thank you!" I called after her, rubbing the sore part of my neck and muttering under my breath, "I'm not *that* scrawny," as she disappeared into the crowd.

"I don't know how scrawny you think you're not"—Devon patted my shoulder—"but you still can't stand up to a cab. Seriously, man, you shouldn't be allowed to cross the street. That's, what, three times some old lady has saved your ass this month?"

Devon was right. Old ladies were my guardian angels in New York. I think they formed a league when I was little. The *Keep Bryant Jameson Adams Alive League*. They'd done pretty well so far. I mean, I had made it to sixteen without ever riding in an ambulance. I don't know why they couldn't have formed a *Get Bryant Jameson Adams a Girlfriend League*, or I'd even take a *Make Bryant Jameson Adams Mysteriously Cool League*.

But, beggars, choosers...whatever. I duly acknowledged my begrudging gratitude for the growing bruise on my neck and got on with my afternoon.

We crossed the street, and Devon chose our post for the next few hours. We sat at one of the café tables in the middle of what used to be Broadway before they blocked the road off so tourists could spend their money without worrying about little things like people needing to drive anywhere that might actually matter.

Devon took off his coat and draped it over the back of his chair. He struck a casual pose, turning his face to the sun. "How do I look?"

"Ridiculous," I muttered.

"Don't be jealous of my swagger." Devon twinkled.

He looked like one of those male models plastered on the buildings, glowering down on us.

"Saying 'swagger' automatically makes you ridiculous. And why do we have to come here anyway? We're New Yorkers. It's our obligation to avoid Times Square like our lives depend on it."

"With the way you walk, yours might." Devon winked at a group of girls passing by, sending them all into fits of giggles. That was Devon's game. Go to Times Square looking like a stereotypical New Yorker—head to toe in black, sleek shoes no sane person would ever want to walk in, requisite coffee in hand—then flirt with all the tourist girls. On a bad day, he'd get winks and giggles. On a good day, he'd ditch me and strut away with a girl on each arm, ready to be their personal tour guide.

I tried my best not to be jealous. After all, it wasn't Devon's fault he was born a naturally muscular, racially ambiguous chick magnet. He couldn't be blamed for that any more than I could be blamed for being a pale string bean with scrawny arms and plain brown hair. I wish I had been born with red hair. Then at least I could blame my pastiness on being a ginger.

I pulled a book out of my school bag. Just because I was lounging in Times Square with Devon didn't mean I needed to watch his attempts at becoming the teen demigod of New York.

"Doing homework isn't cool, Bry." Devon slid the book away from me.

"Neither is failing history."

"Failing is counterproductive," Devon said, giving a slight nod to a passing woman.

"Aw come on, man." I pulled the book onto my lap. "That one was pushing thirty."

"And I just made her day." Devon smiled, sinking back into his well-practiced casualness.

It took two hours for Devon to get his fill of smiling and winking. I finished all my homework before he decided he wasn't going to get lucky that day.

"You know, no one makes you come with me," Devon said as we walked home, interrupting me as I tried to keep my mind on watching for cars.

"Ah"—I shook my head—"but then when one of those out-of-towners you pick up turns out to be a—"

"Harpy?" Devon raised one black eyebrow.

"I was going to say serial killer," I growled, "but harpy works fine. Mythical cause or not, if you go missing, I want to be able to identify which girl you wandered away with so I can help the cops find your body."

"Thanks?"

"I want you to have a proper funeral." I shrugged. "I mean, that's what friends are for, right?"

"Make sure there's plenty of girls crying around my casket, and you've got it covered." Devon smacked me on the back and grinned as I failed to hide that he had made me stumble.

"Tomorrow is pizza and game night at Le Chateau?" Devon asked as we stopped at my door.

"Sure thing." I put the outside door key in the lock. "See you in Chem."

Devon waved goodnight and kept walking. Having a best friend that cool sucked. But when he's your only real friend, you can't be too picky.

The outside door banged shut behind me with its familiar *creak*. Before I could get out the key for the inside door, Mrs. Fortner, the super's wife, waddled out, cramming herself into the tiny safety space between the corridor and the streets of Manhattan.

"Hello, Bryant," she said in her thick accent as her giant boobs knocked into my arms. "Getting home late again? Your mama will worry."

"She knew I was going to stay out," I grunted as Mrs. Fortner squished me into the fake marble wall.

"Mamas always worry." Mrs. Fortner pushed herself past me toward the exit.

I just managed to catch the inside door with my foot and

scurried into the hall, escaping before Mrs. Fortner could pin me in for a talk on why mamas are always right.

The hallways smelled like the same stale Chinese food they had for the last thirteen years. It probably smelled like old takeout before that, too, but we hadn't moved in until then, so I couldn't say for sure.

I ran up the grooved stairs, which matched the fake marble walls, two at a time until I reached the top floor. A fifth floor walk-up might not seem too glamorous, but it was home. And at least my mom had always been able to make rent.

The door flew open as I reached the landing, and my mother's head appeared. I inherited her dark brown eyes and brown hair. On her, the colors looked beautiful and gentle. On me, they looked like someone had spread dog poop on my head.

"Hey, Mom," I called up, knowing exactly how the conversation would go. "School was good. Devon didn't get murdered by a Scandinavian spy masquerading as a hottie tourist. Yes, I finished my homework, and whatever you already made for dinner sounds perfect."

As soon as I reached the door, she pulled me into a hug, ruffling my hair. "Very funny, sir. And we need to get—"

"My hair cut. I know, Mom." I walked through the door, tossing my bag onto the nearest chair, which scared Mrs. Mops, sending her skidding under the kitchen table crammed into the corner of the living room. The apartment smelled like lasagna and cake. My two favorite things. *Not* a good sign.

"Anything else fun or interesting happen today?" my mom asked as she crawled under the table to coo to the shaggy, gray, obese cat, comforting it after my faux pas.

I debated telling her about almost getting hit by another car. But I already had the daydreaming lecture memorized, so I didn't really see the point.

It's not that Mom thought daydreaming was bad. That would

have been really rich coming from a lady sitting under a table talking to a cat. No, she believed in *directed daydreaming*, like writing books or drawing or being an actor. Things I'm not good at. I might have walked around thinking about dragons bursting into school and freeing all us helpless students from boredom, but I wasn't going to go writing a book about it. I already had it bad enough. I didn't need to be designated any more the artsy kid than I already had been. Especially since I don't actually have any artistic talent.

I turned to go to my room.

"Oh, sweetie," my mom said, at her most suspiciously casual, "I know you have a lot of schoolwork, but I volunteered you for the set crew for *Pippin*."

"Mom, I hate—"

"*Hate* is a strong word, sir." She slinked out from under the table and toward the oven. "Besides, you need to be more involved, and Elizabeth will be there, too. She's in the show, so maybe you could talk to her, ask her out for coffee."

"Not gonna happen, Mom." I shook my head, stifling a sigh. "Never gonna happen."

I walked into my room and closed the door behind me, resting my forehead against the cold, smooth wood.

I don't know what's worst—having a mom who runs the drama department at your school, having a mom who reads you well enough to know which girl you've been crushing on for the last three years, or having a mom who's cool enough to try and set you up with said girl and delusional enough to think this beautiful and perfect girl would ever give you the time of day without the threat of a nuclear apocalypse looming over her head.

Whichever way it landed, I was going to be stuck holding a paint brush and trying not to look like a total ass in front of Elizabeth.

"Why, why, why?" I groaned, punctuating each *why* with a thump of my forehead.

"Sweetie," Mom's gentle voice came from the living room, "if you bang your head against the door, you'll end up with a flat forehead."

"Thanks, Mom."

2

"You ready for tonight?" Devon asked me twelve times before lunch.

That was one of the benefits of having a mom on faculty. You could swing it so your best friend was in all your classes. Bonus: you're less likely to get beat up with your super cool best friend around all the time. Extreme drawback: no girl will ever notice you with your super cool, über chick magnet friend around all the damn time. It's fine though. Maybe I'll get a girlfriend when I'm thirty. Or in the nursing home. Either way, it's bound to happen eventually, right?

"So the plans are all set?" Devon asked again as we left school.

I turned to him to ask what the hell plans he thought I should have made, but at that very second, Elizabeth waltzed out the school door and onto the sidewalk in front of us. I don't want to sound stupid or lovesick or anything, but I swear when Elizabeth walks, she glides on the air. Some guardian angel hauls around a giant fan to make Elizabeth's blond, perfect, curly hair blow gently behind her. Her eyes sparkle like she klepto'd stars and uses them as contacts. Except she would never steal anything because she's the kind of girl who saves puppies, runs fundraisers for the theatre department, and helps lost tourists get out of Hell's Kitchen.

Elizabeth Wick is perfection.

"Close your mouth, man." Devon pushed my jaw shut. "Girls don't dig mouth-breathers."

"It doesn't matter what I do." I shook my head, running my hands through my hair, which really did need cutting. "Elizabeth will never think I'm anything more than her favorite teacher's dorky son."

One of the basketball players was chatting up Elizabeth by the fence that covered the school's ground floor windows, his hand on the metal bars, leaning over her like she was his lunchbox. For an umpteenth time, I wished I was...say, a basketball player with a weird-looking letterman jacket who was cool enough to talk to Elizabeth Wick without tripping over himself while managing to say words that could be recognized as a part of the English language.

"Bryant," Devon enunciated, none too subtly indicating he had been trying to get my attention. "Are the *plans* all set for tonight? For Le Chateau?"

"What? Yes. The *plans*. The plans are all set."

"Awesome!" Devon strolled around the corner from school and headed downtown. I trotted to catch up.

We walked in silence for two blocks, cutting south and then east. Away from where all the other kids from school would be heading. It was the rule I set up three years ago when I finally let Devon in on the big secret.

When we got far enough away, Devon hailed a cab. I told the driver the address. As soon as the door closed, Devon launched into his weekly spiel. It was kind of annoyingly endearing. With more annoying than endearing. But what d'you do? It was tradition.

"Man, this one is going to be epic! Are you sure everything we need is going to be there?"

"I put in all the orders online." I watched Central Park whiz by. "Drake is going to have everything we want."

It only took about five minutes in the cab. We could have walked, but it was against the rules. Cabs only when going to Le Chateau.

The cabbie pulled over and let us out. I tossed him the cash for the fare and a hefty tip—because why not—and we headed to the door.

There was a new doorman that night. All dressed up and shiny. "Good evening, Mr. Adams," he said formally even though I had never seen him before. It was kind of funny to think of doorman training involving learning to recognize my face.

"Good evening, Mr. Adams," Drake said from behind his desk as soon as we walked in. "Mr. Rhodes," he added, nodding to Devon.

"Drake." Devon nodded back, looking all stiff. Like any *normal* person, the only time he'd be caught dead in a building like this is when he came here with me.

"I have your order." Drake pulled three pizzas, two bottles of soda, and a bag from behind the desk.

I took the pizzas and sodas while Devon opened the bag.

"Sweet! I told you it would be epic!" He brandished the new video game we had picked for this week.

"Thanks, Drake." I kicked Devon in the ankles to make him move to the elevator.

Le Chateau looked out onto Central Park from the top floor of the building. Well, really, it *was* the top floor of the building. As soon as the elevator doors opened, I saw me. Well, me from two years ago in a portrait of me and my dad he had commissioned for some unknown reason.

"Hey, Dad," I muttered to the portrait. "Good to see you again."

"Go do your rounds, Bry, and let's get started," Devon called as he flicked on the giant TV that sat in front of the big leather couch.

"Yep," I called back before walking to the kitchen.

It was my job to check the apartment every week. My dad's place. He travels all over the world for work, so I'm lucky if I get to have coffee with him once a month. But he kept this monstrosity in New York so I could have a home with him. And since I'm a minor who shouldn't be staying in an apartment alone, I got paid for "weekly chores." I don't know how much. It's all a business disbursement, but the financial advisor he sent me to last Christmas said from the funds I got deposited in my housesitting account, I could get a few doctorates and never eat Ramen.

I walked through the kitchen, checked the empty fridge. Then all three of the bathrooms for water damage. Looked over the guest rooms, my dad's room, my room. I mean, he designated it my room, but really, I only ever slept there the day after my birthday every year, so I don't know why he didn't let other people stay there. He could have made a killing as an Airbnb. Not that he needed more money.

I finished my rounds and headed back to the living room. Devon had already opened the first pizza.

"All good in Le Chateau?"

"All good." I picked up my controller, ready for battle.

W e played for a few hours until the pizza was gone and we knew Devon's dad might freak if we were out much longer. We always had to be really careful not to push it too far. If Devon's parents said he couldn't come with me anymore, I would be stuck hanging out at my dad's all by myself once a week. No one else from school really knew about Dad. Well, I guess they knew I must have one *somewhere*, but no one but Devon knew my dad was super rich. When you're already the dorky outcast, the last thing you want is to be the rich dorky outcast. I mean, sure, more people might be nice to you, but only because they'd want you to buy them stupid things and take them to fancy parties.

Devon was the only one I trusted to know my dad picked me up in a helicopter to take me upstate for Thanksgiving lunch last year without treating me like a human piggy bank.

So, reluctantly, Devon and I went downstairs to catch a cab home. It felt like throwing money away to travel fifteen blocks, but Dad insisted and paid, so I guess it didn't really matter.

There were no cabs lurking out front, and since it was October, it was a little cold to be standing around waiting.

"Let's start walking," I said, and Devon nodded, shoving his hands into his pockets.

"I can arrange for a cab if you'll only wait inside, Mr. Adams," the new doorman said, but I darted past like I hadn't heard him. I don't know if I'll ever feel like a *Mr. Adams*, and I definitely didn't want some dude with polished brass buttons pretending he actually knew who I was.

As soon as we got a block down, Devon and I started hailing cabs. A couple sped past. One slowed down, realized we were teenagers, and pulled away. Devon reached all the way to the back of his vocabulary to cuss out the driver.

"Keep walking, Devon," I said as rain fell in a cold mist.

"We should have waited for the new doorman to call a cab." Devon popped his collar.

"Somebody will stop." I raised my hand again without looking back at the street.

It was like a cue in a play. As soon as I held my hand up, a cab stopped, letting out a guy, who stepped gingerly into the rain as though it offended his sensibilities.

The ex-passenger couldn't have been much older than twenty, but he wore a black suit with a black bowtie and white shirt. His hair was darker than his tie, and his skin an even paler white than mine. He stared right at Devon and me for a second. His eyes were dark, too. The dude seriously looked straight out of a black and white picture. There was no color to him at all.

Devon climbed into the cab while the guy stumbled away.

"Bryant," Devon shouted, "stop watching the drunk dude, and let's go!"

The guy looked back at us for a minute, glowering like he was about to say something. I hopped into the cab and shut the door behind me, giving the cabbie Devon's address. We pulled away as the guy stumbled into a restaurant with a shining purple awning.

"Somebody's having a good night," I muttered.

"Maybe not," Devon said quietly enough to not be heard over the blaring country radio. He flipped his palm to show a phone.

"Everything okay back there?" the cabbie asked.

"Fine." I took the phone from Devon and shoved it into my pocket.

Now, I know what you're thinking. *What about lost and found? Why didn't you turn the phone in?* I've lost enough things in cabs to know that once they go into that logbook in the front of the cab, no rightful owner ever sees any of them again. And, even if the photocopy guy was about to get into a screaming match with me on Central Park West, losing a phone in Manhattan sucks, and I do my best to be a good Samaritan.

But if I had known what that stupid cellphone would lead me to, I would have thrown it out the window of the speeding cab and into the nearest gutter. Not even a rate-jacking, country-blasting, onion soup-smelling cab driver deserved the hell my life was about to turn into.

To be honest with you, I didn't actually think about the phone that night. By the time I got home and past the mom monster, I had completely forgotten about its existence. And I don't mean like, *Ahh! My mom sprouted tentacles from her head and tried to feed me to a God from the underworld!* We're still in the part of my life that was completely boring and normal. What I mean by *mom monster* is whenever I get home from Dad's, Mom gets all clingy for the rest of the night. Like she needs to prove that even though she can't dump ungodly amounts of money into my college fund in a questionable way, she still loves me and I should keep living with her in Hell's Kitchen instead of moving to Central Park West. Not that living on Central Park West was ever really an option. I mean, I'm sixteen, but I'm still a minor. And it would kill my mom if I tried it.

So, I let her stuff me full of even more food and talk about all the things we used to do together when I was little and make plans for family bonding time for the weekend. Which in this case meant me painting sets for hours while she directed at the school. Not really my idea of fun, but whatever.

I didn't really think about the phone again until the next day after school when I was elbow deep in a failed art project.

Our school had a giant set shop next to the stage, which was one of the big perks for our theater program. We used to have students build sets in school with like Stage Craft class and all that. And I really do mean all of that in past tense. The set shop is not so much there anymore. Unless you count a smoldering hole in the wall as a set shop. But at least it was a nice set shop while it lasted.

My mom was doing her thing with the students on stage. Elizabeth was the lead. I mean, of course she was. She was perfect and brilliant and freakishly talented... and perfect.

While I was reduced to painting a giant ring of fire onto a set piece, trying to make it look like the flames hadn't been designed by a four-year-old. As I said before, I'm *not* good at painting.

Something weird was going on onstage. But I was too deep in my pre-school art to pay attention. I'd be watching the show all weekend anyway, so I didn't really need to see a cleaning rehearsal.

Mom called a five, and soon I heard quiet crying and that firm yet comforting tone she always used with hysterical actors.

I swung around. Sure enough, in the far corner, Mom had her hands on Elizabeth's shoulders, talking her off the ledge. Not a real one.

I turned back to my painting. Why did Elizabeth have to look so freaking appealing even when she cried? Not that I'd be caught dead staring. I mean, you don't get much creepier than that. But what if there was something I could do? What if she needed money to pay a loan shark? I could find a way to outsmart the shark and corner him in an alley. I mean really, getting the money would probably be easier. But if I had to find a way to sneak into a loan shark's office under an overpass in the Meatpacking District—

A tap on my shoulder made me drop my brush, leaving a big splotch of orange in the middle of the red flames. I cursed, and Mom stage-whispered, "Bryant Jameson Adams, not in school."

Fine, but did she *have* to use my full name?

"Sorry, Mom," I said before noticing the still-soggy Elizabeth and immediately growing tongue-tied.

"Elizabeth, you know Bryant," my mother said, not bothering to ask if I knew Elizabeth.

The girl of my dreams nodded. "Hey, Bryant."

"Elizabeth is in your Pre-Calc class," my mom said.

"Really?" I ran a hand through my hair, trying to play it cool, before realizing my hand was covered in orange paint, which was now in my hair.

"I sit next to you," Elizabeth said. "I have all year."

"Oh, right, yeah you do."

My mom raised an eyebrow at me. "Elizabeth." Mom gestured for her to step forward.

"So," my one-and-only began, "your mom says you're top of our math class."

I shot my mom a quick glare. Why did she have to make me look like more of a geek than I already managed all on my own?

"I shouldn't even be taking that class. I'm not a math person." Elizabeth shook her head. "My dad made me do it. He said I couldn't do art all the time. But I have a *C* in the class, and if I don't get an *A* on the test on Tuesday, the school is going to pull me out of the show."

"Oh." I nodded.

Tears started to stream down Elizabeth's cheeks again. "I'm trying, I really am, but I don't get it. And your mom said maybe you could help?" Elizabeth's porcelain face turned pink. "You could tutor me this weekend during tech?"

I gawked at her, wanting to say, *Hell, I'll take the test for you if it will make you smile at me.* Or even, *I promise I will find a way for you to ace that test.* But she was standing there all pretty, and words seemed too hard.

"Bryant?" my mom said.

"Uhh, yeah." I stumbled over the words. "I can help. Let me see your homework and tests and then I can figure out—"

"Thank you!" Elizabeth threw her arms around my neck. Her arms. Around my neck. Just to repeat for clarity.

"Take a minute, and then come back onstage," Mom said quietly, winking as she walked away.

"You have no idea how much this show means to me," Elizabeth sighed, stepping back.

I should have hugged her back, but I couldn't figure out how arms were supposed to work, and my hands were covered in paint anyway.

"It's okay." I tried to sound as though spending time teaching her math wasn't going to be the best thing that had ever happened in my life.

"Maybe we can meet right after rehearsal tonight?" she asked. "I mean, if you have time."

"I can work it out," I said.

Devon would just have to return the phone on his own. I didn't think he would mind under the circumstances. But as soon as I thought about it, my pocket started to ring.

It wasn't a normal ringtone. It sounded like a song I had never heard before but somehow knew the melody of. I froze for a minute. What if the vampire guy was calling his phone?

I pulled it from my pocket with my less painty hand.

But as soon as it saw the light, the ringing stopped.

"Sorry. I made you miss a call," Elizabeth said.

"Not even my phone." I pushed the button on the bottom to

try and see the caller ID. But when I held my thumb to it, the phone unlocked.

"I thought you said it wasn't your phone." Elizabeth frowned.

"It's not."

I studied the home screen, trying to go to the missed calls section, but there was no phone icon. Or email icon. There were no weird little games with jewels or freaky llamas.

Only tiny little symbols I had never seen before. One looked like an old book, one like fire, a dragon, and some weird stuff I couldn't begin to venture a guess on.

"Huh," I muttered.

"What?" Elizabeth leaned over to look at the phone. Her hair smelled like sunshine.

"I, umm, the OS is weird." I tapped the fire button, stupidly thinking it might be some sort of emergency call button. A picture of flames appeared on the screen, along with a level bar.

"Is it a game?" Elizabeth asked.

"Maybe." I slid my finger along the bar, making it tip to one side. The flames started to crackle.

"Weird game," Elizabeth said. "Is the phone making that smell?"

She was right. It had started to smell like smoke. And the crackling didn't sound like it was coming from the phone. And it was getting hot. Really hot.

I looked down at the flat I had been painting with grade school style fire just in time to see it burst into real flames.

"Oh, God!" Elizabeth leapt back.

"It's okay," I shouted, sprinting for the fire extinguisher by the stage door and popping the pin like a boss. She stood behind me while I pointed the foam at the base of the flames, calmly sweeping the tube back and forth. It wasn't as good as fighting a dragon, but it was almost like showing off. My years of battling my mother's kitchen fires had finally come in handy.

The only problem was the fire wasn't going out. It was like it was eating the foam, feeding on it to make itself grow.

"We need to get out." I grabbed Elizabeth's hand, towing her toward the stage and pulling the little fire lever on my way past. Instantly, red lights flashed and sirens started to beep.

"Everybody out!" I shouted over the din. "There's a fire in the shop!"

People screamed, running for the door.

"Bryant! Come on!" Cool under literal fire, Mom herded students toward the door, ordering them to leave their bags. "Bryant, go!" She yanked on her stage manager, who was trying to save the lighting board, and dragged him toward the exit.

I pulled Elizabeth along, her hand clasped tightly in mine. Once we broke out onto the sidewalk, the sirens of the fire trucks blared at us as they sped toward the school.

But over the sirens and the screaming, I still heard Elizabeth when she turned to me with panic in her eyes.

"How?"

5

W e were stuck out on the sidewalk for forever. First, we did the whole huddle together and look on in horror thing. Elizabeth held my hand, and we watched the flames grow. I don't think she was really holding my hand on purpose. We both just kind of forgot how to let go. Too soon, she melted into the crowd of crying actors when they moved us all back as the firemen swarmed the scene. They kept shouting and radioing back and forth about how the flames weren't going out as quickly as they should. And then there was the fact that the fire was in a theatre with big heavy lights that were hung by not-so-competent students that could fall on the firefighters any minute.

Mom was being interrogated by the guys at the blockade. They asked questions about everything, and she kept manically counting all the students, making sure she really had gotten all of us out of harm's way. Every few minutes, she would run back and squeeze me hard before talking to the fire dudes again.

About a whole hour later, Devon showed up, pushing his way toward me through the throng.

"Shit, Bry!" He ran his hand through his hair, making it actually not look perfect for once. "Your poor mom."

"She's over there." I pointed to where she was flapping her hands at some guy with a clipboard.

"I mean, I know she made it out." Devon shook his head. "But that theatre was like her *life*."

It was kind of true. I mean, other than me, my mom's whole world was going up in flames. She had been working to build that theatre department since I hit kindergarten.

"She'll be okay." Devon slapped me hard on the back. "We'll figure something out. The school's got to have insurance."

An ear-splitting screech came from inside, and one of the lighting booms crashed down, sending the firefighters running for the door.

"Or maybe your dad can buy a new theatre." Devon shrugged.

I didn't mention that my mom would rather perform for the mole people who live under the subway tunnels than take any help from my dad.

"We need that damn fire to stop!" I pushed the heels of my hands into my eyes so hard, little white spots began to blink in the blackness. "We could lose a lot more than the theatre if it doesn't."

I didn't want to be sent to a different school to spend the rest of my pre-college career someplace strange. Dad would probably try and send me to some fancy boarding school upstate. It's what he had been campaigning for for years. I tried to picture myself wearing a bowtie and living in a dorm. Maybe I could convince him to spring for Devon to come with. Then at least I would have one friend in a hellhole of brats with way too much money.

"Bryant?" Mom put her hand on my shoulder. She looked exhausted, but she was holding it together. She was a trooper.

Elizabeth stood two steps behind Mom, her face all pink

from crying.

How could anyone look that pretty after crying for an hour?

"This is the fire marshal." My mom pointed to the clipboard guy. "He wants to ask you and Elizabeth some questions. I'm going to go talk to the principal. I'll be right back."

Out by the fire trucks, the principal was busy glaring at the firemen like she was going to give them in-school suspension if they didn't get those flames put out soon. Like an hour ago.

The fire marshal led us away from the other students who were all still loitering in the middle of the street watching the theatre burn.

He was shorter than me. Stocky and sweaty with black little eyes like a mole.

"So, you two were the first to notice the fire?" he asked without introducing himself.

Elizabeth looked silently to me.

"Yes," I said, "we were."

"And what happened?" the marshal asked.

"We were talking, and then it smelled like smoke," I said, wondering if I was ever not going to smell like smoke again. "We looked down, and the set piece I had been painting was on fire."

"And you were only *talking*?" the marshal asked.

"Yes." I nodded, not missing his so-thin-it-was-practically-invisible-eyebrow creeping up his face. And I do mean eyebrow, not brows. I'd never seen such a pale, thin unibrow in my life.

He turned said unibrow to Elizabeth. "You weren't playing with any tools? No soldering, no sanders left on."

"I had been painting," I said. "I never even plugged anything in."

"We were looking at a cellphone." Elizabeth's voice shook. "Neither of us was touching anything but the phone, and then...." She shot me a weird look. Granted, this was a weird day. But still.

"I don't know if somebody else left something plugged in or what," I said, needing the marshal to stop glaring at Elizabeth with his little mole eyes. "But neither of us touched anything."

"Figures." The man took more notes on his clipboard. "Theatres are deathtraps. Why anyone in their right mind would want one in a school..." He handed Elizabeth and me cards. "If you think of anything, give me a call." He waded back into the crowd.

I looked back up at the school. The fire was finally settling down. It was just a lot of smoke now. You couldn't see the flames anymore.

"We were playing with that phone." Elizabeth's voice still shook.

"I know," I said. And for some miraculous reason, I reached out and touched her arm. Just kind of laid my hand on her shoulder like I was comforting her. And she seemed to sort of take it like I was trying to comfort her and didn't tell me I was a loser and to never touch her again.

"We shouldn't have been playing with that phone," Elizabeth said.

"I don't think it would have made a difference." I shrugged. "I mean, even if we had noticed the fire a few seconds earlier, I don't think we could have stopped it. I tried the fire extinguisher—"

"That phone started the fire," Elizabeth whispered, stepping close so no one but me could hear. "You opened the fire app, and then that fire! *We* burned down the theatre."

"That's not possible. It's just a phone." I pulled it back out of my pocket and held it out to her. "See?" I tried to pass it to her, but she backed away like she really was scared.

"I don't care what's possible. I don't care if you don't see it." Elizabeth shook her head. "There is something wrong with that phone."

"It's fine." I pressed my thumb to the button, and the phone unlocked. The fire app was still pulled up. And the setting was still on high. The flames on the screen danced around like the Yule Log channel.

"Bryant, don't touch it," Elizabeth said, but I was already scrolling my finger along the bar, pulling the fire setting all the way down. The logs on the screen turned black as the fire disappeared.

"See? No big deal." I held the phone out to Elizabeth.

But she was pointing up at the school. The smoke was gone. And I don't mean it dissipated a little bit. It was gone. There was still a burned hole in the school where the stage used to be. But there was no more smoke, no fire at all.

"Get rid of it." Elizabeth's face was sheet white. "I don't know what the hell that thing is, but throw it into the river. Get rid of it Bryant, please."

I wanted to throw it into the river right then on the off chance she might say thank you or hug me again. Call me stupid, but I didn't really think there was anything weird about the phone. I thought it was a crazy coincidence. Or fate. Or the school board wanting to collect the insurance money. It really seemed more likely that Zeus had decided to smite my pathetic paint job than a cellphone had magically burned a giant hole in our school.

But I didn't care. Elizabeth was looking at me with her sparkly eyes, and I would have done whatever she wanted, even if I didn't buy the whole demon phone thing. I was going to be really daring and ask Elizabeth if she wanted to walk with me to the river right then so she could watch me toss it into the Hudson. But my mom pushed her way back over to us.

"The marshal said he's done with both of you," she said with her *I would rather stick my foot up his butt than listen to anything he has to say* voice. "So you should both go. You're going to have a lot of studying to do tomorrow, and you need your rest."

"Studying?" I asked.

"You are going to help Elizabeth study for the calculus test, she will get an A, and we will open *Pippin* next weekend." My mom switched to her freakishly determined tone she usually saved for customer service people. "The show must go on, and I will be damned if fires or math tests stop us. Go home and rest up, both of you. Bryant will meet you at the library at ten." She turned to Elizabeth, who looked like she wasn't quite sure what to say.

Elizabeth nodded, which was probably her best bet anyway.

"This is going to be one hell of a week, so we had better all be ready for it." My mom stalked away, ready and willing to rally each and every theatre student.

"She's a little scary sometimes," Elizabeth said.

"Sometimes?"

Devon was pushing his way through the crowd toward me.

"I have to go." Elizabeth turned to look at the building. "I don't think I have a math book anymore."

"We can figure something out," I said, wondering how much of the inside of the school was actually left.

"Okay." She nodded. "I'll meet you in the morning. Just...get rid of it." She turned and walked away.

"Did you just have a conversation with Elizabeth Wick?" Devon asked.

"Yep. I'm her new math tutor."

"And she doesn't want you to get rid of the idea that you should ever talk to her again? Or yourself in general?"

"Nope." I shook my head, watching Elizabeth disappear down the street.

"Then what was she talking about?" Devon asked.

I held up the little black cellphone.

6

W e walked uptown toward my dad's. I don't know if it was instinct, habit, or the fact that my keys to Mom's place had been melted by a fire. Either way, Le Chateau seemed like the best bet.

A cab would have been faster, but since I smelled like a barbeque gone wrong, I figured it was better to walk.

Devon started by giving me a blow-by-blow of what the firemen had been doing: running in and out and a lot of hauling hoses mostly. "And then Linda May, sweet little Linda May, was so terrified she needed comfort, and of course she ran to me. I'm telling you man, the fire made 8th Ave crazy."

"You do remember I was there, right?" I asked, trying not to sound snarky even though I was tired enough to curl up on a subway grate and sleep. "I was the one who saw the fire start and pulled the alarm to get everyone out."

"Really?" Devon asked, looking surprised for a second but trying to cover up his shock by punching me in the arm. "Good for you, man! Elizabeth must think you're a hero. This could be the break you've been waiting for. Did you ask her out?"

"What? No, I didn't ask her out!" I ran my hands through my hair. It was gritty from the smoke and orange paint.

Devon grimaced and shook his head, looking down at the sidewalk.

"What?" I asked again, trying not to get angry. "What did you want me to do? Was I supposed to look down, see a fire, and stop on the way to the alarm to ask Elizabeth to be my girlfriend?"

"I mean, *girlfriend* might have been pushing it, but it would have been better than nothing," Devon said.

"Sorry, I was trying to make sure everyone didn't burn to death."

"What about when you two were talking once everyone was out of the theatre then?" Devon said, nodding and winking at a random dog walker.

The poor girl had two mastiffs, three Chihuahuas, and one drooling pug. Their leashes had all gotten tangled, and one of the Chihuahuas was dangling over the bigger mastiff's back. Being a dog walker was on my top ten list for jobs I never wanted in Manhattan.

"I don't know how many more chances you can hope to get with Elizabeth."

"I've never had a single chance," I said as we turned onto Central Park West, "and now she probably thinks I'm a freak, so...." I was screwed. There was something about knowing she thought I had magically started a fire with a cellphone and was now afraid of me that made it seem more true than years of her never speaking to me ever had. My stomach felt heavy and gross.

"Why does she think you're a freak?" Devon asked. "I mean, you just saved the whole theatre class."

I pulled the little black demon out of my pocket.

"She's thinks you're a freak because you forgot to return the phone? Which, by the way, is not cool, man. You don't leave a guy phoneless in Manhattan."

"If you remember, before you *had* to tell me all about how you made out with Linda May while our school was on fire, Elizabeth wants me to get rid of the phone." I slid it back into my pocket. Somehow having it out in my hand made me feel exposed, like a big eye in a creepy tower was watching me as I ran toward a pit of lava.

"So then let's get rid of the phone," Devon said. "We'll take it to the purple restaurant and make it their problem to find the vampire dude, and you can tell her you did what she wanted."

"She doesn't want me to return the phone," I sighed, knowing full well Devon was going to laugh at me. "She wants me to throw it into the Hudson to destroy it. She thinks the phone started the fire."

I started counting to three in my head. Before I got past two, Devon had tossed his head back and roared with laughter. People stared as they walked by.

It took Devon a full minute to speak. "I'm sorry." He wiped the tears from his eyes. "Was there a stray ray of sunlight you reflected off the screen to ignite the mounds of dried grass in the set shop?"

"No." I pushed Devon in the back to make him start walking again, and he promptly skidded on sidewalk goop. "There's an app on the phone, and she thinks I started the fire with it."

"An app. She thinks you started a fire with an app on a phone you can't even open?"

"I did open the phone," I said, "and a fire app thing."

"How did you open the phone? It should have a password." Devon turned to me, his laughter fading a little. "Do you have like post-traumatic stress or something from the fire? Because I mean, we could call your mom."

"I don't have traumatic stress." I pulled Devon into the shade of a coffee shop awning. The place smelled like vegan food and almond milk. "And I didn't use a password." I glanced around before pulling the phone back out of my pocket. I didn't know what I was looking for. No one seemed to care about the two teenagers hanging out by the vegan coffee shop. But I still couldn't shake the feeling that someone was following me. Or that the evil eye was gazing down at me from the Empire State building. "I used my thumbprint." I pressed my thumb to the button, and the phone opened, showing the same funny symbols as before.

"Whoa!" Devon took it from me, but as soon as it left my hands, the thing turned back off. "Aw, come on." He pressed his thumb to the sensor, but the screen stayed dark. "Damn. Battery must have died."

I took the phone back and pressed my thumb back on the button. The screen popped back up. Devon grabbed the phone again, and it was the same thing. Him—phone off. Me—phone on.

"Bryant." Devon's voice was barely above a whisper. "Did you buy a phone and rig it to do that to freak me out? Because I mean, good for you, but that's a lot of trouble for a prank."

"You found this in the cab. And I would never prank you. I know better." And really I did. Devon would take any reason to punk you. If you were five minutes late when you were supposed to meet him, you had to spend the next week wondering what his revenge would be. Pulling a prank on him would be the worst idea anyone in Hell's Kitchen had ever had. Except maybe the next thing I did. That may have been the worst idea anyone in New York had ever had.

Devon was still giving me the *I don't believe you* stare with his eyebrows raised and his arms crossed. And Elizabeth thought I had a possessed phone, and my mom's theatre had burned down, and I had sort of had enough.

"Fine." I dragged him over to a trashcan by the side of the street, then tapped on the app that showed the picture of the fire. There it was—the still flames with the bar below balancing perfectly centered. I held the phone out like I was going to take a picture of the can and tapped the bar, tipping it all the way to the right.

Big mistake.

Flames shot out of the can and flew ten feet into the air like the sanitation department had decided collecting trash was too hard and installing a giant blowtorch was a better use of resources.

People behind us started to scream. Devon cursed and backed away. I stood there, frozen by the sudden heat. I couldn't move. I mean, I know I had gone to the fire app to prove to Devon that I wasn't wandering the city in some PTSD haze. But finding myself in front of a ten-foot-tall pillar of fire, holding a possessed cellphone in my hands, I sort of felt like maybe I had lost my mind. Maybe this wasn't even New York and I was locked in a cell. Or even better, and less scary maybe, I was still in bed, and this whole thing was a dream. I hadn't even gotten out of bed yet, and soon I would wake up with cat ass on my face.

I squeezed my eyes tightly shut and opened them again. There was still a fire right in front of me. No padded white room. No stinky cat ass.

I tapped the left side of the bar and pulled it all the way down. Just like it had sprung up without warning, in an instant, the fire disappeared with nothing but a melted trashcan to show for itself. Well, that and the sour, nose hair-burning stench of flaming crap.

I turned to Devon who stared, petrified, at where the flames had been.

"See? Not a prank."

"What the hell?" he muttered. "Not okay. That is definitely not okay. Burning trashcans is not okay."

The rubberneckers behind us chattered noisily. One woman

shouted into her cellphone, "The fire's gone out, but I think it's a gas line!" She paused for a second. "Back away. 9-1-1 says everybody back away."

People immediately scurried down the street or hugged next to the building, still transfixed in fascinated horror.

"You need to move, boys!" the cellphone lady shouted at us as sirens echoed between the buildings.

"Go!" I pushed Devon so hard his feet finally started to work again. I grabbed his arm and dragged him onto a side street out of view of the fire trucks as they pulled up to the melted trashcan.

Two run-ins with the fire department in one day is not a good thing. Especially not when you might have caused the fires. Even if it was by accident.

We cut back around the block and to my dad's building. The fire trucks had parked down the street, but from here we couldn't even see what all the firemen were staring at.

Drake was behind the desk like always. "Mr. Adams." He smiled. "I wasn't expecting to see you here today."

"Yeah." I tried to put my thoughts into an order that didn't involve a possessed demon phone with the ability to make things spontaneously combust that was currently burning a hole in my back pocket. Not literally. I hoped. "There was a fire at school. Everybody's okay, but I lost my house key, so I'm gonna hang out here until my mom gets home." If my mom still had a house key.

"Of course, Mr. Adams." Drake unlocked the safe beneath the desk. "I would be more than happy to let you into the apartment. I am so relieved you're safe. Have you called your father?"

Drake led us to the elevator and turned the key to go up.

"No." It hadn't occurred to me to call my dad. I mean, how could he be worried about me when he didn't even know my school had been on fire? Never mind the fact that the more time passed, the more convinced I was that I had caused the fire in the first place. But Drake was still looking at me all concerned, so I said, "Not yet. I'm going to call before I shower." And I did need to shower. Even though the elevator was a big one, it was still small enough to trap in the horrible smoke and burning trash smell that was stuck to me.

The door opened to my dad's apartment, and Drake waved us in. "Shall I call for a pizza?"

"Two." Devon half-stumbled into the apartment.

"Very well." Drake closed the elevator doors and was gone.

Devon walked into the living room and collapsed onto the couch. I followed him, a little afraid he might be panicked enough to start throwing up onto the carpet. And having to call the cleaning lady to tell her you got puke in the carpet was never a fun time.

I sat on the metal rim of the glass coffee table and stared at Devon, waiting for him to speak. If he could still speak. I wasn't too sure about that.

"The fire," Devon said finally, his hands shaking as he dragged them over his face. "The phone started the fire."

Elizabeth had been right. She had seen it right away.

"Both fires. And the one at school didn't go out till I put it out with the app."

Devon scrunched his face and let out the longest string of muttered curses I had ever heard. "We have to get rid of it."

"Same thing Elizabeth said. I can take it down to the restaurant and leave it with them."

"No way in *Hell!*" Devon shook his head, looking as pale as I had ever seen him. "You just burned down half the school with that thing. You can't keep it. It's arson evidence, Bry."

"So we give it—"

"We are not giving the damn phone to people who might want to do more damage with it than you've already done! That guy we saw looked evil. He looked like a vampire or demon or something. We can't give an evil dude something this dangerous. What if he lights us on fire? Or decides to take out Times Square. I can't have that on my head, man."

"So, we do what Elizabeth said and dump it into the Hudson," I said, wondering if I could convince Drake to find a guy to take the phone to the river.

No, it couldn't be trusted to a courier. I mean, who wouldn't want to open a package they had been hired to dump into a river. We'd have to do it ourselves.

I turned my wrist over, making my watch blink on. Nearly seven PM. "If we head to the water in a few hours, we should be able to find a place to dump it without getting noticed."

"No way." Devon pushed himself to sit up. "The river's way too risky. What if it washes up and someone finds it?"

"It's a phone. It'll be dead from the water."

"A demon phone that starts fires, and you think water is going to hurt it?" Devon stood up, color coming back into his determined face. "We have to destroy it ourselves. It's the only way to make sure it's done."

7

My dad isn't exactly the type to keep a hammer around. If something breaks, he tells Drake, and Drake calls a guy to get it fixed. Since we didn't have a hammer to smash the phone with, like a normal person bent on destroying the Devil's cellular device, we tried all the other heavy objects in the apartment.

First, we tried stomping on it. Then we hit it with the huge frying pan I don't think my dad has ever used. We dumped it in water and let it sit for twenty minutes while we ate the two pizzas Drake had sent up.

After the pizza was gone and I felt sick from the combination of pounding a whole large pie, accidentally burning down half my school, and the sense that something weird was paying me an even weirder amount of attention, Devon fished the phone out of the water. It looked blank.

He held it out to me. "Do your worst."

I pressed my finger to the scanner. My heart flipped for a split second while the screen stayed black. Yeah, but not so much. The phone blinked on. Creepy apps and all.

"It's just not fair." Devon ran his hands over his face. "I drop my phone two feet, and the screen cracks. We spend an hour trying to kill this thing, and nothing."

"I guess a phone that can make fire can protect itself." My mind raced. I mean, I couldn't turn the damned thing in to the police. They would think I was crazy and maybe arrest me for arson, too. I couldn't tell my mom I had burned down her theatre. My dad was halfway around the world. I thought about asking Drake, but I didn't know if evil demon phone destruction was really in his job description.

"Your dad lets you get away with anything, right?" Hope filled Devon's voice in a scary way.

"I mean, define *anything*."

"If there was a little damage done"—Devon stood—"he wouldn't like cut you off or have you killed or something?"

"We're not gonna pitch it out the window!" I shook my head for emphasis. "It could kill someone, and a murder rap would definitely piss my dad off."

"No one's gonna get hurt." Devon grabbed the phone from my hand and bolted to the kitchen. Before I could catch up, he'd tossed it into the microwave and pressed the popcorn button.

"Devon, no!" I shouted.

Too late.

Tiny little lightning bolts leapt around the inside of the microwave. Smoke drifted out through the edges of the door, accompanied by weird tinny *cracks*. I didn't reach out to try and stop it. I mean, if this would destroy the phone, I would hand out flyers in Times Square to earn enough money to buy my dad his fancy replacement. It took less than a minute for the microwave to give one last pathetic hiss and go black.

I reached for the door and pulled it open. A horrible stink of burned plastic made the already burnt hair on the inside of my nose die a final death.

"Don't touch it! It's hot!" Devon shouted as I picked up the phone.

But the thing was, it wasn't hot. Or cracked, burned, melted. Nothing. The microwave had been reduced to a warped pile of stink, but the phone was fine.

My thumb shook as I pressed it to the button. The phone flashed on even faster than when we had tried to drown it.

"It's the Rasputin of phones," Devon murmured. "It can never die."

"We're screwed." I sank down onto the kitchen floor. "Utterly screwed."

Just when I thought things couldn't get worse, the little fire alarm overhead started to beep.

The callbox by the elevator buzzed. It would be Drake calling up before dialing 9-1-1.

"Tell him everything is fine, we burned something in the microwave." I ran to my dad's room, threw myself onto his closet floor, and popped open the fake air conditioning vent at the bottom of the wall. Six inches back was the safe. Dad had given me the combination years ago in case I needed emergency money, but I had never actually opened the thing. Barely even noticing the stacks of cash, I tossed the phone in and slammed the door shut, then slipped the grate back into place so it looked like an air vent again. I was back to the living room in less than a minute.

Devon was still standing next to the intercom, looking dazed.

"Is he sending people up?" I asked.

"No." He shook his head. "I told him we accidentally nuked a spoon."

"Then it's fine." I sighed. "He'll tell my dad, but it's a good story. I'll email him and say I'm sorry. It'll be okay."

"Bryant." Devon's voice quaked like it was very much not okay. Somehow, seeing that crack in Devon's customary coolness made the immortality of the demon device even scarier than anything else had managed to. "We put the phone in the *microwave*, and it didn't kill it! What are we supposed to do?"

"Go home and think of something else." I pressed the elevator button. I didn't even have a backpack to grab. "The phone'll be safe here for the night, and we'll come up with a new plan tomorrow."

I looked down at my real phone. Mom had been texting for an hour.

At home but I don't have keys. Are you upstairs?

Never mind. Found Mr. Fortner, he let me in.

Please call so I know you're okay.

Don't forget you have to meet Elizabeth at ten tomorrow. Do you have math books in your room?

I hit my head on the elevator wall.

"What?" Devon asked.

"I'm meeting Elizabeth tomorrow at ten," I said.

"Well, at least there's a beautiful blond light at the end of the tunnel." Devon patted me on the back.

"Sorry for the alarm," I said to Drake as we passed to go out onto the street.

I don't remember his response. I was in too much of a daze. Devon was telling me how to put the moves on Elizabeth while teaching her about cosines. Oh, and there was an evil phone hidden at my dad's. And I had no idea what to do about any of it.

"Sorry," I muttered as I shoulder-checked a guy dressed in black who was heading into the building. I wasn't even a good New Yorker. I ran into someone on a mostly abandoned street.

I hope you never have a day where you feel like as big a screw up as I did on that walk home.

But things got even worse. So much worse.

8

M y mom didn't let me go to bed till late that night. We were up sitting on the floor, trying to think of anyone we knew with theatre access who might owe somebody we knew a favor. Finally, I said we could ask my dad to rent her a stage for a day. I knew I shouldn't have said it, but I was tired and knew it would end the conversation so I could go to bed. I mean, he would have rented her a stage if she asked. But she'd never ask so...gotta love parents who won't speak to each other.

She woke me up at eight the next morning, and I guess she wasn't mad about my mentioning Dad buying her out of the theatre problem because she made normal Saturday breakfast: bacon, waffles, and homemade whipped cream. It was sort of our thing.

"Do you have everything ready to meet Elizabeth?" For an actor, Mom was really bad at sounding casual.

"I have my math book from last year." I shrugged. "This year's got burned."

"I'm sure you'll be able to help her," my mom said. "She is such a smart and talented girl."

I really didn't need my mom to explain to me how the girl of my dreams was the most brilliant person to ever walk the earth.

I *mmmhmm*ed a response.

"I'm sure you'll be good friends once you spend a little time getting to know each other."

"Mom," I said, trying to act like my stomach wasn't being shaken by a monkey with cymbals, "you do know how weird it is to make your son tutor a girl to try and set him up with her?"

"Tutoring is a great way to spend time with someone," my mom said blithely.

"So they say. Gotta go, Mom." I stood, leaving my half-eaten waffle on my plate. The monkey with the cymbals that lives in the pit of my stomach and likes to practice for his band concerts when I get nervous was working on the *1812 Overture*. His percussion was winning the war against my desire to eat.

I ran out the door and down the steps, thinking up murder scenarios for the poltergeist phone rather than let my stupid brain psych itself out about my non-date.

The library was two blocks away, so I was there before I could try and come up with anything more creative than putting it on the subway tracks, which could kill people. And I had already gotten way too close to that for comfort.

Elizabeth was sitting outside the library, bag in her lap, and long blond braid draped over her shoulder.

"Hi, Bryant." She stood and smiled at me. Her eyes were all sparkly and perfect.

I opened my mouth to say hi, but somehow "*heyaaii*" came out.

She bit her lips together. It was nice of her not to laugh.

"Crazy day yesterday," she said.

"Yep," I managed, which was a recognizable word, so at least I was heading in the right direction.

"But it's done, right?" Elizabeth's sparkly eyes dimmed for a second. "I mean," her voice dropped, "you got rid of it?"

"I, umm..." I took a breath. This was too important to stammer. "I tried. Devon and I both did."

"What do you mean *tried*?" Elizabeth took my hand and dragged me away from the door. Her hand was so soft and delicate in mine. Like a little butterfly hand. "Bryant!"

"I mean, we smashed it, drowned it, *and* nuked it. Nada." I glanced around at the passersby. Even talking about the phone made it feel like that stupid giant eye was back being a creeper.

"Why didn't you throw it into the river?" Elizabeth asked.

"Because," I said, "we didn't want it to turn into another remake of the *Jumanji* movie. If the thing can't drown and it washed up on shore, what if someone who wanted to cause fires found it?" I didn't mention that Devon had thought of it. Elizabeth didn't need to know he was the one who was actually capable of functionally thinking under pressure.

"So where is it?" Elizabeth asked after a few seconds, taking a step back as though she thought I might have the thing in my backpack.

"Someplace safe," I said.

"Take me there."

"What? Why? There's no point," I said. "It's fine where it is until we figure out what to do with it."

"That thing tried to burn me to death," Elizabeth growled. "If you and Devon can't figure out how to break a damn phone, maybe I can. I'm not stupid."

"I—I know you're not," I sighed, rubbing my hands over my face. "It's at my dad's."

"Lead the way." Elizabeth linked her arm through mine.

Now, I know we were on our way to my rich dad's place that I hated when people knew about, to try and do something I had already failed to do, that could quite possibly do a lot more damage than simply wrecking my dad's microwave. But walking down the street with Elizabeth on my arm felt nice. Like we were on an old-fashioned date. She smelled like flowers, and the scent cut through the usual homeless pee stink of the city.

People looked at me differently. I mean, mostly they were noticing Elizabeth, because how could you miss her? But once they saw her, they looked at me differently, too. Like, *Oh, that dude must have some redeeming quality to have a girl so exquisitely perfect walking with him without a knife to her back.* And it made me feel a little bit better, even if they guy winking at me didn't know Elizabeth was only interested in destroying a dangerous cellphone.

"So, here's the thing," I said as we turned toward the park. "My dad's place is different."

"You mean he's like a painter or something?" Elizabeth raised a blond eyebrow at me.

"Not exactly."

"He lives with a man?" Elizabeth stopped in her tracks. "Because there's nothing wrong with having two dads."

"No, not two dads." I know I might seem a little bit crazy to be so shy about having a super-rich dad. But the only thing worse than having Elizabeth walking arm in arm with me because there's a cellphone that might try to destroy the world, would be having her walk with me because my dad plays golf with former presidents. I can deal with being a dork who only has one friend who only likes me because I've been around for so long he hasn't really figured out guys like him aren't supposed to hang out with guys like me. Having a bunch of fake friends who only pretend to like me so I'll spend money on them would be way worse than having no friends at all. Or even no girlfriend at all.

"So what is it then?" Elizabeth asked after a few awkward minutes. "Does he live in the projects?"

She turned to go down the steps to the subway, but I pulled her to walk along Central Park West.

"My dad lives in a penthouse. He makes more money having lunch with someone than a lot of people make in a year. His doorman gets me whatever I want, and I get paid to check in on his empty apartment. When we couldn't break the phone, I locked it in his hidden safe where he keeps a boatload of cash in case I need it and he's not in the country."

Elizabeth stopped as though her feet had been glued to the pavement. "You're joking."

"Nope." I had to look down at my shoes. Her blinking her sparkly eyes at me all confused like that was too much for me to take.

"But you live with your mom in a walkup."

"Yep," I said. Why did I have to sound so lame?

"You go to a public school. A crappy public school."

"Yep."

"You could be going to a private school in Scarsdale. You could already be at an Ivy League college with how smart you are."

"My mom wanted me to go to her school." I glanced back at Elizabeth, vaguely insulted. "She didn't want me to turn into a yuppie rich brat who doesn't appreciate anything. I'll go to an Ivy League after I've applied like everyone else. That was the deal—my mom picked the high school, my dad picks the college."

Elizabeth narrowed her eyes at me. "The deal, huh? So, what do *you* get to pick?"

I opened my mouth to say, I don't know, something about how I got to pick lots of things in my life. But that was a lie. I had been so happy my parents weren't yelling across the lawyer's desk, I had just said everything sounded great. I had been agreeing to everything that might keep the peace for years.

"I might get to pick my major," I said lamely.

"Well, after we destroy the phone, maybe we can look up some state schools. Who knows?" She took my arm. "You already burned down a theatre, maybe there's a bit of rebel in you yet."

"The school thing was an accident," I huffed.

She held my arm closer now, not so stiffly. "I know. But you got everyone out, and that makes you pretty badass."

"Thanks?"

"*Thanks* is right." Elizabeth smirked, shaking her head.

We were at my dad's building now, with its big carved marble front and the awning that reached all the way to the curb so people could get out of their cars without getting wet.

"Wow," Elizabeth murmured as I led her inside, walking quickly past the doorman as he launched into his, "Good morning, Mr. Adams."

That's the thing about living in Manhattan. You know people have lots of money. You see all the limos and furs. You walk past Tiffany's and Cartier and all the super fancy shops. But it's not until you walk into the swanky building where the rich people live that you really think about rich people having bedrooms and toilets. I mean, my dad lived there, but it still creeped me out. Normal people aren't supposed to have marble floors.

"Hey Drake," I said as I walked up to the desk. He looked at me for a second like he couldn't quite figure out who I was. His eyes were bloodshot, and his face drawn and gray. Worse, his shirt front had a wrinkle in it. I know it might sound awkward, but even one wrinkle was like way weird for Drake. "You okay?" I asked. When was the last time he had had a day off? Did he get days off? Or sleep?

"Fine, Mr. Adams." Drake's words were a little slurred, almost like Mr. Klein's, my old chem teacher's, had been before he was fired for keeping straight vodka in his water bottle.

"You're back again, I see." His eyes drifted slowly over to Elizabeth. "With a new friend. Is Mr. Rhodes not feeling well?"

"Devon's fine," I said, "but I'm tutoring Elizabeth, and we needed a quiet place to work."

"I understand, Mr. Adams." Drake still looked a little confused. "Would you like me to have a pizza sent up?"

"No thanks," I said, instantly regretting it. Having possession of a thing that could spontaneously combust at any second was making me hungry. "But I still don't have a key, so..."

"Of course." Drake peeked below the desk, and his brow furrowed. "Strange."

"What's strange?" I glanced over the high edge of the desk. Papers were scattered across the shining wooden surface, and the lockbox that held all the extra keys hung open.

"Nothing," Drake said, his voice getting bright again as he stood, the penthouse key in hand. "Nothing at all. Rearranging things this morning."

He led Elizabeth and me to the elevator and put the key in the penthouse hole. He turned it, and as we all stood there silently, the elevator *whooshed* up. I didn't know why, but something still felt off. I thought maybe it was Drake being mad because I ruined my dad's microwave and now he was in trouble with the HOA for letting kids run wild. Or maybe he could only take being nice to me once a week. Or maybe it was bringing Elizabeth to my dad's.

The elevator stopped at my dad's, and the door opened up into his apartment.

"Thanks, Drake." I pulled Elizabeth out of the elevator.

Drake nodded silently as the doors closed.

"Was he all right?" Elizabeth whispered.

"Probably." I shrugged. "Drake's a cool guy." I don't know how *cool guy* was supposed to mean nothing was wrong with him, but it didn't matter. Elizabeth had taken a few steps forward and was staring into the living room. I glanced at the coffee table. Someone had cleaned up the pizza boxes Devon and I had left behind. Maybe that was why Drake was mad.

"The park." Elizabeth pointed out the window.

I looked out, expecting to see our landmark on fire. But Central Park was there, looking fine.

"Yeah," I said, not really sure what she was talking about.

"Your dad has a penthouse view of Central Park," Elizabeth clarified.

"Thanksgiving is the only time my mom comes here. We watch the parade from the window. I mean, my dad's not here or anything..."

But Elizabeth had drifted away. "Chandeliers?"

I looked up. There was a big chandelier in the living room and another in the dining room through the door. I never really looked at them anymore. They were just sort of what turned on with the light switch.

"They're a bit much, I guess," I said.

"You bring the same backpack to school you've had since freshman year." Elizabeth moved through the dining room to the kitchen.

"You kept track of my backpack?" I asked, following her.

She ran her hands over the freakishly prefect countertops. They were some kind of fancy something or other, and Elizabeth walked her fingers between the sparkly patches.

"I sit next to you two classes a day." She turned to me, her blond eyebrows squeezed together. "I thought you had noticed."

"I did," I said too quickly. "I mean, I know we have classes together, but I didn't think you'd noticed me."

"I did, and the bright red backpack."

"My mom got it for me," I said. "And there's nothing wrong with a red backpack."

"But you could get a new Gucci bag every day."

"I don't want them." I tipped my chin up. Since when was not wanting to spend money on backpacks a bad thing?

Elizabeth took a step forward, looking straight into my eyes.

"What now? I should have designer eyes? Is brown not good enough for a rich kid?"

"No." She retreated. "I was thinking there might be more to you than a geek with a cool mom." She sounded annoyed now. "Where's the phone? Let's get this over with."

Why did I have to snap at her? That, right there, is why I had never had a girlfriend. The second a girl looked at me not as a walking calculator and was willing to stand within a foot of me, I turned into a dickwad.

"Look, I'm sorry," I said, feeling stupid as my face got hot, and I knew it was turning pink.

"Let's just get the phone."

I led Elizabeth back through the master bedroom and into the closet.

"Wow," she breathed. I didn't have to ask what she was talking about. I mean, my dad's closet was bigger than a lot of bedrooms in Manhattan.

I knelt and pulled out the back grate.

"If your dad has passports and foreign currency in there..." Elizabeth said as I opened the safe.

"Nope. Just a ton of American money." I pulled the phone out of the safe and locked it back up, sliding the grate in place. "Here ya go."

"I don't want it!" She backed into my dad's arranged-by-color suits. "I can't even open the damned thing."

"And I can't break it." I pressed my finger onto the button. The screen flashed instantly to life. I tossed it on the closet floor and stomped on it. "See? Nothing." I picked it up and bashed it against the metal piping the clothes were hanging from. "Not a crack." I held the phone out to Elizabeth. "It's perfect. I can't break it, so if you want to try, you're going to have to touch it."

At that second, a ding echoed through the apartment.

"What was that?" Elizabeth asked, her voice quiet like we were hiding from something.

"It's the elevator," I said. "Drake must be coming up for something."

"Maybe because you're alone with a strange girl in your dad's empty apartment," Elizabeth whispered. "Did you think he was really going to buy the tutoring thing?"

"But it's true," I said. "My mom wants us to—"

Right then, the elevator doors whooshed open. I reached over and shut off the closet light, pulling Elizabeth into the shadows. I don't know why, but something felt weird. Like Drake was going to have me banned from my dad's house for bringing a girl up here. A few footsteps carried from the living room.

My brain was telling me to call out and tell Drake where we were, hiding was only going to make everything worse. But my gut kept me pinned to the shadows.

More footsteps, and a man came into view. A man who made me instantly decide never to doubt my gut again. The evil vampire who owned the cellphone from Hell was standing in my dad's living room, large as life and twice as pale.

9

He looked just like he had when he had gotten out of his cab. Dressed in an all-black suit, black shiny hair, unsettlingly white skin.

"Who is that?" Elizabeth breathed in my ear so softly, I could barely hear the words.

"The phone guy," I whispered back, turning to her. We were nose to nose in the closet. I had her pinned to the wall, her heartbeat pounding against my chest. The man's eyes flicked our way, and both our hearts stopped for an instant.

He glanced down at his wrist before walking farther into the living room and out of sight.

"We've got to get out of here," I said.

"He's next to the elevator," Elizabeth pointed out with her trademark, if badly shaken, reasonableness.

"Another way." I took her hand in mine, pulling her out of the closet and into my dad's room as the man's footsteps echoed from somewhere around the kitchen.

I led Elizabeth down the hall to my room. It was on the river side of the apartment even though all you could see from my window was a sea of buildings. There were four doors—one to the hall, the bathroom, the closet, and our way out.

We had gotten to the far side of the bed when a voice called out from the hall.

"Bryant."

I froze in place, but Elizabeth yanked me down to the floor behind the bed.

"Is that your name? Bryant?" The voice sounded angry and also younger than I had thought an evil demon vampire's would. He sounded like the condescending college kids who think they have dibs on every coffee shop in my neighborhood.

"Well, *Bryant*"—he kept inching toward the door—"you have something of mine." The footsteps stopped. "A phone you stole from me, actually. It's as silly as that. Whether you took the thing to pawn it or to try and earn your wretched way in the world, I don't really care. The only thing that matters is that it's useless to you and priceless to me. The only way you can possibly hope to survive long enough to leave this apartment is to give me what I want. So toss the phone out to me, and I'll be on my way. And you and your girlfriend can get back to...whatever it is you were up to."

My stomach purred. He thought Elizabeth was my girl-friend. But then I remembered *he* was an evil man in my dad's apartment, and, even though Elizabeth smelled like sunshine and flowers, the purring disappeared.

"Are you going to give me back my phone, Bryant?" the intruder asked. "Or am I going to have to take it from you?"

"Don't do it," Elizabeth mouthed.

"Any ideas?" I mouthed back.

Elizabeth held the phone up to my face.

I pressed my thumb to the reader, and the light blinked on. There was the fire app, but I didn't really want to risk setting a building full of people on fire...again.

I looked at the different squares, trying to sort through what each of them might do.

"I'll give you to eight," the man said.

"I don't know what to do," I whispered.

"Aren't you supposed to make it ten?" Elizabeth shouted.

I looked at her, but she pointed to the phone. She was trying to buy me time. She was so smart, and bold, and beautiful, if I hadn't been terrified of us being murdered, I wouldn't have been able to look away from her.

"They speak!" the man said. "At least the girl does. I'm surprised you're letting her do the talking for you, Bryant. Is she more of a man than you?"

I tried to ignore him as I scanned through the symbols. There were the ones with letters I didn't recognize. A purple ball of light, promising.

I scrolled to the next screen, and there was a red square with the letters FF emblazoned in white.

"You really think men are braver?" Elizabeth asked. "What century are you from? And what kind of freak breaks into an apartment looking for a phone? What are you anyway?"

"I'm no thief," the man snarled, "and as for *what* I am, I don't think that's any of your concern."

Something in my gut told me to click the red box, and since I had just decided that maybe my gut was the smartest part of me, I did it.

Four choices popped up on the red screen. *Offensive at a Glance, Defensive at a Glance, Quick Escape, Last Resorts.*

I clicked on *Quick Escape.*

"I think it is if you want your phone back," Elizabeth said.

"Funny for a girl hiding behind a bed to press her luck like that," the man shot back.

"Fine then," Elizabeth said. "What's your name?"

The man chortled. "Eric Deldridge. What's yours, blondie?"

"Not going to tell you," Elizabeth growled.

There was a list of words I had never seen before. Each of them had a link next to it, but I didn't have time to look at descriptions.

"Then I'm done with you, in three—"

There was a note in bold at the top of the list that said, *Remember to speak clearly.*

"Two."

Aarantha was the first word on the list.

I heard Eric begin to say "one" and beat him with, "*Aarantha.*"

A weird wind whooshed through the apartment before Eric shouted, "What did you say?"

"*Aarantha!*"

It was like Dad's place had become a tornado, and I was stuck in the eye. The pictures flew off the walls and swirled around the room. The bed ground along the floor, making a terrible *shriek* I could barely hear over the wind. I sat and stared for a minute, but as sparks flew from the ceiling when the chandelier pulled loose, Elizabeth screamed, and I came back to my senses.

I yanked her toward the fourth door in my room.

There was a lock in the door handle, a dead bolt on top, and a stop peg on the bottom.

I started fumbling with the locks, my hands shaking so badly I couldn't grip the bolt. Eric screamed at me, but I couldn't make him out over the wind. I looked behind. He was holding onto the doorway with his fingers, his feet streaming behind like some sort of a creepy human windsock.

The eye of the storm had followed me to the door, but the wind still raged. Eric was glaring at me, looking like he wanted nothing in the world more than me dead.

"Let's go!" Elizabeth shouted. She had undone the locks while I had been staring stupidly at Eric.

I grabbed the door and swung it open an inch, but then it slammed shut like a giant hand had pushed it. Elizabeth and I both pulled together, but the door wouldn't budge.

I glanced back at Eric. His lips were moving like he was muttering something.

"He's blocking the door!" I screamed.

Elizabeth looked terrified, and I mean, who wouldn't be, trapped in a whirlwind that was now ripping chunks of drywall the size of my head from my bedroom walls?

I checked the phone again, the handy *Defensive at a Glance* tab. *Abalata* was the first word my eyes landed on.

I went with it.

For a split second, the wind stopped, and I thought I had done something stupid. I had killed the only thing that was keeping evil Eric from murdering us!

But then my hand tingled like I had touched a lamp with a short in it. I looked down, and saw myself holding a cloud of black.

"You!" Eric pushed himself to his feet. "Who are—"

I didn't let him finish. I threw the black cloud with all my might, and somehow I managed to hit him square in the chest. But the blackness didn't leave my hand. It stretched as it pushed Eric away. He flew backward down the hall and toward the living room window. He was going to fly out the window. I moved to run after him to do I don't know what, but it only accelerated the inevitable. Right before he hit the glass, he screamed something and stopped. I could feel him pushing against my hand, fighting to move.

He screamed something else, and a wave of purple flames streaked toward me.

"*Aarantha!*" I screamed when the fire was a foot from my

face. The wind swept the inferno away, sending it crackling to the walls.

"Bryant!" Elizabeth pulled on my sleeve, spinning me to the door. The flames covered the handle, but as I reached for the knob, the wind pushed them out of the way. I yanked the door open, then let it shut behind us once Elizabeth and I were through.

I looked around the stairwell. Plain concrete stairs. I couldn't even hear the fire or the wind. It was deceptively normal. I wanted to curl up and catch my breath or wait for my mom to come and get me.

"Mom!" I yelped as Elizabeth broke the glass over the fire axe and shoved the metal handle against the doorknob, blocking Eric's path. "That freak knows my name. He'll be able to find my mom."

"We have to go." Elizabeth motioned toward the stairs. "Bryant, let's move!"

The apartment was on the fiftieth floor and going down that many stairs is no quick thing. We ran as fast as we could, not saying anything. Just running. I kept waiting for the fire alarm to go off. Or for Eric to come chasing us down.

My mind raced. How had he found me? Would he go after my mom?

"He knew my name," I panted, my words jostling in my chest as we ran. "How the hell did he know my name?"

"You really don't look properly, do you?" Elizabeth said. "Your doorman was acting all weird, his papers were tossed around like someone had searched through them, and then an evil dude walks into your dad's place knowing your name."

"You think Drake gave out my name?"

"*Gave out* might be the wrong term," Elizabeth puffed. "Try and keep up."

When we got to about the tenth floor, the red lights started flashing. There was no way it had taken the fire alarm that long to go off. Except maybe purple fire doesn't smoke as much as the normal kind?

"Slow down," Elizabeth hissed, still holding my hand and slowing to a trot as other residents started moving out onto the staircase.

They were all murmuring angrily like someone had interrupted their pinochle game with a stupid question about Go Fish. I kept glancing up the staircase, waiting for Eric to shower some horrible thing down on us from above.

Soon, we were out in the lobby. Drake stood outside the window, looking up in horror. The brass button doorman shook next to him.

"Stay calm," Elizabeth whispered as I pushed through the crowd to get outside to see whatever it was that was freaking Drake out.

My pulse pounded in my neck as we waddled out onto the pavement. Seriously, I have never seen people move so slowly while alarms blared. Rich people are weird.

As we made it onto the sidewalk, everyone stopped and stared up at the same place Drake did. There was barely any room to stand.

"Watch out!" I shouted at the fat sweaty man trying to shove through us.

The man's face turned the shade of red exclusive to angry New Yorkers, and for a second I thought I was going to be screamed at while being packed in like a sardine with people who didn't have the sense to keep moving away from the burning building. But right after he opened his nasty, garlicky mouth, the woman behind him screamed, "Jared, look!" and fat Jared turned to gawp up at the building.

I followed his gaze, and judging by her gasp and the fact that her hand slipped into mine, I guess Elizabeth had, too. Flames leapt out of the top floor of the building. Right out my dad's front window. But the flames weren't red or orange. They were purple. The same purple Evil Eric had shot at me. Only from down here, they didn't look dangerous at all. They looked beautiful. Inviting.

There were sirens wailing up the street again, but I almost liked their weird song. It sounded calming and strangely normal. Someone stomped hard on my foot, and I looked around. Elizabeth was glaring at me and trying to drag me sideways through the crowd.

"We have to go," she growled.

"But it's not spreading." I wanted to look back at the purple fire. The strangeness of it was magnificent, a shock of brightness breaking through the posh dullness of the Upper West Side skyline.

"We have to warn your mom." Elizabeth stomped hard on my foot again. "Remember your mom? The one you were so worried about?"

I cursed so loudly, fat Jared's lady friend gasped and opened her mouth to berate me. But the enchantment was broken.

I pulled out my phone. My real phone, not the evil devil cellphone that had destroyed my dad's apartment. I dialed my mom as Elizabeth steered me past the fire trucks and down a side street.

"Give me the phone, Bryant." Elizabeth held out her hand. I didn't need to ask to know she meant Eric's. The disgust in her voice made it clear, but the fear was tamped down by purpose.

She pressed her thumb to the print reader. The thing stayed dark.

"Open it." she ordered.

I pressed my thumb to the button, and the phone flashed on. She touched the screen, and it went dark again.

"You'll have to do it." She passed the phone back to me.

"I need to call my mom."

"This first," she said so firmly, I didn't dare argue.

I unlocked the phone. It was still open to the list of defensive spells.

"Go back to the home screen," she said.

I flipped back to the page with all the strange squares.

"Go to settings."

"Settings?"

"Just do it." Elizabeth steered me by the elbow down side streets and through breezeways between buildings.

I scrolled through the icons, fairly certain *this* phone wouldn't have a settings button. But sure enough, there was the little square of cogs looking annoyingly normal.

"Found it," I said.

Elizabeth led me into a bodega and paused for a moment, looking really interested in the Twinkies before shaking her head regretfully and whispering, "Turn off the *find my phone* feature."

"What?" I asked, but before I could say the demon phone didn't have said feature, I noticed the little green toggle and pushed it over to red.

Elizabeth glanced at the phone before lacing her fingers through mine and leading me back out onto the street, then through a hotel lobby and catty-corner from where we had been, toward the park.

"How did you know?" I stumbled on random goo as I stared at her.

"He was looking at his watch," Elizabeth murmured. "He had a smartwatch. He was tracking the phone."

"So, when I pulled it out of the safe," I said, feeling stupid and numb, or stupidly numb, whichever.

"He found us," Elizabeth said. "Now call your mom."

I put the black phone away and pulled out my scratched,

non-homicidal model. It had a tiny chip in the corner and a geeky Doctor Who case my mom had bought me for Christmas. I had never appreciated how normal and important my non-fire-starting phone was until that very instant.

Mom answered on the second ring.

"Bryant honey, how's the studying going?" she said in a voice I knew meant that wasn't the question she really wanted to ask.

"Not now, Mom. Where are you?"

"I'm out looking for a theatre space—"

"I'm invoking Family Agreement, Article Seventeen. You can't go home, Mom."

There was silence on the other end of the line.

"Bryant honey—"

"Article Seventeen states that in a true emergency no questions will be asked and no punishment given if the son approaches the mother with a genuine fear," I quoted the thirty-page document we kept in the kitchen drawer. "You can't go home, Mom. It's not safe. Go to Aunt Tina's and stay there. No looking for theatres, no going to school."

"Bryant, what's going on?" My mom's voice was crisp with fear.

"Article Seventeen. There's something weird going on, and I don't really know what. You can't go home, Mom." The reality of it sunk in as I said the words, the weight nearly crushing my chest. "Neither of us can."

"Bryant, meet me at Tina's," my mom whispered, "if someone is after you."

"No," I said. "I'm safe where I am. You go to Tina's and stay there. I'll call when I can." I hung up without waiting for her to argue. I wish I hadn't, but as Elizabeth dragged me across the street and into Central Park, it seemed like the right thing to do.

10

The air in Central Park felt different from the air on the street. It was like all the relaxing things New Yorkers had done on its grass over the years had created a permanent cloud of calm. I wanted to sit and rest. But if I squinted up the street, I could still see the purple flames wafting out of my dad's apartment. I took the lead toward the castle, pulling Elizabeth along since she had taken out her bright purple phone and started texting one-handed.

"No, go south," she said, without looking up.

I didn't argue. She had saved my life twice within the last hour. Arguing seemed like a dumb idea. Instead, I focused on trying to look like I wasn't running away from someone who had tried to kill us by esoteric means. Really, if you had added in some ice cream, you could call it a date.

We slowed down a bit when we hit the paths that led south. Elizabeth shoved her phone back in her bag. We were still outpacing the tourists, who plodded along like walking had never been used to get anywhere and was meant more as an exercise in slowly shifting your weight from one leg to the other while trying to see how little you could move.

"What's Article Seventeen?" Elizabeth said as we skirted a tourist who stopped in the middle of the path to tie his shoe.

"Oh," I said, feeling stupid. "I—I decided we needed a constitution after the first time I got grounded. I didn't think it was fair that she had punished me for doing something that had never been expressly forbidden, so we locked ourselves in the apartment for the weekend and wrote up the articles."

"And one of them was in case your life is in danger, you can tell your mom to run, no questions asked?"

"Not running per se." I shrugged. Mom had insisted on the rule in case I was stuck at a party that got crazy. I had never been to a party that got crazy. "Dangerous life-saving trust in general."

"Bet you didn't think you'd need it for a magic phone and an evil wizard," Elizabeth snorted, dropping her bag by a fountain and sitting on the stone ledge. Her gaze swept over the throng.

"The phone isn't magic." My words came out strangled and small. "It's some kind of super advanced technology. Or something."

"Bryant"—Elizabeth took my face in her hands and stared deeply into my poop-brown eyes with her sparkly perfect ones—"you read a spell off of a magic cellphone and made a tornado that saved us from a magical purple fire that is probably still burning in your dad's luxury penthouse."

"But—"

"Bryant." She leaned in. "It's magic. Wielded by you. And a wizard named Eric. You're supposed to be smart, so please catch up on this."

She was close. So close. Her breath tickled my cheeks. If I moved forward an inch, I would be kissing Elizabeth Wick.

"Okay?" she said.

My mind raced back to the purple fire and the list of defensive spells at a glance.

"Magic." My throat instantly dried out.

"Bryant!" a voice shouted from the sidewalk as Devon waved high above the crowd.

"He *has* to shout," Elizabeth growled, dragging me to my feet. She was a lot stronger than she looked.

"Devon, what are you doing here?" I asked as my BFF looked not so slyly at Elizabeth's hand holding mine.

"I texted him." Elizabeth stepped forward to throw her arms around Devon's neck.

My heart sank. Actually no, it didn't sink. My heart turned to ice, then sank, hit my kidney, and shattered.

"Hey, you okay?" Devon asked, looking over Elizabeth's head.

I opened my mouth to shout that no, I wasn't okay, my best friend was hugging the girl I'd been desperately in love with for three years, but Elizabeth was already talking.

"That phone is magic. I went with Bryant to his dad's to try and get rid of it, but the owner showed up—"

"The vampire?" Devon asked.

"He's not a vampire. He was out in daylight," Elizabeth said without hesitation. "He's a wizard, and he was going to kill us. So Bryant used a spell from the phone to save us, but it caught his dad's apartment on fire. And now we're on the run from Eric Deldridge the murderous wizard, and quite possibly the police for setting another building on fire."

Devon took a step back and bent double, running his hands over his face. "Okay." He stood up. "What do we do now?"

"We?" I burst out, lower and angrier than I had meant to. "Why are you even here?"

"I told you, I texted him," Elizabeth said.

"Why? He wasn't there. Why should he get involved?" I growled. "And why do you even have his number?"

"I've had his number since I've had a phone," Elizabeth's voice hardened. "Not that I see how it's any of your business. And I thought Devon was your best friend, not to mention a guy who knows more places to legally lay low than anyone else I know. So since someone is trying to kill us and probably your mom, too, I thought your good ole bestie here would be able to help." She turned to Devon. "Unless you want to go home and pretend you've never met Bryant, which I wouldn't blame you for."

Devon turned to me without skipping a beat. "Your mom? How is your mom involved?"

"Evil Eric—"

"Evil *Wizard* Eric," Elizabeth corrected.

"Evil *Wizard* Eric found my name. It won't be hard to find our address." I ran my hands through my hair so hard it hurt. "I told her to stay away from the apartment, and she will. Maybe."

"Article Seventeen." Devon nodded. "So Ms. Miller is safe. Do you still have—"

I patted my pocket.

"And the wizard owner who set your dad's apartment on fire is going to be coming after it?"

"Yes."

"Right." Devon glanced at Elizabeth, his face losing its default devil-may-care confidence for half-a-second. "I don't know how you want me to help. Not that I'm being a chicken-shit, but I have no wizard-fighting experience. I only found out about wizards two minutes ago."

"We need a quiet place to think where Eric can't find us," I said. It felt like every person walking past was a threat.

"Quiet hidey-hole out of the way in Central Park." Devon smiled. "I've got you covered."

He led the way back up and deeper into the park, Elizabeth next to him, and me taking the rear, trying to feel grateful and pretending I didn't want to punch Devon in the back of the head. We were being chased by a murderous wizard. Betrayal-by-best-friend would have to take a backseat to possible death.

Finally, Elizabeth pulled out her purple phone and speed-dialed, grimacing at Devon as it rang. "Hey Dad, a bunch of theatre kids are going to try and help Ms. Miller wrangle a space for the show next weekend, can I camp out for the night and help?" She paused for a moment as Devon led us off toward a clump of food carts. "Yes, I'll study, and yes it's only girls. Well, mostly. Besides it's a theatre group, Dad, nothing to worry about on the boy front."

Devon scowled and pulled out his own phone, texting someone before slipping it back into his pocket.

"Love you too, Dad," Elizabeth said before hanging up.

"Did you have to insult the masculinity of theatre in order to make an excuse for staying out?" Devon asked as he passed a twenty to the hotdog cart guy, who seemed to wordlessly know exactly what Devon wanted.

"If he knew I was with you," Elizabeth said, "he'd never let me stay out after dark, and I feel like it might take more than a few hours to stop the evil wizard from, you know, triple homicide."

"Touché." Devon grinned.

The hot dog man chortled and shook his head like running from wizards was some kind of hip slang with the wacky youth. It was a true chortle, too. I wished I could have filmed it for my mom to show her students. Pain shot through my stomach at the thought of her running scared to Aunt Tina's.

"What about your parents?" Elizabeth asked as the man handed us ten hotdogs and some sodas.

"I texted and said Bryant was having an existential crisis and needed me there." Devon shrugged as he led us off the path and through a thick stand of trees.

"I suppose realizing you can use magic counts as an existential crisis," Elizabeth said as Devon lifted a branch out of the way so she could climb under. He let go of the branch, and it hit me smack in the face. Somehow it felt like the tree knew how my day was going and just wanted to emphasize the point.

I've never been one to wander the wilds of Central Park. I have a well-instilled fear of finding a dead body in the bushes. Or of becoming the dead body in the bushes. Devon, not so much. Judging by the way he wove through the unmarked trees, he'd been here a lot. Probably with girls. Bile rose in my throat. Hopefully not with Elizabeth.

He stopped at a tiny clearing barely big enough for all of us to sit comfortably around the giant mound of hotdogs.

Elizabeth grabbed the first one and took a huge bite. "So," she said, after downing the entire hotdog in less than a minute, "we have the phone. Eric wants the phone."

"If we give Eric the phone," Devon mumbled between mouthfuls, "he could use it to kill us or destroy Manhattan like a bad movie scene."

"If we don't give him the phone"—I took a bite of my own dog. It was mostly cold and a little rubbery, but somehow running for our lives made it taste good anyway—"he'll chase me and my mom. And since he knows where I go to school and he's seen both of you...."

"He'll be after all of us." Elizabeth lay back on the grass and stared up through the trees.

"We could call the cops," I said lamely. *"Hello, NYPD? I have a magical phone that starts fires, and I think someone may be trying to kill me to get it back."* No one laughed. Not even me.

"We need a plan that's daring but won't get us killed," Devon said.

Elizabeth nodded. "Why do you think I texted you, Dev?"

Dev? No one called Devon *Dev.* My stomach squirmed.

"Don't you specialize in stupid without getting killed?" Elizabeth asked *Dev* with a smile.

"Just about." Devon grinned stupidly with his stupid face before turning back to his tray of stupid hotdogs.

We sat in silence for a minute.

"The restaurant with the purple awning," Devon said finally.

"The one Eric went into?" My stomach tightened at the thought of finding the phone. I should have let the cabbie hock it. I set down the third hotdog I had been lifting to my mouth.

"I say we go case the place."

"*Case the place,*" Elizabeth said, mocking Devon's tone. "What are we, jewel thieves?"

"And how do we *case the place*?" I looked away as Devon playfully swatted her ear.

"We find different clothes so Eric won't recognize the geek and the blond in the dress. Then find the purple awning, see who's coming and going—"

"And if anyone is pigmentally-challenged, we follow them," I finished for him.

"Stalk albino wizards, and hope they don't figure it out." Elizabeth rested her arms over her face. "Sounds great. Wake me up when it's time for the shopping trip."

11

I watched Elizabeth lying on the grass. Her breathing went steady, and her arms relaxed as she fell asleep in the fall sun.

"You okay, man?" Devon asked after we had been sitting silently for a few minutes.

"Fine." My voice came out all weird and high like it always does when I'm lying. This is why I never did well in acting classes.

"We'll figure it out, Bry." Devon sounded cool and confident like always. It made me want to punch him in the face.

"I said I'm fine." I pulled out the black phone. More for something to look at that didn't make me want to scream than because I actually wanted to play with it.

"I don't know if that's a good idea," Devon said. "I mean, I really like this spot."

"I won't light it on fire." I pressed my thumb to the button.

The screen blinked on, and I flipped back to *Defensive Spells at a Glance*. I thumbed down, rolling all the strange syllables on my tongue. I had only ever taken Spanish, but I knew about roots of words and none of these looked like any language I had ever seen.

I tapped on one of the words. *Pentceena.* A new screen popped up.

Pentceena—A spell that will cause water to boil and explode. When done properly, the boiling water can be directed at your opponent for maximum damage.

WARNING! Water will boil and explode from ALL nearby sources, and directing the stream may be difficult. Proceed with caution and concentration.

I swiped my thumb and went back to the list of spells. All of them were underlined and led to descriptions.

Calimarta dropped things onto your opponent's head. *Dothranta* made everything go black. There was even a note under it, advising the user to be sure to know their way out before attempting the incantation. Too bad I hadn't seen that one at my dad's place. Then maybe my dad would still have a place.

"Let me see." Devon sidled up next to me, reaching for the phone.

"It won't work." I handed it to him and watched the screen go immediately black.

Devon tried to turn it on before handing it back and shaking his head. "Weird."

"Yep." I turned the screen back on and scrolled through the different icons.

"So, does this make you"—Devon paused, scanning the trees—"like, a witch or something?"

"No." I snickered for a split second before stopping. "I mean, I *can't* be a witch. I'm from Hell's Kitchen, and my mom is a drama teacher."

"But you did magic, dude," Devon whispered.

"The evil phone did," I said, feeling a lot defensive and, I hate to admit it, a little afraid. "I just have a thumbprint it likes."

"Do a spell." Devon pointed to the phone.

"I thought you said you didn't want me to burn down your little corner of Central Park?"

"It's an experiment. Just don't pick a fire spell."

There was a glow in his eyes. The one that meant I should say no to whatever he was suggesting. But I wanted to see if I could do another spell. And I wanted to show Devon maybe there was something I could do that he couldn't.

"Fine," I said, choosing the most innocent looking icon I saw. It looked like a teeny tiny forest. The whole picture was in shades of green, and the longer I stared at it, the more variety jumped out at me. Light green, dark green, puke green, greens I'm sure there were fancy names for but I couldn't tell you what they were. After a few more seconds, the trees started to look like they were moving, swaying with a wind that existed only inside the phone.

I tapped on the picture to make the motion stop. It looked like the inside of the *At a Glance* App, but this time there were pictures on the tabs. A rock, a stream, a tree, and a little white rabbit.

"Cute bunny." Devon laughed. "Can you pull it out of a hat?"

I shrugged and tapped on the bunny.

A list popped up with more words I didn't understand, but this time I couldn't tap on the word to get more information. "I don't know what they do."

"Just try it. Come on *witch man*, make the bunnies happen."

I looked down the list.

Eruntulia. I mouthed the word silently. I liked the way it rolled around in my mouth. It didn't feel hard or scary like the other two spells.

"Do it," Devon whispered.

"*Eruntulia*," I said softly. I waited for something to happen. For the trees to burst into flames or some other kind of scary death to come chasing us. But instead, my eyes fixed on some silver vapor. It was like breathing mist in winter, but the vapor pouring out of my mouth was thicker and shinier. As it floated away from me, it narrowed into a thin strand that hovered in the air for few seconds, twisting around itself like it was looking for something, before separating into three threads and diving off silently into the trees.

Part of me wanted to chase it to see what it would do, but Devon had already punched me in the arm. "It's okay to have a dud spell. Try another one."

I wanted to throw the phone at him and tell *him* to 'try another one' if he didn't think my witch-ness was good enough. Except, and it was a big *except*, by every reasonable standard I could think up with my mind racing so fast it felt like I had pounded three espressos before gym class, I had just done magic. Deliberately and somewhat successfully, I had done magic.

I looked back at the phone, to the little picture of the water. "*Stilgarna,*" I whispered.

A warning sort of gurgle came from right underneath me. I jumped to my feet just as water bubbled up from the ground where my butt had been only a second before.

Devon rolled to his side, laughing silently. "You made a magical bidet. Let me try one." He leaned over my shoulder to look at the phone. "Pull up a cool one."

I flicked to the flower screen as the water trickled downhill only about a foot away from the sleeping Elizabeth.

"A flower, dude?" Devon snickered.

"You want to try one or not?"

"Okay, okay." Devon took a deep breath and pointed dramatically at a tiny blue flower by my feet. "*Milkawa.*"

My heart leapt to my throat as he said the word. I don't know if I was more afraid that it would work, or that it wouldn't. I didn't have time to figure it out because Devon started gagging in my ear.

"The demon phone is cursed," Devon coughed. "That word tastes like shit."

"Words don't taste." It was my turn to laugh.

"*You* try it." Devon swished his mouth out with soda and spat it on the grass.

"*Milkawa.*" I tried to keep my voice clear and firm like it had said to do with the *At a Glance* spells as I glared at the tiny flower Devon had been pointing to, which remained completely ordinary. "The word doesn't taste like anything. You've lost it."

"Close the phone and try it again," Devon said. "Maybe you have to be holding—" He never finished his thought.

The tiny wildflower by my feet had started to twitch and squirm. Devon and I bent down to look at it. I squinted to try and see what the leaves were doing, but suddenly the leaves were easier to see. So, I stopped squinting and almost fell over in the grass. My eyes hadn't gotten better. The flower had grown. A lot. In less than a minute, it was up to my knee.

"Umm, Bryant?" Devon pointed to the ground around the flower. The grass had started to grow too. Shooting up like the flower had. Devon dragged me back as the stalks under our feet started to writhe as they tried to grow under our shoes.

"Elizabeth!" I screamed as the flower pushed her head up in its inexorable upward momentum.

She sat up, gazing around with a look of fright on her face. "What did you do?" she shrieked as the grass swallowed her legs.

I dove forward, grabbing Elizabeth under both arms and dragging her to her feet. But even after her legs were free from the grass, she kept screaming. There were words. I know she was screaming words at me. It was something about a death wish. Or me wanting to kill her. But I couldn't listen. I was too busy staring at the flower.

The tiny flower that had started out no bigger than my little finger was as big as me. Bigger than me. A linebacker version of me. And it showed no signs of stopping.

Devon grabbed my arm and spun me around, dragging me back through the trees, Elizabeth leading the way. I could still catch words like *dumb* and *maniac*. I was about to shout something back, but I looked behind. Huge mistake. The flower now towered over the trees.

All I could think of was Jack and his magic beans. My mom had directed *Into the Woods* for a summer program a few years ago, and here was this flower, with its giant blue petals, looking way better than the flat she had made me paint that no amount of fancy stage lights could really make look like it was touching the sky.

Devon pulled me onto the sidewalk, and we weren't the only people running. Everyone was running. Women in business dress and men who owned hotdog carts. Nannies and dog walkers and their respective charges. Running for their lives. Terrified of the deadly blue flower.

We didn't stop until we reached the very bottom of the park. Tourists lined the sidewalk, packed thick like the flower was some sort of fancy show Central Park was putting on just for them.

Elizabeth caught onto Devon's hand that didn't have a death grip on my wrist as we waded through the crowd.

Soon, we were out by the department stores. Devon dragged us across to the Plaza as more cop cars raced up the street. The NYPD was probably having the strangest day on record, and it was all my fault. I felt myself cackling before I heard the sound or even knew I'd decided a flower looming over Central Park causing 9-1-1 calls was funny.

Soon my sides ached I was laughing so hard. Devon was still dragging me down the street. A tug on my arm spun me right before Elizabeth slapped me hard across the face. I stopped laughing as I rubbed my stinging cheek.

"Look, I know you're a crazy person," Elizabeth hissed, "but I would really appreciate it if you could keep the hysteria in check. You turned Central Park into *Jumanji*—"

"I love *Jumanji*," I said softly.

"Do you really think Eric isn't going to know that was us?"

Devon turned to look at her, his eyes wide with fear.

"We need to get out of sight. We find new clothes, and then we follow Devon's plan." She set off down 5th Avenue before rounding on us again. "Because at least Devon has the sense not to try and get us killed."

I looked at Devon. I thought he would tell her he had said we should try another spell. Or at least say I hadn't meant for anything like this to happen. But he was already trotting next to Elizabeth, not defending what we both had done or even checking to make sure I followed.

Lagging ten steps behind, I cut through the oblivious tourists all transfixed by the park and to the revolving door of a department store. Elizabeth and *Dev* were out on the other side of the door before I had even made it into the glass circle of doom.

It was different inside the store than it had been on the sidewalk. Everyone was calm and quiet. Clearly, they hadn't noticed anything or even heard the sirens over the music pumping in through the speakers.

"We're looking for black and cool." Elizabeth rounded on me. "Not burglar chic." She turned away for a minute to locate the escalator before looking back. "And you're paying."

I felt my pockets. My wallet was still there. And in it would be the black credit card my dad had given me on my twelfth birthday in case there was ever an emergency. I had never tried to use it. I knew it wasn't expired, but I didn't know if it would actually work. I didn't mention that small fact as Elizabeth stepped off on her floor and headed toward the girls' section.

"Meet you in fifteen," Devon called after her before turning toward the guys'.

I hated shopping. Even under the best of circumstances. Shopping to stalk a deadly wizard was even worse. Devon tossed some clothes at me, not asking for my opinion or size. I trudged after him into the fitting room, locking the door behind me and not looking in the mirror as I pulled on the dark jeans and button up shirt.

I didn't want to see myself. I had done magic. I should look cool. Weird cool. But what if my face had gone white like Evil Eric's? Or I was all normal and poop brown like I always was? Either way, I didn't want to know.

"You okay?" Devon called over the door.

I opened the sliding lock.

Devon looked even cooler than usual in a brand new dark ensemble with tags still dangling off the individual pieces like a new round of fawning admirers desperate to cling to the glory that was Devon Rhodes.

"You look good, bro." He smiled. "Very non-magical and ready to blend into the night. Elizabeth's gonna dig it."

Heat and anger bubbled in my stomach, and I wanted to punch Devon. Not in the arm, in the face. Hard enough to break his racially ambiguous nose.

"I don't think she'll care." I backed into the dressing room.

"You gotta look good for the ladies, Bryant." Devon examined himself in the mirror.

"*You* gotta look good for the ladies," I snapped. "*I* have to be ignored by them. And the only person who's going to give a shit how I look is also trying to kill me."

"Elizabeth isn't trying to kill you."

"Elizabeth doesn't care if I'm alive or dead." Blood pounded in my ears. "The only part of me she cares about is the evil cellphone that's trying to destroy Central Park."

"You had her in your dad's penthouse," Devon said. "You can't tell me that didn't do some good."

"What does it matter, *Dev*?" I shouted, enjoying hearing my voice echo through the empty dressing rooms. "Hasn't she been to your apartment before, *Dev*? And how am I supposed to compete with the great Devon Rhodes? Money? Magic? They're nothing compared to his raw animal magnetism."

"What the hell are you tal—"

"She texted you!" I shouted. "The girl I've been in love with since we started high school texted you to tell you we were being chased by an evil guy from Hell! And how did she get your cell number? Been hooking up with her after school? I mean, we spend so much time together, it must have been quite a feat for you to find time to make out with your best friend's dream girl!"

Devon stood staring at me as I panted, glaring at him, waiting for him to tell me the truth that would end our friendship forever.

"I never hit on Elizabeth," Devon half-growled, half-whispered after a minute had passed. "I never made out with her. I never chased her. Because she's the one girl my best friend wants. She has my number because we've done scene work together before, and she's terrified of your mom. She texts me when she thinks your mom hates her, and I tell her your mom doesn't think she's a talentless hack who will never go anywhere.

"And do you know why I've never hit on her?" Devon took a step in so he was really close enough for me to clock him. "Because my best friend is in love with her. And I would never do anything to hurt my best friend. Even if he is a total moron who has a tendency to destroy things. And by the way, jealousy because a girl texted a guy *friend* is a real dick move, Bry."

Devon stared into my eyes, daring me to punch him.

My chest crumpled as my heart disappeared into oblivion. "It's not about her texting a guy. It's about her texting my best friend. The one guy I thought I didn't have to try and compete with. I thought you were on my side, but who the hell was I kidding? She would take you over me any day even if you're not trying. You're the coolest guy in school. You even have a rockstar name. Every girl in school wants you. And Elizabeth—"

"Is off limits," Devon said. "Always has been. And you're a better catch than you give yourself credit for. I would have tried to set you up with her last year if I thought you could have formed a sentence in front of her, but now you're all magical *and* capable of real English speech. You've got it made, brother." Devon shook me by both shoulders. "We're stopping an evil wizard and getting you the girl, Bryant. Because that's the sort of best friend you have." He hit me on the shoulder harder than usual and turned back to his dressing room, disappearing behind the shutter.

I huffed out a half-guilty, half-relieved breath. Maybe going Goth and stalking wizards wouldn't be a total deadly waste of time after all.

12

Elizabeth waited for us by the register, wearing new clothes. The salesgirl was glaring at her. Maybe because she was wearing clothes she hasn't paid for yet. Probably because Elizabeth looked gorgeous. She wasn't wrapped up in a fancy dress. Just dark pants and a flowy, black top, complete with a floppy knitted hat and big sunglasses.

"You do know the sun will eventually go down, right?" Devon pointed to Elizabeth's sunglasses as I stepped forward with my black credit card in hand.

"I'm paying," I said. The shop girl raised her eyebrows as we all started pulling the tags off our clothes.

"For the record," Elizabeth whispered over the quiet *deeping* of the scanner, "I know it's going to get dark. I also know Eric has seen my face, and I really don't fancy having to tell my parents they need to evacuate our apartment. We don't have articles of confederation in my house."

"It's constitution," I muttered.

I tried not to listen when the girl jabbered out the total. I still had to explain to my dad how I magically burned down his Central Park West penthouse. Well, not me, but a magic guy who wanted to kill me, which didn't seem to make the whole *no more Le Chateau* thing feel any better. A few hundred dollars on a credit card couldn't really make things too much worse.

When we got on the escalator to go back to the first floor, Devon managed to sidestep so Elizabeth and I were riding together.

I looked back at him, and he winked.

I should say something.

I knew I should say something. This was my time to say something cool about being a witch, or how I would protect her, or hey, even *wow Elizabeth, you look awesome!* But no. I walked next to her out of the building and onto the sidewalk, not saying a word. Because that's the sort of loser I am.

We turned to go north, and I stopped. Devon walked into me. But I was too stunned to even stumble forward. The damned flower towered over Central Park.

News vans lined the sidewalk. Every face on the street was turned to look up at the blue mammoth. It was like a disaster scene in a movie or even on the news where everyone is stuck, not knowing what to do or how to process something crazy.

"Let's go." I finally pushed the words through my dry throat. I grabbed Elizabeth's and Devon's hands, weaving them through the frozen crowd. When we got up to the news vans, I overheard the reporters talking into their microphones.

"It's been a day filled with strange, dare I say, impossible occurrences here in midtown," a young woman with long dark hair spoke earnestly into the camera. "We began this morning with a shuddering halt to our metro system after two trains were nearly shaken off their tracks by seismic activity scientists are still struggling to explain. Then came the fire on Central Park West. The fire chief has told News 1 exclusively that, although the fire has been contained, the firemen at the scene have yet to find a way to douse or even approach the strange purple flames that can still be seen flaring from the side of the building.

"And now the latest development. A flower has taken over Central Park. Yes, you heard that right, folks. Over the last hour, this flower has grown more than one-hundred feet, towering over the trees that usually dominate the park. The rangers have yet to make a statement on the cause of this plant's incredible growth. Rumors on the street are explaining what has been dubbed *Big Blue* as everything from miracle of God to biogenic terrorist attack. We can only hope the source of these disturbances can be determined quickly so our park, and our city, can be safe once again. Stay tuned to News 1 as I interview eyewitnesses, coming up next." The reporter's eyes swept the horde.

I led Devon and Elizabeth away as the woman's eyes locked onto Devon. He certainly looked the part, and his eyewitness account of the birth of Big Blue would make her career. Not that the reporter knew that. And there was no way I was going to let her find out. We cut to Central Park West and headed uptown, examining every awning, searching for the something shiny and purple.

Devon and I muttered back and forth, "You sure it was purple?"

"Yes, it was purple. Neither of us is color blind."

"You sure we were still on Park?"

"For God's sake!" Elizabeth stopped in the middle of the sidewalk. "Neither of you even knows where the hell this place is or if it exists, or if you'd even know it if you saw it?" Elizabeth's voice came out as a whispering shriek.

"We'll find it." I took a step forward. "I promise."

"Because you're so good at keeping your word. Like how you weren't going to try and use the magic that, I don't know, might get us noticed?" Elizabeth batted my hand away as I reached for her. "This isn't a game, Bryant."

She turned and cut through the crowd, finding a seat on a bench with her back to Big Blue. Her face was in her hands. She had every warning sign. Red cheeks, shaking hands, tense shoulders. She was girl angry. Girl angry is way worse than guy angry. Guy angry might get you shoved into a locker or punched in the face. Girl angry could get your soul ripped out and your spirit broken beyond repair.

"You should talk to her." I nudged Devon forward. "Tell her we're sorry for playing with the phone."

Playing with the phone sounded better than using magic that had all of New York panicking.

"You're the one who's desperately in love with her," Devon said. "You go talk to her. You're never going to have a girlfriend if you run away every time a girl gets pissed." He planted both hands on my back and shoved me forward. "This is for your own good."

I balled my hands into tight fists and sidled up to Elizabeth. I could do this. Maybe there was a spell in the phone for dealing with angry girls.

The second I thought it, she looked up at me, glowering, like she had heard me think about using the phone.

Even though she looked like she might kill me as soon as speak to me, her eyes were still all sparkly, and she was still beautiful.

"Elizabeth." And there it went, my face traitorously turning red as my voice shook on the one word I had managed to say. "I'm sorry. I shouldn't have been, you know...with the phone."

"We shouldn't be involved in any of this," Elizabeth said. "All I needed was a freaking math tutor, and now I'm looking for a purple awning to try and find a guy who wants to kill us before he manages to get to my favorite teacher."

"We won't let him get to my mom." I swallowed hard as my

stomach crawled at the thought of Eric being within ten blocks of my mother.

"I'm sorry!" Elizabeth clamped a hand over her mouth. "That was terrible. I know she means more to you than she ever could—"

"It's fine," I said.

Elizabeth stood up and took both my hands in hers. "It's *not* fine. None of this is fine. But if I'm going to help you, you can't decide to do dumb things behind my back. I'm not following you around Manhattan to be your cheerleader. I could go hide out at a friend's place and wait this whole thing out. But you need me. I can help. I may suck at calculus, but I'm not stupid."

Her eyes had gotten extra glisteny. I could see tears forming in the corners.

"You're not stupid," I said as a tear slid down her cheek. And something happened. I don't know if it was human instinct or reckless abandon from almost being killed that morning. But I reached up and brushed the tear away with my thumb. Her skin was soft, and she didn't back away or wince when I touched her. It even made her smile a little. I stood silently for a second, trying to figure out what I had been saying. "You're the one who realized how Eric found us. You're the one who figured out what the phone was doing. You saw it right away. If I had believed you then—"

"Then Eric would have the phone by now," Elizabeth said, "and we could be looking at something a lot worse than Big Blue. But we're a team, all right? All three of us together."

"A team." I nodded.

She smiled, threading her fingers through mine, and towed me back to Devon. Her palm was pressed into mine. Not like before, when she had been holding my hand like I might as well have been her grandma or a kid she was babysitting.

She and Devon were talking about something. But I couldn't

pay attention to anything but Elizabeth's hand held tightly in mine.

"Sound good, Bryant?" Elizabeth asked.

"Yes," I said, not sure what I was agreeing to.

"Then lead the way," Elizabeth said.

"I, uh..." I gave Devon the look that said, *by the Bro Code, you must save me from whatever I just walked into.*

"I'll lead the way." Devon punched me in the arm a little harder than necessary. "Bryant here has never been good with directions. Now, I know we walked south and we didn't go more than six or seven blocks."

"But that means we should have found it by now," Elizabeth said. "You said it was packed in with other restaurants?"

"It's there." I pointed before I really realized I had seen it.

Elizabeth grabbed my arm and lowered it for me while I stared at the awning.

"No, that one's black," Devon said.

And it was. The awning was made out of weird, shining fabric like extra shimmery silk. And in sunlight, it looked black. But walking past it, it had seemed purple. Except, if I squinted and tipped my head a little...

"Squint at it," I told Devon and Elizabeth.

They both bunched up their eyes.

"It's purple," Elizabeth said after a few seconds. "Or at least it would be under street lights."

"I still don't see it." Devon shrugged. "But if you think it's right, you can stay here and watch this place while I go look around a little more."

"No," Elizabeth said. "We stay together. Right, Bryant?" She looked at me.

"Right." I nodded. I swear Devon smiled for a split second before he sighed.

"Fine, we wait at the *black* awning and see if it turns purple or if any creepy, pigmentally-impaired people show up. And look, there's even a nice place for coffee." Devon pointed to a bistro two doors down from the purple/black awning.

He was right. We would be able to see the door to the awning place from there.

As I stared at it, thinking of the black credit card sitting in my pocket that was about to get used again, I noticed faint letters glimmering on the silk.

The Consortium.

It sounded like something out of Star Trek.

"The Consortium." I tasted the word in my mouth. It felt dark and powerful.

"Huh?" Devon asked as we played Frogger with cars that didn't seem to care about the stoplight or the crosswalk. The drivers were all too busy gaping at Big Blue.

"The Consortium is the name of the restaurant," I whispered as we sat down at a café table, pretending to stare at Big Blue while really watching for people walking toward the purply-black/blackly-purple awning.

"How do you know?" Elizabeth asked quietly, trying to read the menu and watch the street at the same time.

"It says it on the awning," I said. "But I could barely read it."

"The *black* awning didn't say anything." Devon's face transformed into his signature grin as the waitress approached. She was probably twenty-five, but when did that stop him?

Elizabeth stared at me while we all ordered and didn't look away once the waitress left.

"What?" I asked, finally turning to her.

"I think there might be something wrong with you." She leaned in close to me.

"Wrong with me?" I managed to say. I wanted to be offended, but somehow I couldn't get away from the feeling that Elizabeth was right.

"I mean different," Elizabeth corrected.

Devon snorted.

"You can make the phone work," Elizabeth said after a *thump* came from under the table that I'm pretty sure meant she had kicked Devon in the shin judging by his grimace. "You can read words on the awning neither of us can see. I don't think it's just that the phone likes your thumbprint. What if you're a witch and just never knew it?"

"You have always been weird," Devon agreed.

"It's just the phone," I said as the waitress brought out our food. "Nothing to do with me."

We all sat and ate, falling in and out of silence as Big Blue crept higher into the sky. When the food was gone, we ordered more coffee. And then more coffee again after that. My hands were beginning to shake. I'm not sure if it was from the enormous amount of caffeine I had consumed, or if I was getting twitchy from being still for too long.

"There," Elizabeth said, not pointing but looking directly at a woman trotting down the street, her gaze fixed on The Consortium.

The woman's skin was stark white, but unlike Evil Eric, her hair was white, too. And since I couldn't see any trace of eyebrows on her face, I could only assume they were white as well. The woman wasn't old enough to have white hair. She looked younger than my mom. It was like someone had dunked her in a vat of bleach.

"Well"—Devon took a sip from his coffee—"either the place is a meeting hall for Pasty Folks Anonymous, or that lady is into the whole weird—"

"Magic," Elizabeth inserted.

"*Magic* thing, too," Devon finished.

"But what can we do about it?" I dragged my fingers across the lattice of metal holes in the tabletop. "Should I walk in there and say, *Hey, your friend Eric tried to kill me this morning, and I have his cellphone that's rapidly destroying New York. I would give it back to him, but then he might kill me even faster. Got any ideas that don't end with us dying?"*

Elizabeth bit her lips together as she studied her fingers. I knew that look. It was how she looked when we were working on math problems in class.

"Never fear." Devon patted the table, making my coffee slosh. "I'll take care of everything."

"What do you mean *take care of*?" Elizabeth asked before I could say anything.

"For all we know, Eric is in there right now. I'm the only one he hasn't gotten a really good look at, so I'll go in, see what the deal is." Devon grinned.

"See what the deal is?" I asked, trying to convince myself I should feel incredulous even though I knew he was serious as Shakespeare.

"See how many children of the corn are in there." Devon swiveled to the café window to fix his hair in the reflection. "See what the hell that place is for. The usual."

"And when they figure out you're snooping and turn you into a toad?" Elizabeth's eyes narrowed.

"Not gonna happen," Devon said. "Remember, I'm the best actor in school."

It was true. Devon couldn't sing or dance to save his life, but he could play a role that would rip even the evil lunch lady's heart out.

"How will we know if something's gone wrong?" Elizabeth asked.

"I'm assuming the building will catch on fire," Devon said, "but I'll call you, put my phone on speaker, and you dolts stay on mute."

"You saw that in a movie, didn't you?" I asked as Devon stood up.

"Sure did." Devon smiled. "And it worked, too."

"This isn't a movie, Devon," I said. "You can't just pretend to be some big hero. You could get"—he was already too far away to hear me without shouting—"hurt," I muttered as my phone rang right before Devon disappeared into The Consortium.

13

It was Devon's number on the screen. I opened my mouth to tell him to stop being an idiot, but voices were coming from the other end of the line.

"May I help you?" It was a woman speaking. If she was surprised to have a random teenager show up, I couldn't hear it in her voice.

Elizabeth leaned in close to listen, our faces a breath away from touching.

"Just wanted to check the place out," Devon said in his *I'm so cool, I only listened to half of what you said* voice.

"Are you interested in a meal?" the woman asked.

"No." The sound of fabric rubbing on the microphone distorted a few of the words. "...creepy guy, and I was hoping he'd be here."

"I don't know whom you're speaking of." The woman's voice was decidedly tenser now.

"Funny," Devon said, "because I saw him come in here a few nights ago. I was looking for him because he lost something. And what with the weird fires and that"—there was a sound like tapping on glass—"giant flower outside your window, I thought maybe it had something to do with Mr. I-like-to-leave-things-in-cabs Eric Deldridge. But if you don't know him, I guess I'm in the wrong place."

"What did he lose?" A different woman spoke this time, her voice high, thin, and angry.

"Don't suppose it matters since you don't know the guy anyway," Devon said.

"Perhaps I was mistaken," the first woman spoke. "We do have so many customers."

There was a pause. "Really? It looks pretty dead in here to me."

Silence again.

My heart leapt into my throat. Did Devon *have* to insult their business savvy?

"Our clientele come and go at all hours," the first woman said.

Elizabeth leaned in closer to me, her cheek pressed into mine.

"Any idea when Eric might be coming back?" Devon asked. "Or where I could find him, maybe?"

"None," the high-voiced lady said. "But if you leave whatever he lost here—"

"Naw. If you don't know when he'll be back or how to get a hold of him, I probably shouldn't leave his phone here."

The sound of glass smashing was followed by a low chuckle. "Did the glass piss you off, ma'am?" Devon said. "Anyway, I'll just have to find Eric some other way."

"Leave the phone here," the high-pitched voice growled. "It doesn't belong to you."

"You either." If I hadn't known Devon since forever, I wouldn't have been able to hear the fear in his voice.

"You have no idea the lengths to which Thaden will go to

retrieve his property," the first woman spoke. "Be a smart boy. Give us the phone."

"Wouldn't even if I could." Fabric whooshed against his cell again. "Besides, don't have it on me anyway." There was silence for a few seconds. "Mind if I grab a takeout menu? Your kitchen smells amazing."

"Thaden will find you," the high-pitched woman warned.

"Well, have him bring along some takeout," Devon said.

The door under the purple awning swung open, and he stepped out onto the street.

I started to lower the phone from my ear. "Well then," Devon said, louder than he had been speaking in the restaurant, "better head down to my bro's name place. Wouldn't want to miss such an awesome evening."

I glanced down to see the screen flash on as Devon ended the call. I stared at the phone for a second before looking up, just in time to watch him turn the corner and swagger out of sight, a woman almost spilling out of The Consortium on his heels.

"She's following him!" Elizabeth sounded like someone was strangling her.

"He knows." I scribbled my name on the bill before leading her in the opposite direction of where Devon had disappeared.

"We...we can't!" She tried to pull me back. "We have to help him. What if..."

"I know where he's going." I dragged her to the curb, raising my arm to hail a cab.

"What? How?" She stepped in front of me and signaled as well. The first cab that passed skidded to a stop in front of her. Not surprising.

"His bro's name place." My stomach sank as I crawled into the cab. "Bryant Park," I called up to the driver. "We have to get to Bryant Park."

14

Three sets of clothes, dinner for three, and a cab ride through midtown traffic. That wasn't too bad. Right?

While the horns honked as the cabbie tried to take us down Broadway, I played out the conversation in my head.

Hey, Dad, how's wherever it is you are?

Fine, son. Have you decided between Harvard and Yale yet? Both are fine institutions, and I have good friends on both acceptance boards.

No. Sorry, Dad. I didn't have time to think about my future today. I was too busy fighting an evil magic dude who was trying to kill me and the girl I'm desperately in love with who thinks I'm an idiot. And I kind of trashed your apartment, so you might want to reconsider the whole paying my way through college thing.

How did my only son get involved with the dark deeds of...witches?

I found a phone and decided to do my best impression of a pyromaniac. And I've gone on a spending spree with the emergency credit card, and I don't see it ending any time soon since Mom is now on the lam. Oh, and a state college sounds good. If we make it through this alive.

I tried to imagine my dad getting mad at me. Maybe yelling at me for destroying part of Central Park. But I didn't really know him well enough to know what him mad would look like.

"You okay?" Elizabeth asked.

I nodded.

"Do you think Devon's okay?"

"He's spent more time chasing girls and then giving them the slip than any other sixteen-year-old in the city." I sighed as the cabbie pulled over. "He's got it covered." My voice sounded confident, but my stomach was still a heavy, squirming mass of terrified worms.

I let the cabbie run the black card and turned to the park. There was no movie or concert on the lawn that night, but even still, people had spread out their blankets and were sitting under the streetlights enjoying the cool night breeze.

We found an empty bench under a tree. I scanned the crowd, searching for Devon or Eric. Or anyone else with creepy bleached skin.

Couples dotted the grass. Some eating food, some kissing. Kind of a lot of kissing.

"Are you really named after the park?" Elizabeth asked.

"Me?" I asked stupidly like there was someone else she could be talking to. "Yeah. I am."

Elizabeth stared at me for a few seconds. "Why?"

"Oh, my parents met in Bryant Park. Mom was performing here, and Dad thought she was amazing. When she was done, he asked her to share his picnic blanket." I smiled, looking out at the park. They had fallen in love here. Which meant they must have been happy in this park. "Anyway, she was going to say no. But he had a bottle of Jameson, so...."

"And that's where the middle name comes from?" Elizabeth grinned.

"You know my middle name?"

"Your mom always uses your full name when she's mad at you in rehearsal," Elizabeth said. "And I'm really good at memorizing. So…"

"Buttons." I laughed. "Lots of button sewing tonight." It's what my mom would have said. It was her favorite line when her students started an excuse with "so…." I tried to think of an excuse I might be able to give her for this whole mess. My brain immediately fizzled, so I went back to scanning the park instead. I kind of needed my neurons in working order.

The streetlights glowed overhead, casting the whole place into shadows. But somehow the park's shadows didn't seem scary like the ones in my bedroom that had given me nightmares when I was little. If the shadows in my room were filled with monsters, the shadows here were filled with possibilities. A thousand different paths hidden just out of sight. You only had to be brave enough to step into one and find out what was there.

"When did your parents split up?" Elizabeth asked, pulling me back to the present.

"When I was three." Maybe I should have felt sad about it, but I never had. "Dad had been on a *corporate is evil* kick when he and my mom met. But then she had me, and all he wanted was money. For things like Harvard and private schools. She didn't like that all he did was work. He didn't like that she didn't care about money. And then it was over."

"Sad," Elizabeth whispered. "Sad that stupid money broke them up."

"More ideals than money." I ran my hands over my hair. God, I wanted a shower. Catching things on fire and running for your life really makes you long for creature comforts.

"Still sad," Elizabeth sighed. She turned to me, looking into my eyes. And, I know this is going to sound crazy, but it felt like, for the first time, she was seeing *me*. Not my mom's son. Or the smart kid who sat next to her. *Me*. The product of a dark park, a bottle of Jameson, and a divorce. The guy whose parents can't stand each other and who doesn't know enough to care. Me who catches his dad's place on fire with magic but thinks the most amazing thing that's happened this year is sitting on a park bench with Elizabeth Wick. We stayed like that for a moment.

I hated the word *moment* until that bench.

It had always seemed too indifferent. Too romantic. Like you were confusing a measure of time with a state of being and trying to make something quantifiable. But once you have a moment, you understand what a moment is. Because the world stops, and magic doesn't matter. And you're not afraid to be alone with Elizabeth, or of Eric, or magic, or even of the moment passing and never coming back again. Time freezes, and there you are, drinking in the most beautiful girl who's ever lived. And that moment is perfect.

"Am I interrupting?"

I gasped as Devon stood above us, his hands on his hips, his face showing his judgment. "Because if I'm interrupting, I can go. I mean, it's not like I raced across town to lose my tail from Un Café du Magic. Or found out vital information about the evil cellphone that is bent on destroying Manhattan. So I'll just go. Let you two kids go back to staring into each other's eyes."

Heat rose to my cheeks, and I was glad the streetlights wouldn't show their color. I tried to think of something witty to say and had finally settled on, *Glad you're not dead, dude,* when Elizabeth spoke.

"You're sure you weren't followed?"

Because of course even after our moment in the park, she'd be all practical like that.

"Triple sure." Devon nodded.

Elizabeth stood up and threw her arms around his neck—then hauled off and punched him hard in the shoulder. "Don't you ever go all rogue like that again! You could have gotten yourself killed. You could have gotten all of us killed, and for what?"

"I will tell you *for what*." Devon rubbed his arm. "We learned three very important things. First, the ladies of The Consortium didn't know that Eric had lost his magic mobile. Second, Eric's missing phone really scares them. And third, some dude named Thaden is probably going to kill all of us for even knowing about the phone."

"Kill us?" Elizabeth choked.

"This may be hard to believe, but I tell you, when I mentioned the phone, the white chicks got even whiter," Devon said. "Whoever this Thaden guy is, I think he might be the boss. Or at least the creeper the boss is scared of."

I looked up at the sky. Somewhere high above the skyscraper lights were stars. Hidden by the ambient light, but always there. And the way out of this mess was like the stars. There and possible to reach, if you could only see beyond the immediate. Good God, one moment in the park, and my brain had turned into romantic mush. Not that Elizabeth was really interested in me. I mean, maybe. But no. No way ever.

"So, we find Thaden," Elizabeth was saying when I finished giving myself a mental beating for being a romantic sap.

"And if he's the guy who wants the phone," Elizabeth said, "I say we give it to him. We tell him Eric is a nutbag, and if Thaden promises to make Eric leave us alone, aren't we golden?"

Devon shook his head slowly. "I don't think so. The way those ladies were talking about him...Eric is stupid. Thaden is evil."

"How do you know?" Elizabeth tipped her head to the side, narrowing her eyes.

"Because beneath this charming exterior lies a deep and very perceptive soul," Devon said seriously. "Well, that, and I've spent tons of time studying people for acting class."

"I thought you were girl trawling?" I said.

Devon smiled. "Same thing. Either way you swing it, anyone who can make the magic albinos that scared is not a dude we should be trying to make deals with."

"So we're back at the beginning." Frustration seeped into Elizabeth's voice.

"No," I said, and did something brave and stupid. I took Elizabeth's hand in one of mine and brushed the perfect blond hair away from her face with the other. It was like being in a movie. Sitting in the dark romantic park with my dream girl, being all strong and comforting as danger crept closer. But in the movie I was supposed to have a plan. And right then, I had nothing. "We'll... we'll figure this out," I said, trying to sound like that was actually a promising thing.

"Okay." Elizabeth squared her shoulders, her perfect eyes becoming hard and bright, like diamonds. "Then we find a way to tell Eric we know about Thaden. He's got to be getting desperate. We make a deal for the phone, tell him if he doesn't agree, we go straight to Thaden."

"We don't know how to find Thaden," I pointed out.

"Eric doesn't know that." Devon grinned.

"It's the best we've got." Elizabeth shrugged.

"But it's not good enough. It still has Evil Eric ending up with the phone." My mind raced, trying to find an option that didn't involve trying to find the guy who was trying to find us. "I say we go to The Consortium, explain everything, and let them deal with their problem child."

"Unless they tell Eric to take care of us, and then we won't know he's coming," Devon spoke over me.

Elizabeth held her arms up between Devon and me to silence us. "We need to try and find out more about The Consortium and go from there."

"We can't wait!" Devon ran a hand over his face. "This is the time for action."

"We have to find out what the hell is going on. It's not just about getting rid of the phone. It's about making sure no one gets hurt, including us!" I ended in a whispered shout.

"How long do you want to camp out in the park, Bryant? Weeks? Years? Is being homeless a part of this plan, too?" Devon whispered. "You can't sit around and wait for life to get safe, Bry."

"Devon, if you would try and think for a minute—" I wanted to shake my best friend until he realized that maybe being the coolest kid in school wasn't going to keep us from being killed.

But I never finished the sentence because the phone rang. I looked down at my pants, terrified. But it was a normal ringtone. The geek chic one I had picked out for my phone.

The phone screen said *Mom* in big, bright letters.

"Maybe we should ask her to come up with a plan," Devon said. "Maybe she—"

I tapped the screen, fed up with Devon's ideas. "Hey, Mom. Are you at Aunt Tina's yet?"

"No, she isn't at Aunt Tina's," a voice lilted from the other end of the line, freezing my insides at the first word. "Your mother is at home. And, Bryant, you had better hurry. Crazy day today, never know what might happen."

"Leave her alone," I growled, sprinting toward the street. The pounding of footsteps followed me until I stopped at the curb.

"Gladly," Eric said. "I want nothing to do with your mother or your tiny apartment. You're the thief, remember? Give me back what's mine, and your mother won't even need to know what her son has become scrambled up in."

There was a pause on the other end before Mom's terrified voice screamed, "Bryant honey, call the police! Don't come here!"

"Don't call the police," Eric said, and I could hear the sneer in his voice. "We both know the police can't help you. The only way to fix this—"

"Fine," I said as a taxi pulled up and the cabbie eyed me out the window. "I'll be there in a half-hour. Don't hurt her."

"Don't worry," Eric said. "I, unlike you, am an honest man. But be careful, Bryant. I may cross the line if you push me."

Mom shouted something else before the line went dead. I wrenched open the taxi door and three of us piled into the back of the car.

"Where to, kid?" the cabbie asked, supremely unconcerned with the less than savory topic of my conversation. Clearly, this was a lifelong New Yorker.

"10th and 57th," I said, watching the cars speed by as the cab nosed out into traffic.

"I can get you there in ten," the cabbie said happily. "I thought this was going to be a long trip."

"No, sir." I pulled the black phone out of my pocket. "Just needed to buy myself a little time."

15

I t only took us ten blocks in traffic to work out a plan. It wasn't the best plan, but I had never been a part of a magical hostage situation before. Devon and Elizabeth agreed with everything I said. I don't know if it was because I had suddenly formed a commanding personality, or if I just looked that close to the edge.

"Neither of you has to do this," I whispered when the cab was only a block from where I asked the driver to stop.

Elizabeth said, "We know," at the same time as Devon said, "Yeah, we do."

"We're not letting you go in there without backup, Bry," Devon said.

"And we're too far in this thing to back out now," Elizabeth murmured as the cab stopped.

I let the man swipe the black card. He kept it in hand until the others climbed out. "Listen, kid," he said, "I don't know what you're into, and I don't want to know. But it sounds like you're in over your heads. I know the cops have a bad rap sometimes, but"—the man paused, shaking his head—"it's better to ask for help, while help is still possible."

I really looked at him for the first time. He was old enough to be my grandfather. His eyes were filled with concern, and somehow that made everything feel so much worse. I wanted to stay in the back of the stranger's cab and tell him everything. Make him come up with a plan and save the day. But even the most concerned stranger wouldn't believe everything that had happened. And curling up in a ball wouldn't save my mom.

"Thanks, sir." I pasted a smile on my face. "But it's not that bad. Honest." I took the card from his hand and slid out onto the street, then watched the cab edge back out into traffic.

"You got the plan?" Devon asked.

"I came up with the plan." My voice faltered in my throat.

"See you up there." Elizabeth kissed me on the cheek. Like she really was worried. And like maybe she really did want to see me upstairs. Maybe it wasn't love. But she wanted me to not die. My chest began to feel all warm and glowey.

"Be careful, Bryant." Devon punched me on the shoulder in lieu of a kiss and, together with Elizabeth, disappeared around the corner while I walked up the two blocks to my apartment.

I almost strode. I was Don Quixote. A demented knight walking into a dragon's lair with a stupid black phone instead of a sword and shield. Mom's artistic soul would like that.

Cliaxo, cliaxo, cliaxo. I thought the word through a few times to make sure I had it right before saying it out loud.

"*Cliaxo*," I said firmly, watching the keyhole on the outside door of my building. The lock twisted around like I had inserted and turned an invisible key.

For once, Mrs. Fortner wasn't there to try and squish past me in the tiny vestibule. I ran up the grooved steps two at a time, only slowing when I reached the last flight before the stairs that led to the roof. My stop.

The door looked normal. No weird shimmering words. No

purple flames. Just home. My lungs ached as I took the biggest breath I could manage.

Should I knock? Should I do the spell and walk in?

Screw him. It's my house. I'm not knocking.

"*Cliaxo.*" The lock turned, and I walked into the apartment. At first glance, all I noticed was the mess. Like my mom had decided to have all her students over for a post-show pizza party. But then I saw her standing in the corner, her face sheet white and Mrs. Mops growling in her arms.

"Bryant!" Her voice sounded far away like I was underwater and she was trying to yell at me for not getting out of the pool. She raised a finger, pointing behind the door to the chair.

"Hello, Eric." I swung the door halfway shut. He lounged in the chair, still all in black, his pasty skin incongruous against the vibrant colors of my apartment. "Glad you've made yourself at home."

"At home," Eric sneered. "This place is filled with unnecessary clutter. I would never deem such mundane environs my home."

"Then I'm sure you won't mind leaving," I growled.

"As soon as I have what's mine," Eric said, "we can begin to discuss my departure."

Departure. I didn't like the way he said the word. It sounded permanent.

"Fine." There was a stack of books on the floor. I pushed them to the door with my foot, propping it open, and stepped farther into the room, closer to my mom. "But before we discuss anything, you let her go."

"That isn't the way this works." Eric stood up. He looked taller now than he had when he had tried to kill me in my dad's apartment. "You give me what I want, and then I see how generous I'm feeling toward the thief."

"I never stole anything," I shot back. "And I'm not giving you anything until you give me my mom back."

Eric smiled. "*Conorvo.*"

My mom screamed. The air around her shimmered and contracted, pushing her tightly into the corner. Mrs. Mops yowled as she was crushed into my mother's chest.

"How small do you think I can make their cage?" Eric said. "*Conor—*"

"You think because you can do magic, you make the rules, is that it?" I shouted, cutting off Eric's spell.

"That's *exactly* it." Eric smiled. "I'm glad you're catching on so quickly."

"But you see, I don't agree with you." I inched over to my mom. "See? I'm the one with prize." I pulled the black case out of my pocket.

"Give it to me!" Eric took a step forward.

"Maybe," I said. "But maybe I don't want to."

"You don't have a choice."

"Sure I do." I forced out a laugh. "I can take it to Thaden, see if he'll give me a better deal."

Eric's face turned pink as he glanced toward the door. "You know Thaden?"

"Yep." I smiled broadly, sticking my hands in my pockets and tucking that which must not be named safely back in place. "And I don't think he's too happy about you losing the phone."

"I didn't lose it," Eric spat. "You stole it, and now you're trying to frame me."

"Like I said before, I never stole anything. You left it in a cab like an idiot when you stumbled drunk into The Consortium. All I wanted was to return the damn thing." I stood up straight, puffing my chest out as much as I could. "But how can I return a magic phone to a guy who's trying to kill me?"

"It doesn't matter anymore." Fear shook his voice. "If Thaden knows you've seen the phone, we're all done for. He won't make a deal. Not with you, not with me. We're all dead. It's only a matter of time."

"But—"

"Give me the phone. If I have it, I can make a run for it, maybe lead him away."

"You just said it would only be a matter of time before Thaden killed us."

"I could buy myself a few good days of happiness." Eric took a step forward, his arm outstretched. "You can barely form a spell. You can't hide from Thaden, not for an hour."

"I managed to get away from you, didn't I?" I said. "And Thaden might want to hear me out. So, I think I'll take my chances with him." I crossed my arms and watched Eric's mind race.

"Fine," Eric said. "I'll let your mother out. Then you give me the phone. Tell Thaden I lost it. Tell him I stole it from you and ran. Tell him whatever story you like. Just give me the phone."

"Sounds good." I smiled even though my stomach was still trembling. A door creaked open somewhere outside the apartment. The pink that had crept into Eric's face disappeared as he glanced toward the hall.

"*Vanexo*," Eric said.

I spun around in time to see my mother stumble out of the corner and the cat yowl and dart off under the table.

"Now your end of the bargain." Eric reached for me.

"Sure thing." I pulled the phone from my pocket and tossed it to him.

He glanced up at me, and for a second, I thought the plan had gone horribly wrong. Eric was going to murder my mom, me, and Mrs. Mops right there in our tiny living room.

But instead he murmured, "Best of luck, fool," and hightailed for the door. He disappeared into the hall right before a dull *thunk* and a heavy *thud* carried into the apartment.

"Got him!" Devon called as I turned to my mom.

"Are you okay?" I asked as she half-collapsed, half-sat on the floor.

"I know I promised not to ask questions," my mom said, shaking her head, "but Article Seventeen or not, I need to know what the hell you have gotten yourself into, Bryant Jameson Adams."

The sound of my mother using my full name was almost as terrifying as Elizabeth and Devon dragging the unconscious Eric through the door.

"Nice hit," I said to Devon as he kicked the door shut behind him.

"Thank you," Elizabeth said. "I think I did a pretty good job."

"*You* hit him?" I grunted as I helped Devon hoist Eric into a chair.

"Well, he did try to kill me this morning." Elizabeth shrugged. "So, I figured I had first right to *bashing the bastard over the head* duty."

Devon pulled the blue-covered cellphone from his pocket and tossed it to me. I pressed my finger to the button and watched the screen flash on. All the funny square icons were still there.

"He didn't even bother to make sure you gave him the right one?" Elizabeth gave Eric a sharp kick in the shins. "Dolt just sees a phone in a black case and thinks it's his. You so had him pegged."

"I'm sorry," Mom said from behind me, "but I've been pinned to a wall, my son was negotiating with a crazy person from a black and white film, and now it looks like that same crazy person is my son's prisoner. I'm really going to need someone to do some significant explaining."

"How about we make a cup of tea and I'll fill you in, Ms. Miller?" Devon took my mother's elbow, gently leading her to the side of the living room that served as the kitchen.

"It's bad enough for a cup of tea?" she asked faintly.

"Afraid so." Devon patted her on the back.

"Should I find rope?" I asked Elizabeth while we stared at the unconscious Eric. His head lolled onto his chest, his arms dangled limply at his sides. "He isn't dead. Is he?"

"I don't think so." Elizabeth cocked her head to the side. "But if he is, well, he *was* trying to kill us…"

I tried hard not to think about finding a place to hide a murdered witch in Manhattan. I suppose I could have made another flower to hide the body.

"The phone," I whispered more to myself than anyone else as I pressed my thumb to the button and tapped my way to the list of *Offensive Spells at a Glance*. "There has to be some sort of trapping spell here." I spent a minute working my way down the list, clicking on the different spells.

"He's going to wake up before you decide what to do with him," Elizabeth said.

"Well, then hit him on the head again." My eyes flicked up to Elizabeth's face.

She grinned. "I guess I can do that."

"Bryant Jameson Adams, you destroyed my theatre, your father's apartment, and grew the alien flower in Central Park?" my mother half-shrieked from her seat on top of the kitchen counter.

"Yes, but only the flower was really my fault," I said. "Consider it a science project on new plant species."

"Bryant." My mother's voice was low and dangerous.

I clicked through the list of spells faster.

"Sip the tea, Ms. Miller," Devon said. "It probably feels way worse to you right now than it really is."

"No, I think she has about the right level of panic, confusion, and anger," Elizabeth said.

"You're not helping," I grumbled as I clicked on *Parapus.*

Parapus—A spell to bind one's opponent. May be used on multiple subjects if they are all touching when the spell is cast.

Note—The opponent must be stationary at the time of casting.

Note—Parapus is not a permanent spell. Your opponent will break free in time.

Counter Spell—Xorus.

"Well, that sounds a little useless," Elizabeth said as she finished reading over my shoulder.

"Yet oddly applicable." *Parapus.* I mouthed the word, testing out how it should sound out loud. "*Parapus.*" Long, thin bands formed in the air in front of me, like the lines on a piece of notebook paper. They hovered for a moment, then shot off toward Eric so fast, they *whooshed* before hitting him with a dull *clang* like metal on metal.

I took a deep breath, trying not to look afraid of what I had just done. Slowly, I stepped forward. My heart raced in my chest, like I was walking up to a lion to see if it really was asleep and not interested in chomping my head off.

The thin, black lines that had hovered in the air were draped across Eric. But they didn't seem insubstantial anymore. They looked hard and rigid. I reached out to touch one. My hand shook and my head told me not to do it, but there went my hand, reaching out to poke the guy who wanted me dead. The line felt like cold iron molded perfectly to fit, pinning his arms to his sides and binding his legs to the chair.

"I never thought I would need to ban magic in my home," my mother said faintly from behind my shoulder. "No candy from strangers, don't play with matches, always follow the crosswalk signs. It never even crossed my mind to tell you not to use magic on home invaders."

"I'm sorry, Mom," I said.

"Are you two…" My mom turned to Devon and Elizabeth who stood huddled together in the corner.

"I told you, Ms. Miller," Devon said. "It all sort of spiraled."

"But both of you have been using magic?" My mom said *magic* like it was a street term for cocaine or meth.

"Neither of us can." Elizabeth shook her head. "The phone will only open for Bryant."

"And Eric apparently." My mom turned to our uninvited guest. "We had better wake him up and find out exactly who this Thaden is who's supposed to be killing us within the hour."

I looked down at the phone. A wake up spell probably wouldn't be in the *At a Glance* list, but there should be one somewhere.

Smack!

My mom hit Eric hard around the face. With a squeaky grunt, he woke up, struggling wildly to break free from the metal lines.

"Or you could hit him," I mumbled as my mother took a step back.

"Now listen, you," she said in a tone that resembled nothing less than an angry lioness. "I don't care if you think my son stole your damn phone. I don't care who the hell wants you dead because you can't keep track of a stinking thing I have to pry from the hands of my students like it is their damn prized possession every day. The only thing I care about is that you broke into my home. You held me prisoner, and you threatened my son. Now you are going to tell him everything he wants to know, or, magic cellphones aside, I will kill you and dump you into the Hudson."

My mom stalked to the kitchen and pulled out the biggest knife from the kitchen drawer. The blade glinted in the light as she walked back over to Eric and sat down cross-legged on the couch, the tip of the knife only inches from his face. "All right, Bryant. Why don't you ask him your questions so I can get this filth out of my home?"

Every once in a while, I forget my mom was raised in the Bronx. Watching her calmly pointing a knife at a guy who had tried to kill us without her hand so much as shaking made me appreciate my New York heritage. Truly, we're a species unto ourselves.

"Well." My voice came out small. Mom raised an eyebrow at me, and I started again. "First things first. Who is Thaden?"

"You know Thaden," Eric said. "You know exactly what he is."

"Sorry, that was a little bit of a fib," Devon said. "I went to The Consortium, poked around a bit. They mentioned Thaden. We've never met the guy."

"You lied?" Eric said, his face melting from relief to anger in a second. "Then there might still be time. Who did you talk to?"

"I'm the one asking the questions," I said, "and I want to know why Thaden would care enough about a phone you lost to try and kill us."

Eric glared at me, and I held his gaze. I could feel him sizing me up, looking for a chink in my shoddy armor. "Because it's his." He sighed, sort of deflating. "He gave it to me to test out. No one was supposed to see it. Not until he was sure it would work. There have been rumors, but he didn't want anyone to know the prototype was ready for beta-testers. He trusted me above all the others. And I failed him." Eric's eyes went wide with fear. "You only get to fail Thaden once."

"Let me get this straight," Devon said. "A deadly guy gives you something he'll kill you for losing, so you lose it?"

Eric dipped his head low. "I never meant for that to happen. It seems as though fate is conspiring against me. For the thing to fall out of my pocket, and for someone like you"—Eric looked up at me, his eyes boring holes into mine—"to find it."

"Someone like me?" My heart pounded like it was determined to sprint out of my chest. Blood tingled in my fingertips.

"Not just anyone could open that phone," Eric said, his eyes still creepy intense. "Not just anyone could use *parapus* on me. Surely you've realized you are not like your associates."

"You mean," I said, trying to push past the sudden dryness that was making my tongue feel four times its normal size, "I'm a witch?"

Eric tipped his head back and laughed, speaking to the ceiling. "I've been captured by an idiot. No, you're a wizard. Unless you wish to identify as female within The Consortium, which is acceptable, of course. Not that you'll live long enough to become a real wizard as I sincerely doubt any of us will make it through the night."

"I'm sorry. You're saying Bryant's a wizard?" My mom stepped in front of me. "I know my family, and I've met his father's parents. I can assure you, you rude little fear monger, that my son is charming, intelligent, and lovely. He also has nothing to do with this *Consortium* business, and quite frankly, if this murdering Thaden wants you dead for being an idiot who can't do a simple thing like hold onto a dangerous device without letting it fall into the hands of teenagers, then I say let him have you. We'll leave you tied up next to the giant flower in Central Park with a sign that says *free to an evil killer* and call it a night!" She was puffing with rage. I hadn't seen her yell like that since the last time my dad sent me my birthday present two months late.

"You can leave me in the park," Eric said, "but that won't keep your son alive. Thaden will kill anyone who's seen the phone."

"And how do you think he'll find us?" I said. "You think we'll leave a return address?"

Even as the words slipped from my mouth, the apartment grew cold. It was as though the air conditioner had turned on full blast, minus the noise. And the cold didn't invade all at once. It crept up my ankles, tingling my calves, making me shake before I knew I was afraid.

16

"They're here," Eric said, his voice wispy and terrified.

"Thaden." My chest iced up, like the magic in the air had imbued the very name with danger.

"The Ladies of the Consortium." Eric glared up at Devon. "You spoke to them. You told them about the phone."

"I lost them on the subway!" Devon shook his head, backing up into the corner.

"And you thought the Ladies wouldn't sniff you out?" Eric whispered as the mist around my feet stretched and thickened into billowing clouds.

"Guys, take my mom and Mrs. Mops and run!" I slid open the window that led to our ancient fire escape. I had never even been tempted to play on the rusted steps, but now they seemed safer than the mist that had crawled up to my knees.

"I'm not leaving you, Bryant." Mom took my shoulder.

"Neither are we," Elizabeth said.

"None of you can help," Eric said. "The best thing you can do is run. You could outlive him by a few hours if you go now."

"No!" my mother growled. "I will not leave my son!"

The door to the hall rattled on its hinges.

"Too late," Eric breathed as the door burst open. There was a blinding flash of blue light. I saw it coming for me, but my mother knocked me to the ground. I heard her grunt before she fell to the floor.

"Mom!" I screamed. But there were footsteps coming up the stairs. Slow, creeping footsteps. "Mom!"

"Stop them, Bryant!" Eric commanded, still bound to the paint-chipped chair. "Say *abalata!*"

"You say it!"

"You've tied me to a chair, Bryant. *Abalata* requires use of your hands," Eric explained with this false sort of calm that was scarier than his shouting had been.

I turned to the hall. There were shapes in the mist. White shapes with arms and faces.

"Now, Bryant!" Eric hollered.

"*Abalata!*" I shouted back so loudly, the word tore at my throat.

The black sprung out of my palm and stretched toward the mist. I thought it would pass straight through the white, but it made contact with something hard that shrieked as it tumbled backwards.

"She's breathing." Devon knelt by my mom.

"You two," Eric said to Devon and Elizabeth, "take Ms. Miller out of here."

"But those things..." Elizabeth's perfect face was nearly as white as the mist.

"Go the way you came in," I said, helping lift my mother into Devon's arms. He was so big, and she looked so tiny, lying still in his arms. "Get to the roof and then head for the street."

"What about you?" Elizabeth asked.

"We'll find you." I shoved them out the doors and to the roof steps, while the terrible feeling settled deep in my chest that I would never see them again.

Please let my mom be okay. If I can only have one thing, let her be okay.

"Block their path so the Ladies can't follow," Eric said.

"I don't know how." I shook my head. The mist was creeping up in the apartment again, this time churning like a stormy sea. And somehow I knew that meant the Ladies were angry. Like it was a fact written in a science book. The Ladies wanted me dead.

"Are they through?" Eric asked.

I nodded, unable to think of words to express, *yes, I've just sent my unconscious mother away.*

"*Portundo.*" The air shook with Eric's command.

I gasped and blinked at the place where Mom, Devon, and Elizabeth had disappeared only seconds before. Where there should have been a rusty door complete with broken alarm, there was nothing but solid wall.

"Let me out," Eric said as the mist turned cold again. "I've helped you. Now free me so I can fight. I will not die strapped to a chair."

"How do I know you won't run off and let the mist get me?" The words came out strangled, like my body was trying to keep the vapor from contaminating my lungs. "How do I know you won't just try and buy yourself a *few good days of happiness*?"

"There is a rather large difference between abandoning enemies and allies, however unwilling the allies might be."

"I let you go, we get out of this together, and you don't leave me here with them."

"I give you my oath as a wizard." Eric's words rung in the air as though he had shouted into an empty cavern.

"*Xorus.*" As soon as I said the word, the black lines around Eric dissolved, and in a second, he was standing. "We should go out the fire escape." I moved back toward the window.

"Never leave yourself hanging when the Ladies are coming for you." Eric sneered at the door.

"Then what do we do?" I asked as the shapes reformed in the mist.

"We fight our way out." Eric raised his hands, pressing his palms against the swirling white. "You know what, six spells?"

My mind raced. "Three that might be useful."

"Wonderful." Eric's voice turned strangely businesslike as fingers joined onto hands growing out of the mist. "Use them however you think won't end up getting either one of us killed."

"Right." I nodded as a face peered right at me from inside the haze. "*Abalata!*" The black sprung from my hand, but two other shouts echoed over mine as the black hit the white with a clang that echoed through the hall. The black ricocheted, striking the wall and crumbling the fake marble façade. A shriek of pain blared from within the mist as it clenched around me, pinning my legs together and drawing my arms to my sides.

"*Erunca,*" Eric shouted, and lightning struck from the ceiling.

"*Tudina,*" a high voice wailed from the mist.

"Duck!" Eric shouted.

A whooshing, whirring sound buzzed over my head as I ducked, screaming, "*Calimarta!*" before I even looked up.

A *crack* shook the hall like a bomb blast. And then everything was still for a moment. Like all of us had frozen, waiting to see what the noise could mean. But before I could take a breath, the ceiling crumbled on the stairs in front of me. Screams of pain and fear far more human than any sounds that had come from the mist before carried over the *crash* of falling debris.

I covered my head as dust and ceiling stuff fell. But a hand closed around my arm, dragging me forward and onto the rubble that had been the stairs to my home. We clambered as fast as we could over the bits of concrete and drywall. The lights of the skyscrapers beamed down on us from above. There was no more roof to keep Manhattan out of the building.

Mrs. Fortner is going to kill me. The irrational thought echoed through my head as we made it down the stairs to the landing.

Something white reached out of the thick chunks of concrete. An alabaster hand that curled its fingers in the air as though grasping for help. Or a fellow victim to drag down with it.

"Run faster!" Eric shouted, pulling me down another flight of stairs and then another. We were almost to the ground floor.

"Bryant Adams!" The voice shook the hall as we reached the lobby. "What in Hell's hot blazes were you doing on the top floor?" Mrs. Fortner took up most of the hall in a nightdress that looked more like a circus tent than a garment meant for a human. The bright red and yellow stripes added to the illusion. Hysteria bubbled up into my throat, and I was laughing. Not chuckling or giggling. Guffawing, like this was a funniest comedy shtick ever.

"Not now," Eric growled.

"Don't you walk out that door," Mrs. Fortner called after us. "You and your mother have been tenants for years, but I won't allow teenage shenanigans to ruin this building! I don't care if you always pay your rent two days early!"

Eric pulled me through the inside door. The lock clicked loudly behind us. But he had committed a cardinal Hell's Kitchen sin. He hadn't looked through the outside door before trapping us in the tiny vestibule. Waiting on the street was the woman we had seen walk into The Consortium. Her skin shone white in the orange of the streetlights. Mist flowed from her hair. And she was smiling as she stared at us through the glass.

I turned to the door behind us. Of course, the keys might have been handy.

"*Cliaxo!*" I shouted, but even as I did, the metal frame of the door melded into the walls. There was no more lock for me to jimmy. I turned to Eric. His eyes were trained on the woman outside.

"Why would you cross The Consortium?" Her voice filled the vestibule as though she were crammed in with us right behind my shoulder.

"I have crossed no one," Eric said.

"Thaden's device." The woman's mouth was moving even as she projected her voice. "He seeks to destroy The Consortium. And you aid him. You assist in his blasphemy."

"The Consortium is built upon knowledge," Eric said. "The phone would bring it to the masses."

"Masses for Thaden to control." The woman tipped her head to the side. "Masses that would rise up against The Consortium. That would bury in darkness the Ladies who have protected our kind for so long. Is that what you wish, Eric Deldridge? To have the Ladies sink into the earth? After all we have sacrificed to protect Magic and all its practitioners, you would draw the craft out of the shadows to destroy us?"

"I know nothing of Thaden's plans." Eric's voice was frighteningly even. "I would never cross The Consortium or the Ladies. Knowledge is my only pursuit."

"Then pursue it you shall. To the grave."

The back of my neck tingled as a high wispy voice filled the vestibule. I spun around. There was another Lady in the hall, this one older, her face sagging and ancient, her skin so white, it defied definition.

"You should have known better than to cross The Consortium, foolish child," agreed the sidewalk Lady. I looked back and forth between the two. We were trapped in my own doorway.

"May your eternal rest be filled with the peace of the darkness," both Ladies intoned as mist poured into the vestibule like water into a tank, sloshing around our ankles. A scent of fresh wild flowers drifted into my nose. If this was death, it wasn't so bad. Warmth and sleep.

"I didn't even think we'd make it down the stairs," Eric sighed, taking in a deep breath of the mist.

The stairs. I had sent my mother up the stairs. My mother, Elizabeth, Devon. The Ladies had scented out Devon. They would...

"*No!*" My scream echoed in the tiny space, making my ears ring. "I won't let you find them! *Aarantha!*"

Obediently, a cyclone formed, like the one in my dad's apartment, only smaller, much smaller. The mist swirled inches from my face, the wind grabbing the oxygen from my lungs. I didn't want it near me. I didn't want any of it near me.

I screamed in rage and fear, pressing my hands into the whirlwind. And the cyclone spread out. I gasped in clean air and kept pushing, the tornado whirling away, even when my fingers could no longer reach it. Right through the walls of the vestibule. Onto the street. The Ladies screamed as the tempest caught them. The mist in the wind thickened as though it had substance of its own.

"We need to get out of here!" Eric shouted over the clamor. He swung open the outer door, and I moved with him, keeping both of us in the eye of the cyclone. Together, we sprinted out into the night, the Ladies' shrieks morphing into howls of anger.

"Now what?" I asked.

"You drop the spell, and we run like hell," Eric said. "Follow me on three!"

"One."

I was going to chase a wizard into the night in Hell's Kitchen.

"Two."

There were probably worse choices I could make at night in Hell's Kitchen.

"Three!"

17

I dropped my hands as he said the word. Part of me expected the storm to keep blowing, for us to stay trapped by my own stupid magic. But the spell dissolved, and the mist shrunk into the night as I launched down 10th Avenue after Eric.

The people on the sidewalks stared at us as we ran. Stared behind us, too, so I chanced a glance back at my building. The façade was...well, kind of missing. The place looked like an open-front dollhouse. Mrs. O'Leery who lived on the second floor was in her giant underpants and pink hair curlers, staring out at the street below her, looking more annoyed than frightened. I caught a glimpse of Mrs. Mops glaring at me from what had been my living room before Eric dragged me around the corner and out of sight.

"We need to find Devon and Elizabeth," I puffed as we pelted toward the water. I wanted to say I needed to make sure my mother wasn't dead, but even thinking that felt like tempting fate.

"Where are they?" Eric asked, breathing easily even as we ran.

"No idea."

"Call them," Eric said as he led me through a creepy alley.

I reached into my pocket and pulled out my phone. Then forgot to breathe until I heard Devon's voice on the other end of the line.

"Are you alive?" he asked.

"No, I'm calling from beyond the grave," I snarked. "Is ah... everyone with you?"

We were running through a dirty hotel lobby now. Eric turned left and cut through the kitchen. The staff swore at us as we tore past.

"Elizabeth is here," Devon said, "and we have your mom. She's still breathing, but I can't wake her up."

Breathing was good. Breathing meant alive.

"Don't let them take her to a hospital," Eric said as we erupted onto the street, and I dutifully panted out the message.

"Yeah, okay," Devon said. "Tell Mr. Obvious we may not be able to use the stinkin' phone, but we're not stupid."

I relayed that, too, as we burst into a butcher shop and paused for a moment, backing out before the man chopping meat could tell us he was closed for the day.

"We need to meet them in a safe place," Eric said.

"And where would that be?" I asked as we sprinted down the street.

"Tell them to meet us at the waterline. Level with 40th," Eric said.

"Presumably with no further explanation from tall, scatter-brained, and pasty?" Devon growled on receiving *that* message. "Fine, bro. You do what you gotta do. The girls and I'll get there."

The phone beeped as he hung up.

It's not that I'm out of shape. I mean, I've never been an athlete, but I do gym and even tap class when my mother makes me feel guilty for having no theatrical talent. But chasing Eric through Midtown at night was on a whole new level. My legs seized up. My lungs burned. I thought I was going to throw up on my shoes. And still Eric ran, weaving circles toward the water. Uptown then downtown, inching around dumpsters.

If it weren't for the fact that at the end of this parkour session I would get to see the very three people in the world I actually cared about seeing, I would have sprawled out on the sidewalk and laid there until morning. Or until the Ladies got me. But I had to get to them. So I ran. And ran. And when I thought there was no way I could run anymore, we started running next to the water, and then Devon and Elizabeth came into sight, flanking a bench, and made all the running worth it.

"Where have you guys been?" Devon demanded as soon as we reached the pool of streetlamp light around the bench where my mom lay unconscious.

"Going around in circles," I puffed, but Elizabeth threw her arms around my neck before I could catch my breath enough to continue with, *because Eric is a sadist who wants to kill me.*

Elizabeth held me tightly. She smelled like heaven and didn't seem to mind that I was sweating worse than a kosher Jew holding cheese-covered bacon. "I thought you were dead," she whispered before Eric cut in, and no, he didn't sound out of breath at all.

"We were laying a trail for the Ladies to follow. If they scent every step we took, it should be long after the sun rises before they ever get here."

"Mom," I breathed, disengaging from Elizabeth to kneel next to her. She looked like she was sleeping. Like she was the cleanest, best dressed homeless person to call a park bench her bed. "What happened to her?"

"The Ladies tried to stop your heart." Eric squinted at my mom. "The spell didn't hit her properly. If we can get her to someone who can care for her, she should theoretically survive."

Theoretically.

"Okay, where are we going?" I lifted Mom into my arms. My muscles shook, and my legs burned like they would give out after the endless running.

"How sweet that you think you will carry her to safety," Eric said. "But that's no way to escape the Ladies."

"So, you run us all over town just so we get to live until morning and then get snuffed out by evil death-shooting mist?" Devon stepped in so he was close enough to punch Eric. "Wait and see if Ms. Miller gets to feeling better in this refreshing Hudson River night air? You know, I think I misjudged you, Eric. You're not only a murdering witch, you're also an optimist."

"I have never murdered anyone—" Eric began.

"So you're a failure, too," Devon said. "Well, keep trying, you might get it right." He didn't even flinch when I kicked him.

"And I have no intention," Eric continued, "of any of us waiting around for the Ladies to find us."

"So then, what do you have in mind?" I asked.

"We're going somewhere the Ladies can't scent us. You carry your mother, and I'll worry about the lot of us living until sunrise." Without a backwards glance, Eric turned and strode to the water's edge.

He stood squinting for a moment at the Hudson, as though trying to make out something in the reflection of the city lights. After a minute, when my arms were really starting to shake from holding my mom, he bent down and picked up a handful of pebbles. One at a time, aiming carefully, he threw them into the river.

"Can I ask why you're throwing stones into the river?" I grunted after another minute.

Eric worked his way south, moving one torturous step at a time. "To save all our lives," Eric said quietly, not stopping whatever passed for his progress.

"Are they magic stones?" Devon lifted Mom easily from my

arms. "Do they smell like you? Are they leading *the Ladies* off our scent?"

"No," Eric said, supremely unbothered by the snide tone. "I left myself an escape route a few years ago, and quite frankly, this whole park looks the same, so it can be difficult to find things you've hidden."

Devon opened his mouth to snark at Eric again, but I socked him in the arm, carefully avoiding Mom's head.

We walked for another minute, listening to the tiny splashes barely audible over the nighttime hum of the city and the lapping of the river.

But then, when I was finally sure the shadows under the park benches would rise up and go for our throats, Eric threw a stone and there was no tiny *splash*. Instead there was a dull *thud*.

Eric's face split into a smile. He threw another, bigger rock, and there was another, bigger *thud*. Then the rock disappeared. No ripple in the water. No hovering in midair. It was gone.

"Perfect," Eric said. "*Todunis elarus promotus.*"

His voice rang strangely in the night, and before I could shake the tingle from my spine, a boat wove itself into existence in front of us. Not like a canoe or a yacht. It was one of those little sailboats that have just enough room on them for a bed and a sink below deck. The ones people claim to live on, even though they're smaller than the tiniest New York apartment.

"Wow," Elizabeth breathed.

"If you don't mind," Eric said, gesturing to the boat, "I think we should all get aboard. Right now." He stomped twice on the bank, and a slat of wood appeared, making a gangplank.

"And what's to guarantee you don't throw us overboard and watch us drown?" Devon asked, his voice shaking so slightly I could barely hear it as he glanced between the open water and Eric.

Eric tipped his head to the side, examining Devon. "Well, I

suppose you could go for mutual benefit. The exquisitely correct *the enemy of my enemy is my friend.* There are two different groups who would like us indiscriminately eradicated, and survival is seemingly in all of our best interests. But then there is the cold, hard truth." Eric turned to me. "Bryant saved my life. He could have left me for the Ladies to kill, but he didn't. A debt like that has to be paid. I always honor my debts."

"We're supposed to believe you're a good guy now because Bryant didn't leave you to die?" Elizabeth asked.

"I never said I was good." Eric pinned me with his creepy, blue eyes. "I said I always honor my debts. I know enough to understand that if I let the Ladies hurt you, the world will exact a far greater payment than my trying to keep you alive will cost me."

"And if we all die together in your boat?" Elizabeth asked.

"Then I will die with a clean slate." Eric turned and walked onto the boat, his shoes making an odd, hollow sound as he crossed the plank. "Better that than to live owing fate." He didn't turn around until he was on the deck of the boat. "We're in this together, whether we like it or not. Now, shall we idle in the dark, waiting for the Ladies to follow our trail, or attempt to survive?"

Devon and Elizabeth both looked at me like they were waiting for me to make a decision. My mom was unconscious in Devon's arms, and there were mist Ladies coming to kill us. Taking a deep breath and hoping I looked brave, I stepped out onto the plank and crossed onto the wooden sailboat floating in the Hudson.

18

A s soon as I was onboard, Devon followed, and then Elizabeth. She didn't take her eyes off Eric as she walked onto the boat. It was like she was daring him to drop her into the water.

I helped Devon lay my mom down on the deck, moving rocks and garbage out of the way.

"Typical New Yorkers," Eric said, punting the beer cans and burger wrappers overboard, "tossing things into the river and not worrying about what the river will do to them in return." He grabbed a rope I hadn't noticed before, leading from the bow to the shore before disappearing into nothingness.

"But didn't you just kick garbage into the river?" Elizabeth took off her bag and knelt, wedging it under Mom's head as a pillow.

Tears burned in the corners of my eyes.

"Occasionally, when one is fleeing for one's life"—Eric gave the rope a giant tug, pulling it free from the rocks on the shore. The rope hit the Hudson with a *splash*—"concerns like properly preserving one's environment must be left behind. As excellently demonstrated by Bryant when he destroyed both his parents' homes today."

I wanted to say something about how it was all his fault any of it had happened in the first place, but I couldn't move past the rope he was hauling onto the boat. It was at least fifteen feet long, even though only six feet of it had been visible a minute before, and it was landing on the deck bone-dry and clean.

"Creepy," I muttered as Eric grabbed the rudder and steered us out onto the open river, no sail catching the stinking wind or whirring motor pushing us forward.

"The Ladies can't find us out here?" Devon asked. "Does mist hate water or something?"

"The Ladies track by scent," Eric said. "You can't scent on the water."

He looked antique standing on the stern, the rudder in hand, the wind blowing his coat and hair around like he was some kind of hero.

"So, we going someplace?" Devon asked, crossing his arms and glaring at Eric. "Fun as this is, we can't stay out here forever."

"We're going someplace they can fix my mom." My voice sounded low and hollow even to my own ears. "Someone can fix her, right?"

"There is a place," Eric said, not unkindly. "It might not be pleasant, but she should be able to help your mother, and The Ladies would have to be desperate to enter there."

I nodded. I wanted to say thanks or something about how if they couldn't fix my mom, I would kill him, but all that came out was, "It's not fair. She wasn't supposed to be in the apartment. She wasn't supposed to have anything to do with this."

Elizabeth wrapped her arms around me, laying her head on my chest. Somehow that made me feel even more helpless.

"Life isn't fair." Eric's voice was barely loud enough to carry over the lapping of the river against the boat. "Magic isn't fair, and fate has definitely never been called fair."

"Fate?" Devon pushed out an angry laugh. "It's got nothing to do with fate. It has to do with you holding Ms. Miller hostage."

"I thought her son was a thief." Eric shrugged. "I was mistaken. But your mother going back for the cat. The Ladies showing up just as we might have come to a peaceful understanding. The strings of fate will draw the things you need close to you at the right moment and pull safety from you just when you think it is near. It's that way in all the world, but the strings are wound tighter when you walk in the world of magic."

"So this sort of thing happens to you all the time?" I asked, too upset to even worry that my voice went all crackly. "You get chased around and blow things up and try to get yourself killed? This is a normal Saturday night for you?"

Eric smiled, suddenly looking younger, like he was barely out of high school. "Exactly."

"This is crazy," I said.

"Crazier than figuring out you're a wizard because you found a phone in a taxi cab?" Eric raised one black eyebrow. It was freaky how the other one didn't even move. "Sometimes the most absurd things in life are the most valid."

We were out in the middle of the river now. It was bright where we were, the lights of New York City on one side and Jersey City on the other.

"So a magic cellphone that destroyed my life is the most valid thing in the world? That's great, just great." I squeezed my head in my hands, wanting to squeeze the past two days right out of existence. Or, just for the pounding in my head to stop, I wasn't picky.

"No, it's valid that the phone found you so you could find your magic," Eric said, sounding like he was explaining to me that morning was when it got bright out.

"To destroy my life, more like." I pulled the solid black culprit out of my pocket. "I could throw it overboard. I should have done that in the beginning, damn piece of magic crap."

"Perhaps." Eric shrugged. "But it's far too late now. The Ladies know we have it, and getting rid of it will only leave us one less card in hand. And by the way, the phone's not magic."

"Is too." I pressed my thumb to the button and watching the screen light up.

"How very mature." Eric snorted as he steered us south toward the tip of Manhattan. "Be that as it may, you are a wizard. *You* possess magic. The phone recognizes it, so it can turn on."

"I am not a wizard!" I shouted, making Eric raise one black eyebrow at me again. "I'm not magical. I'm Bryant Jameson Adams from Hell's Kitchen, and there is nothing extraordinary about my life. Or at least there wasn't until you dragged fate and this magical cellphone freak show into it, and made it all...freaky!"

"You are a wizard." Eric spoke calmly as though I hadn't been screaming at all. "And you were born a wizard. Magic always pounded through your veins, but you never had the cause to feel it. Many are born with magic—fate simply never asks them to use it."

"But my parents are normal." I tried to shout again, but it came out more like a whimper. "I mean, really weird, but normal. I'm not magical."

"You are, Bryant," Elizabeth whispered. "Listen to him."

"Listen to him say what? That the evil lunch lady could be a witch if life had only given her a shove in that direction?"

"I've never met your lunch lady, but yes, that does seem to be the right idea." Eric nodded.

"And when the lunch lady accidentally uses magic to light the cafeteria on fire?' I squeaked.

"If that were to happen, I would assume it would mean she

had figured it out." Eric shrugged, like burning down another chunk of my school would be no big deal.

"Wouldn't it be better for you to, I don't know, warn people they have magic superpowers before it turns their lives into flaming death holes?" Devon asked.

"Not at all," Eric said. "At least not for those of us who already live in the mystery that is magic. No one has time to hunt down everyone who might one day produce a spell or two, and the overcrowding would be terrible."

"So burning your way into magic it is," Devon said.

Eric pursed his lips. "I prefer the term *trial by fire.*"

"So if you hadn't been an asshat who lost his phone, I could have lived my life as a perfectly normal, completely invisible guy who no one cares about enough to kill." I reached over and touched my mom's hand. She always hated it when I called myself *normal.*

"If by normal you mean toiled in anonymity, yes," Eric said. "But you still would have held magic inside of you, and if fate wants you to leap in blindly now, it probably would have happened even if I had chosen to walk to The Consortium that night. Fate will have its way. The phone just so happened to be the stone that got thrown into your path. Extraordinary though it may be, you are the one who wields it. What's inside the phone is nothing more than a digital library with a few bells and whistles—"

"And by whistles you mean tornados that destroy penthouses." Elizabeth held my mom's other hand.

My heart swelled a little, and my throat got tight.

"Cyclones, yes, and fire," Eric said, blithely ignoring the whole *destroyed my dad's place with a twister worthy of Oz* part. "There's also a section for potions. Using digital ingredients, of course. I must admit, I never really got around to testing that portion. I've never really been one for potions myself."

"And you put all sorts of spells, and"—I forced myself to say the word—"potion things on a pyromaniac's dream device? Who thought that was a good idea?"

"Thaden," Eric said simply.

As he spoke the name, a cold breeze blew across the deck of the boat.

"Why does that keep happening?" I asked as a shiver ran down my spine.

"Please don't say fate," Devon interrupted as Eric opened his mouth.

Eric shrugged and stayed silent.

"Why would Thaden—" I waited for the gust of wind, but there was nothing more than the constant airstream over the river. Maybe I wasn't important enough for fate to send breezes at. "Why would he want to put all that on a cellphone?"

"That's a very long and complicated tale, which involves a bit of sordid history of wizard-dom, and years of a quietly waged war filled with shadows and deeply hidden magic," Eric said.

"We seem to have time while we run for our lives from the mist sisters." Devon leaned back on his arms. "Please, do tell," he added in a formal tone, mimicking how Eric spoke. If I hadn't been terrified and tired, it might have been funny.

"Their preferred term is the Ladies." Eric twisted the rudder, correcting the course toward Manhattan. "And I'm afraid we don't have time, as we're nearing our destination, and I'm sure Bryant will want to get his mother into Lola's care as quickly as possible."

"Who's Lola?"

Eric didn't answer my question as he ran up the nose of the boat and lifted the long, coiled line. I looked back at the rudder. It was moving like Eric was still holding it, steering us toward the shore.

"This is too damn weird," Devon muttered as he followed my gaze.

There was a grunt from the bow as, with a giant heave, Eric tossed the rope to shore, where it connected to the giant stone blocks as though pulled by a magnet, and began to haul us in. But the rope didn't get slack or coil up. The rock absorbed the rope, sucking it in like a kid slurping spaghetti.

"Too damn weird." I nodded to Devon.

With a hollow *thunk*, the boat knocked into the stones.

"If one of you wouldn't mind carrying Ms. Miller." Eric stomped on the deck and the plank appeared, making a way for us to climb ashore. He was on land in two quick strides, and stood, his arms behind his back, studying the night, not bothering to make sure we'd followed.

"I really don't like that guy," Devon said as he picked my mom up and carried her off.

I had always sort of hated Devon a little for having an awkwardly gangly stage that lasted approximately seventeen days during July of the summer before 7th grade. But having a best friend who could easily cart around your unconscious mother was bound to come in handy eventually.

It wasn't until I had followed Elizabeth onto solid ground that I really looked around at where we were. I guess I was expecting a wharf or a dock or something. But we were near an overpass. The stink of the river and the stench of rotting trash were mingling together in a horrible combo that made me want to add eau de vomit to the mix.

"This way." Eric started along the water toward the overpass while his boat disappeared.

Cardboard boxes, old shipping palates, and torn up tents had been turned into shelters flanking the concrete wall, which rose up to form one of the supports for the road twenty feet overhead.

Eric led us toward the tent city, not slowing at all when the residents started inching out of their sad shelters. A dozen dirty faces stared at us.

When we neared the first tent, the people rose up, all silently facing us like something out of a horror movie. Elizabeth gasped, and I reached out without thinking, taking her trembling hand in mine.

The big man closest to us raised an arm, blocking Eric's path, glaring silently.

"I'm here to see Lola." Eric's voice sounded calm, steady, but I wished I could see his face to know if he really wasn't afraid as the tent dwellers all walked toward us.

I slid sideways a few inches, trying to hide Elizabeth behind me.

"We've met many times, remember? Lola is an old friend. I'm having a rather trying evening, and this woman"—Eric gestured to my mom—"is in need of Lola's help. Tell her Eric Deldridge would love to pay her a call and see if she is up to company. I'm happy to wait."

The big guy nodded to a kid behind him, and the boy shimmied up the slope of the concrete wall like it was nothing. At the top of the wall, he blended into the shadows.

We waited silently, the homeless staring at us, us staring at them.

The big guy was probably about the same age as my mom, but he wasn't the oldest person by a long shot. There was a shriveled old lady whose skin sagged away from her tiny frame. I think the youngest was probably the kid who had run up the wall. He couldn't have been more than ten.

I wanted to say something like *I can look up a food pantry for you.* Or better yet, *when my mom's better, she'll make you all dinner.* But somehow it felt like talking might break the spell that was the silent truce Eric had made with them.

It seemed like forever but was probably only a few minutes before the boy sprinted back down the wall, right to where the big guy could see him, and silently nodded. The man nodded back, and as though he had given an order, the people all crawled back into their sad homes. In less than a minute, we were standing alone in the tent city.

"What was that?" I whispered as soon as I figured out how to talk again.

"Lola's guard." Eric started forward, walking the same path the boy had run.

"Those people are her guards?" Devon whispered.

Elizabeth gripped my hand like she was terrified she'd get dragged into one of the tents.

"Those weren't people," Eric said.

"Just because they're homeless—" Devon started.

"I mean they aren't human." Eric threw over his shoulder as he leapt onto the steep wall.

"What are they?" I looked back at the still tents.

"Some of Lola's secrets are best not spoken of in darkness." Eric reached the top of the wall near the shadow.

I took two steps up to get above Devon so I could help him carry my mom, but climbing here wasn't like climbing at all. I took another step forward. My eyes told me I was scaling a nearly vertical wall, but my legs and my balance told me I was on a flat surface.

"Whoa," Devon murmured behind me.

I wanted to turn around to make sure he was okay, but this really was like navigating a funhouse tunnel. It was all I could do just to stay upright and slog one foot in front of the other.

With a sudden movement that made my head spin, Elizabeth let go of my hand and ran past me. I looked up to the top of the wall, and she was standing there next to Eric. I swayed trying to look up/out at them.

"Take it at a run," Elizabeth said. "It's a lot better at a run."

Devon took her at her word.

I took a deep breath and thumped after him. Elizabeth was right, faster was better. My feet didn't have time to notice they weren't where my eyes thought they should be. And before I could freak out about how weird the whole thing was, I was on the ledge at the top, between Eric and Elizabeth.

"Well done." Eric's gaze searched Elizabeth's eyes before he turned and walked off into darkness.

"Allons-y!" I plunged into shadows after him. Unable to see an inch past my nose, I held my hands out, expecting metal or concrete. But there was nothing.

"Bryant," Elizabeth whispered behind me.

I reached back and squeezed her fingers, still forcing myself forward, my free hand stretched out, looking for solid wall.

After a few more steps, my heart jumped up into my throat. This was a trap. Eric had tricked us, and now we were going to be stuck wandering in the darkness forever.

"Don't worry, love," a light voice with a deep resonance purred right in front of me. I stopped and felt Devon smack into my back. "Two more steps, and you'll be out of the dark."

Reaching my toe out in front of me to make sure there was solid ground, I edged forward.

The voice laughed lightly at me.

Taking a deep breath and squaring my shoulders, I forced myself toward the voice.

19

L ight filled my eyes, revealing a space so strange, I had to blink for a few seconds to make sure I was properly seeing what was around me.

There were no windows in the room. All the light came from six mismatched lanterns hung from the ceiling, their flickering flames casting the place in a warm glow. Not that it really needed a warm glow. Every surface was colorful. The table in the middle was draped in purple cloth, which looked soft enough to curl up on and sleep right between the steaming pot of tea and the bowl of skittles that sat out like an interrupted midnight snack.

There were big armchairs and fainting couches scattered around the room in no order I could see. Long strips of fabric in every jewel tone I had ever heard of covered the walls, leaving no trace of a door to anywhere else.

I turned to look for Devon and Elizabeth. They were both behind me, Devon still carrying my mother. And staring down into my mother's face was a very...striking woman.

She had dark skin and high cheekbones to go with her angular jaw. Her long black eyelashes fanned out like flying butterflies when she blinked, and shimmering eye shadow reached gracefully up to her perfectly shaped brows. Her lips were painted on like a showgirl's, and she wore a turban on her head with a jeweled clip attached to the front.

The woman reached out to touch my mom's face with her long, deep-purple nails.

"Don't touch her," I spat automatically, shouldering forward.

"Now, love," the woman said, smiling gently at me, "how on earth am I supposed to heal your mother without touchin' her?" She raised one highly arched eyebrow.

Was that like a thing with magic people? Did they go to eyebrow raising school? *Lesson one—How to control magical fire. Lesson two—How to do a perfect skeptical/creepy eyebrow raise.*

"You'll have to forgive Bryant, Lola." Eric stepped in, though I hadn't seen him in the room before. "He's only been a part of our little circle for two days now and has had rather a rough time of it."

"Looks like it," Lola said. "Anyone who ends up finding a way to see me this quick is clearly fated for somethin'." She started toward the table in the center of the room before looking back at me. "I'm not sayin' what that somethin' is, but I don't think you'll ever have to worry about your life being boring. Good Lord, I should've known this day was going to be long when Beville started shakin' badly enough for the folks topside to notice."

I wanted to ask what Beville was, why it was shaking, and what that had to do with my mom. Not to mention if I didn't have to worry about being bored because I was suddenly going to become ridiculously cool and have awesome adventures or because I was going to be killed by the Ladies come morning, but something in the air made me afraid to ask.

"Lay the poor mama down." Lola patted one of the fainting couches.

Devon looked at me, and I nodded. He walked over and carefully laid my mom down. When he stood up, Lola caught his chin in her hand.

She stood for a moment, staring deep into his eyes. "Well, now, that is a twist. Haven't seen one like him in ages." She turned back to my mother, leaving Devon looking stunned.

"It always is the mama," Lola said like she hadn't done anything weird. But then maybe to her, calling my friend a twist was normal. "I know it's because they all love their babies so much, they would do anything to protect them. But then if the kids manage to survive whatever the mama was trying to protect them from, they come dump a dying mama on my sofa."

"She's not dying," I growled, quivering with an almost physical need to run to my mom and shake her, make her wake up and tell Lola to stop being creepy.

"Oh, this mama's not, love," Lola said. "But if you keep her tangled up in your mess, it's only a matter of time before you haul her back here with a problem I can't fix. Mamas with no magic don't last long when fate pushes their babies around in the world. A mama's love is strong, but there is nothing as strong as fate."

"So, you can fix her?" Elizabeth asked. I was grateful she said it. My head was spinning too fast to make words other than *Fix* and *now*.

"This time, sugar." Lola walked to the table and started pouring cups of tea. "You all want cream and sugar?"

"Can't we have tea after you fix Ms. Miller?" Devon said.

Lola turned to examine him again.

"Sweetie, I think I like you. But there are some types of magic I prefer only to play with when the sun shines. So we might as well have a nice cuppa and a snack while we wait for sunrise."

It wasn't until Lola mentioned food that I realized how

desperately hungry I was. Right on cue, my stomach made a horrible, embarrassing grumbling sound.

"Next time you take people on the run"—Lola rounded on Eric—"you should pack some snacks. I swear you are going to end up eating me right out of house and home."

"Why pack snacks when your food is better?" Eric winked.

Lola smiled and walked over to the emerald green curtain and disappeared through it. And I don't mean pushed it aside. She walked through it like it wasn't there.

"What is she?" I whispered, staring at the fabric, which hung motionless though a person had just disappeared through it.

"Lola is..." Eric sat down in one of the comfy chairs, rubbing his chin. "Well, since you're completely unaware of how the hierarchy of magic works..."

"Thanks," I grumbled.

"It would be easiest to classify her as a seer, a bit of a black market healer, and a witch, of course," Eric said. "She's never quite fit into the binary mold, has excellent taste is cheese, and is also one of the finest people I know."

"Then why is she living like a bridge troll?" Elizabeth asked.

"I'm the most fabulous troll I've ever heard of," Lola said from right behind my shoulder.

I spun around and nearly knocked the tray out of her hands.

"I-I'm sorry," Elizabeth sputtered, "I meant no disrespect."

"Sugar," Lola laughed, setting down the tray and taking Elizabeth's face in her hands, "don't you ever be sorry for seeing things in this world for what they really are. Some folks will hate you for it, but the truth that lies underneath always comes out in the end. I should know. I've paid my fair share for seeing the truth."

"For being a psychic?" Devon asked.

"Psychic?" Lola quirked that eyebrow of hers. "The things those city folks stuff in their children's heads! I don't see the future. That would be like trying to read a book the author hasn't finished yet. I see what hides in the shadows. In the deep tunnels under the city and in the darkest places of a man's heart." Lola's eyes pinned Eric's for a long moment before she turned to me. "And sometimes people who are scared of what they want to keep hidden, they try to hide you. But exile isn't so bad."

Lola went back to the table and poured herself a cup of tea before settling down in a blood-red armchair.

Elizabeth, Devon, and I all stood still, watching her take slow sips.

"I thought you lot were hungry?" she said after a minute. "Eat, my little refugees, eat."

I glanced at the silver tray. There were still the skittles and the tea, but it was also now laid out with cheese, meat, and olives.

"Some things never change." Eric snagged a few cubes of cheese. "Not that I would ever want them to."

I poured myself a cup and covered the saucer with bits of cheese and meat, then plopped down at my mom's feet. Even though she was unconscious, it felt better to be near her, like somehow she could keep me safe from whatever hid beyond the drapes on Lola's walls.

We sat quietly for a few minutes, me wishing there was a clock ticking nearby if only to make the silence less complete.

"You were banished?" Elizabeth asked, staring down at the untouched cup she had balanced on her lap.

"I was," Lola said.

"Is that why," Elizabeth said slowly, like she was testing waters, "you're so...colorful? I mean not"—she glanced at Eric—"bleached out like this guy. And the Ladies."

Lola tipped her head back and laughed. "Oh sugar, you are smart. I have never allowed myself to turn into one of those color-challenged witches, not even before I was banned. But my darlin' Eric likes to wrap himself up so deep in magic, it pulls bits of him away, starting with color."

"I used to have freckles." Eric made a little moue, whether of regret or disgust I couldn't say.

Lola took a long sip of tea. "And those Ladies hell-bent on killing all you hold dear, love"—she looked right at me, her eyes boring holes into mine—"they've pushed magic further than it was ever meant to go. So white mist is all that's left of them."

"So using magic steals the color out of you?" Devon asked, an olive paused half-way to his mouth.

"The black, the white, hell, my fabulous lair, it's only an outward sign of the magic within. Like playing with finger paint too long, some of it is bound to get stuck to your skin."

"Am I going to change like that?" I said, relieved that for once my voice didn't wobble.

"You'd have to live through the weekend first." Eric grimaced, and Lola tossed a green skittle that hit him right in the temple.

"You would never get all scary white like the Ladies, love." Lola squinted at me appraisingly. "But if things go well, that charming brown hair of yours might darken up a bit. Don't worry though, you'll still be a handsome little thing. Now eat, eat! I lay out food for the famished masses, and everyone is talking instead of gobbling it up. Explaining the whole colorful spectrum that is magic, my, that would take days, and we do not have that kind of time."

Silence filled the room again. I munched on cheese and meat, waiting for it to be okay with Lola to speak again. She didn't say anything until the whole silver tray was empty.

"All right, now that everyone has been fed, and we all feel like good ole friends, darling, how about you tell me what sort of shit storm you dragged through my front door." Lola turned to

Eric. "I've got a damaged mama, a boy who's just figured out he's got magic in him, one that fate just can't wait to get its hands on, and one that will change the way fate works. I'm feeding very confused teenagers who don't know which end is up and which end gets them dead. You know I love you, darlin', but this one is going to take some explainin'."

Eric took a deep breath and put his cup down on the table.

"Do you remember—"

"When your *friend* Keadred Thaden asked you for a little favor?" Lola said. "I remember telling you to steer clear of the hurricane that man is trying to stir up."

I waited for the ominous wind or creepy goosebumps which usually accompanied Thaden's name, but just my luck, there was nothing. Still, Lola pointed to me.

"Even little love new wizard here knows enough to be scared of Thaden. You should learn from the new kid, darling. At this point he might outlive you."

"There wasn't any creepy wind that time," I said.

"You invoke an evil man, and yes, darling"—she glanced over at Eric—"Keadred Thaden is evil, but saying his name isn't going to get you a big movie style *dun-dun-bwa-na*," Lola sang. "It *will* invite some bad strings into the web of fate. You aren't going to feel all creepy every time you mention the evil unmentionable, 'cause that fate has already crept in the back door. He doesn't need to announce himself again."

"If Thaden is so evil"—Elizabeth leaned forward to swipe more skittles from the bowl, which didn't seem to have emptied at all—"why would anyone want to get involved with him?"

"I would love to hear the answer to that question." Lola leaned back in her chair and crossed her legs, staring at Eric.

"Can't you see the answer?" Eric smiled, but it looked like he didn't mean the smile. Like he was trying hard to be suave but it wasn't worth the effort.

"What I see and what you believe don't always line up, darling. If it did, you wouldn't be in this mess." Lola took a sip of her tea and waited, her gaze fixed on Eric.

"Just because Thaden is evil doesn't mean he's the worst thing in this city," he said with a hint of pleading in his voice. "Thaden may be dangerous and heartless, but at least he believes in freedom. The way things are now, we all live in shadow, constantly afraid to stick a toe out of line. In Beville, no one even dares to speak against the system. Anyone who is deemed other—"

"Gets a nice taste of banishment?" Lola's eyebrow rose again. "Darling, I know."

"Precisely!" The entreaty in Eric's voice morphed into anger. "We should be free to live our lives away from The Consortium's rules. Magic shouldn't be doled out based on favor."

"And we should all ride unicorns in Times Square." Lola sighed. "Darling, even if The Consortium didn't control the pages, someone else would step in with a system we would all grow to hate just as much. And some of those someones would leave us with an even bloodier mess than we're already stuck in. There is no such thing as a true Utopia. I've read the book. It had *slaves*."

"I'm sorry." My head spun. Maybe it was because I was tired. Maybe it was because I had no idea what they were talking about. "Can someone please take me through why the evil dude who wants to kill us is better than the evil Ladies who want to kill us? It sounds sexist, but I don't think that's what you're talking about."

Lola waved a hand at Eric. He leaned forward in his chair and locked his creepy, blue eyes on mine.

"Magic is controlled by The Consortium. That restaurant your friend so brazenly walked into is the only outpost of magic aboveground in New York. The Ladies control The Consortium.

The Consortium controls all the spell books, and with them all knowledge of magic. If you want a spell to do something, you have to petition the Ladies for it. And they dole out spells in the most perverse and miserly way. It keeps us under their thumbs. Experimenting is banned by penalty of death. Searching for lost knowledge is banned by penalty of banishment. So, we all exist by The Consortium's will.

"Except Thaden. He's buried himself so far in the darkness, even the Ladies won't follow him. He doesn't want The Consortium to lord over all of us, hiding that which is essentially our birthright. So, he came up with the idea of the phone. The entire contents of The Consortium's archives on one, normal-looking portable without any of the rules of impartment the Ladies have forced upon us. The knowledge of centuries right in your pocket. Freedom. Gaining the spells from the Ladies was...difficult."

"You mean stealin' the spells, darling—"

"And creating a way around impartment was worse," Eric pressed on. "But Thaden created the phone. His greatest weapon, a way to equip the wizard masses to fight the Ladies."

"And those masses end up beholden to Thaden," Lola finished. "Which made this *such* a grand idea you agreed to help him with it?"

"I thought I was helping us all." Eric pinched the bridge of his nose, scrunching his eyes. "I thought I was standing at the front of a fight for all our freedoms. But the phones were only ever meant for those who would serve as his henchmen, helping him build an army that wouldn't be offering anything but a new name for oppression. I wasn't serving freedom, only darkness."

"And it took getting wasted and losing the item of doom to figure out you weren't exactly working with the angels?" Devon asked. "Great, just great."

"First, I have never pretended to be a hero," Eric said flatly.

"Second, not that it's any of your business, but it wasn't until I had gained his confidence, to whatever extent, that I quite realized the endgame."

"Did you really think you would come out of this in one breathing piece?" Lola asked.

"Better to die free than to live oppressed. No matter the face of the oppressor," Eric said, "and with friends like you, Lola, perhaps I stand a chance."

"You're not going to have friends long if you get everyone who likes you even a little killed, darling. You come to me lookin' for miracles, and I only deal in magic." Lola sighed. "Darling, you took a shiny piece of forbidden skittles from a monster, and you lost the damn pack. I can't save you from this one."

Elizabeth froze with her hand halfway to her mouth with another batch of skittles.

"I was talking metaphorical skittles." Lola turned to Elizabeth even though she couldn't have seen her freeze. "I don't believe in enchanting food. A world where you aren't even safe to eat something sweet? That's a world I don't want to live in, sugar."

Elizabeth turned bright red as she popped the skittles into her mouth. Somehow her blushing made her even more beautiful. "Thanks."

"So, now that you made friends with the hornet and went and kicked in the side of his nest, what exactly do you plan on doing, darling?" Lola confronted Eric again.

"Not dying was really where I was starting from." Eric took a slow sip of tea. "And considering we all made it here, I'd say we're doing pretty well so far."

"Don't say things like that, darling." Lola looked to the bit of fabric we had all entered through. "You don't want fate to decide she needs to prove you wrong."

"And what do you think we should do?" Eric asked. "You

know more about everything in this city than I ever could hope to."

"And you know flattery will get you just about anywhere with Lola." She rolled her eyes and walked over to the nearest lamp.

I hadn't noticed until then that she was wearing glittering, six-inch heels. They were blue, green, purple, red, and as she moved, the way the colors danced was mesmerizing. Even when she stopped, I couldn't look away until she spoke.

"Thaden is buried deep in the darkest places where the mist doesn't go." She was staring into the flames of one of the lanterns. It was like she was reading the fire as it danced. "He doesn't want to come up to the light, the Ladies don't want to go down to the dark."

"So, I should stay in the middle?" Eric joined Lola by the lamp, staring into the flames over her shoulder. But somehow the way he looked at them was different than the way she did. With him, it was like he was puzzling out a book in a language he couldn't read.

"The middle—where it ends." Lola's voice dropped two octaves. The glorious woman had been replaced by a sad and ancient man. "The middle is where you get penned in. Trapped like a pig for slaughter."

The room was silent for a moment. Funeral silent.

"The only way forward is down," Lola murmured. "Go into the dark and drag the light down after you. You can't fight in the city where the light rules, or down in the pits where Thaden reigns. But if you fight in the middle, even the shadows don't know what will happen." A tear rolled down Lola's cheek.

"A chance is better than death." Eric smiled.

"Not for the ones left waiting and banished," Lola whispered.

Eric reached out and took her hand. "You know I've always been good at fighting. It's one of my better features."

"Most people don't consider their better feature something that's likely to get them killed every other month." Lola and Eric stood silently for a moment.

Part of me wanted to leave them to...whatever this was, but my mother was unconscious on the couch, and I didn't know how to get out of the room without going back through the non-human, homeless guards anyway.

"Now then, everybody's had a snack, you might as well get a little sleep," Lola said, all traces of fear and sadness gone. "I won't be able to get to work on mama for a few hours, and rest is exactly what Lola's ordered. Come on, littlelings." She nodded toward the right wall, the one opposite where she had gone for the snacks. "You walk right through the blue strip, you'll find a nice, cozy place to sleep. Mama can rest on the couch till sunrise."

I stood up and walked over to the blue cloth. The color was somewhere between sapphire and the dusky shade of the ocean at sunset. I checked to make sure Elizabeth and Devon were behind me before girding my loins.

"I'll wake y'all up in the morning," Lola called after me as I stepped through the curtain.

20

I t felt more like pushing through a cobweb than anything else. The fabric dragged along my face, but it didn't stop me or cling. It was just there, a light thing caught on my nose. Then I took another step, and it was gone. Everything had gone dim for a moment while I walked through the curtain, but once I was past, I was in another room.

There was one light that looked like a giant, glittering chandelier in the middle. Tiny candles burned all over it. But instead of there being clear, diamond-ish hangings, this chandelier was hung with reds, blues, purples, and greens that threw off dancing reflections on the walls as the flames flickered through the crystals.

"Wow," I breathed. It was like Fourth of July fireworks made babies with a laser show.

"I call right side," Devon said from behind me.

It took me a minute to realize what he was talking about. The only furniture in the room was a king-size bed.

"What?" Devon asked when I spun to look at him. "I always sleep on my right so I can see my alarm clock."

"Whatever makes you happy," Elizabeth mumbled, almost falling on the left side of the bed. "As long as no one tries to light me on fire, chase me, or kill me with mist, I'm good."

Which left me to crawl up the middle.

I kicked off my shoes and scrambled up from the foot of the bed, trying not to make it bounce too much since Devon and Elizabeth seemed to have conked out already.

I knelt on top of the sheets. They were soft and silky. I yawned, and then, *You'll be under these sheets with Elizabeth*, a terrified voice in the back of my head said.

You're running for your life from the Ladies who control the magic books and the dude who believes in free knowledge because they all want to kill you. Where you sleep really shouldn't be a priority, the other voice sighed.

It doesn't matter. She held your hand. She thinks you're brave, the first voice crowed.

I lay down, staring at the back of Elizabeth's head.

Brave doesn't mean she would date you. You don't even know if wizards date, the second voice said.

She thinks you're brave. She doesn't want you dead. She even held your hand.

I slipped into sleep before my brain could finish duking it out.

———

"Where's Elizabeth?" Devon's question yanked me into the waking world.

"Wha d'ya mean?" I sat up, blinking at the colorful lights that still danced on the walls. Everything looked the same as when I had drifted to sleep. But Elizabeth was gone. The covers on her side of the bed had been thrown back.

I swore so badly Devon muttered, "Damn, dude."

"Let's go." I pushed myself to the bottom of the bed and slipped on my sneakers. Part of me wanted to pull the phone out of my pocket. But somehow I didn't think picking a spell at random would really help if Lola wanted to keep us separated and trapped here.

I held my breath as I stepped into the blue fabric, half-expecting to be stuck in its folds for the rest of my life. But I passed back out into the front room as easily as I had left it.

Elizabeth was sitting on the red fainting couch next to Lola with her back to me.

"I still don't see why this has anything to do with me," she said, unsteadily lowering her teacup onto its saucer.

"It's the seeing that got you tangled up in all this." Lola wrapped her arm around Elizabeth's shoulders. "And don't worry, it's not all living like a bridge troll with fabulous shoes. You're not magic, Sugar, you're simply not as easily deceived. Even my darling Eric can't see my beasties outside for what they are."

Elizabeth shuddered hard enough I could see it shake Lola's arm.

"Fate dragged you into this mess to see what that pack of helpless boys can't." Lola took Elizabeth's face in her hands and tucked her blond hair behind her ears. "It's funny how a girl like you can't see how very special you are." Lola glanced at me. "Good thing Bryant here knows."

My cheeks burned as Elizabeth looked over her shoulder at me.

"I'm only here because I suck at Calculus," Elizabeth said. Bright tears balanced in the corners of her eyes. "If I hadn't needed a tutor, I wouldn't have seen the fire start, or gone to Bryant's dad's, and Eric never would have seen me. I'm only here because I'm stupid."

"You aren't stupid." I crossed around to the front of the couch. My mom still lay there, like she was taking the best nap ever. "You're great at lots of things. You're really good in all your other subjects. You're great on stage. And you're beautiful, and nice, and incredibly brave. You figured out the phone was magic and you didn't try to run away. You wanted to help, that's what landed you here."

My heart soared up into my throat as Elizabeth smiled at me, blushing the gentlest pink. "You're brave too, Bryant. And really, pretty great."

My throat was too tight to form words like *thanks* or *I love you.*

Luckily, Devon took my terrible non-word sigh as a cue.

"And you could be good at math if you wanted. Your dad wants you to be a math genius and not an actor"—he took Elizabeth's hands in his—"and then suddenly you can't do math anymore. You aren't stupid. You're rebellious. That makes you cool in my book."

"I don't suck at math on purpose." Elizabeth shook her head.

"Don't argue with the boy." Lola shook a finger at Elizabeth. Her nails were a brilliant bright blue this morning. "He knows more than those good looks give him credit for. And besides, even if you were top of your class in every subject the world has ever seen, you would still be in my sitting room right now. 'Cause that's how fate works, sugar. The Devil's in details. But fate, she don't give a shit."

"Eloquent as always." Eric walked through a strip of scarlet fabric. "I thought I heard the dulcet tones of teenaged angst."

"I would be nice about the suffering of their tender young hearts if I were you, darling, since you barely managed to escape being a teenager yourself," Lola said.

"Surviving twenty years of this life has been a feat, hasn't it?" Eric smiled.

"You're twenty?" I asked, louder and maybe a little more disbelievingly than I should have since everyone but my unconscious mother spun to face me. "What?" I sputtered, flushing for the second time in two minutes. "You just seem older."

"Surviving below will steal years off your life, add years to your soul, and never let you die in peace," Lola said.

"And that is why you in your grandeur escaped." Eric poured himself a cup of tea from the pot on the table and took a biscuit from an overflowing tray.

It wasn't until I saw the steam rising from the biscuit that I noticed the wonderful smell, and my mouth started watering.

"Go on." Lola waved at the tray without looking at me. "I made them for you all. And you should be grateful my banishment, which you so lovingly call escape, left me alive and topside, or you would be huddled under a bridge with a dead mama. If you had even survived this long without my help. Which I highly doubt would have happened."

"Not in a million years." Eric smiled, lifting his cup to Lola. "My savior."

"As long as we agree on something." Lola stood up and walked over to the little desk in the corner. Her long, silk, embroidered bathrobe swished at her ankles.

"My mom." I froze with the hot biscuit in my hand. "Is it light out now? Can you fix her?"

"Fix her?" Lola laughed as she rummaged around in the drawers. "Isn't it cute how he says *fix her* like she's an engine with a bad spark plug?" Lola reached down, and her arm disappeared up to her elbow in a drawer that was at most six inches deep. "I can heal her. I can use my immense—" there was a clattering of things toppling over. "Damn those little things. Where was I?"

"Your immense..." Eric prompted.

"Thank you, darling. I can use my immense magical prowess, power, and knowledge to save your mama's life." Lola stood up, holding a handful of something. "But if you want to talk about the very woman who gave you life like she's an automobile, that's fine with me. I'll *fix* her for you."

"Thank you," I said sheepishly as Lola started pulling things out of her fist. It was like a magic show where the magician keeps drawing yards and yards of scarves out of her hand. But instead of scarves, there were glass vials filled with sparkling liquid, two silver trays, a violet and a pale blue candle, a wooden mortar and pestle, and a silver spoon.

"Darling, you come be my mixer." Lola poured some of the liquid into the wooden bowl.

Eric obediently popped the rest of the biscuit into his mouth and walked over, picking up the pestle and lazily stirring as Lola added a few drops of blue, then purple, then red.

I wanted to ask what she was doing, but something in the pale pink smoke rising into the air kept me silent.

After about a minute, she moved on to the first tray, dripping the ingredients right onto the surface. After a few different vials had added their contents, she picked up the spoon to stir what was on the tray. I thought I would hear the scrape of metal against metal, but instead the spoon sloshed like it had been dipped into a bathtub.

Another few minutes passed before Lola tapped the spoon on the edge of the tray, knocking off the few stray black drops that had clung to it. Eric stopped stirring in the wooden bowl, too.

"Did I tell you to stop?" she snarked as she picked up the violet candle and stuck it to the middle of the tray.

Eric rolled his eyes and kept stirring.

Lola started mumbling at the candle. I tried to listen to the words, but they were all strange. Lower and more guttural than the ones I had found on the phone.

When she finished, the tip of the candle burst into flame,

making lights dance in my eyes as the glow settled down to normal. Well, normal except for burning pink. She took the wooden bowl from Eric and whispered something into it before dumping its powdery contents onto the second tray and picking up the pale blue candle. A puff on the tip, and a gentle teal flame shimmered to life. Lola smiled and settled the candle onto the middle of the second tray.

"*Erbracina*," she said loudly, and with a popping *hiss*, both the candles puffed out and their smoke drifted down, flowing onto the trays.

"Nicely done." Eric cocked an impressed eye at the trays.

"You know how I love praise for my excellent work." Lola lifted the candles, laying them on the desk before picking up a tray in each hand and carrying them to the table in the center of the room. "Now comes the hard part."

"Hard part? What else do you have to do?" I asked.

"Oh not me, love. You." Lola pointed at the trays. "You have to pick which one you want to give your mama."

I looked down at the trays. One had a pill on it, a capsule filled with pale blue powder. The other—a tiny stone so purple, it looked almost black.

"What's the difference?" My heart raced in my chest as I imagined all too vividly having to solve some terrible riddle or do something magical when I didn't know anything but how to whip up a tornado.

"One wakes your mama up"—Lola indicated the stone—"and the other keeps her sleeping." She pointed to the blue pill.

"Then give her the stone."

"If that's what you want, love." Lola nodded. "But what happens when she wakes up? You have enough folks out to kill you that getting dead shouldn't be too tough. Do you think your mama's gonna let you just waltz out there on your feet or in a box and not do anything to try and stop it? Do you think if she's with you, she won't end up getting hurt again?"

My throat was so tight I couldn't make words. I looked at my mom. Sleeping on the couch. Halfway to dead because she had tried to save me.

I shook my head.

"The pill," Lola said, "it'll cure what the Ladies did to her, but it won't let her wake yet. She'll stay asleep and safe here till you come back and get her up and running."

"What if I don't make it back?" I croaked. The reality of the words shattered me inside.

I had to follow Eric to survive. Following Eric might get me killed. I would never get to see Mom again.

"Then I'll wait to give her the stone. Even if it takes a hundred years for the Ladies to lose her scent. I've got the time and the house room. I'll make sure she stays safe."

"And wakes up in a hundred years to find out her son's dead?" Devon shook his head. "You can't do that to her. It would kill her just as much as the Ladies would."

"This isn't your choice." Lola held up a hand to stop Devon from talking. "It can only be Bryant's. Even I can't see who makes it out of the shadows that crawl around under our feet. But I know mamas, and I know what it's like to watch yours die."

The room fell silent. Everyone stared at me as I looked at my mom. I wanted her eyes to open. I wanted to talk to her and ask her what I should do. But I knew what she would say. She would tell me I couldn't go underground, especially not without her.

"You'll keep her safe?" I asked, not bothering to hide the tear snaking from my eye.

Lola nodded. "I won't let anyone get to her, love."

"Blue pill."

Lola lifted it off the tray and slipped it into my mom's mouth. Blue haze poured out from between Mom's lips, wrapping itself around her. The haze got denser and heavier, so thick I couldn't see her face anymore, so thick I wanted, *needed* to rip it away. To hug her and tell her I loved her and I was sorry for every mean thing I had ever said and for every time I had been a pain in her ass. But the haze would keep her alive. So I sat and watched my mother's face disappear behind its veil.

Tears ran down my cheeks as the haze turned into a cocoon, shimmering as it solidified.

"Take her to the low room, darling," Lola said.

Eric stepped forward and lifted the cocoon with one hand, pushing it in front of him like it weighed nothing. He walked out through an orange patch of curtain.

"The low room is the safest place I have," Lola said.

Elizabeth slipped her hand into mine. Three days ago I would have given anything to have her hold my hand. But right then I would have given anything to go back to how things were before, when the worst problem I had was figuring out how to get the most beautiful girl in New York City to give me the time of day.

"You two aren't coming either." I glanced at Devon. "I'll go with Eric, but you can't—"

Elizabeth and Devon lit into me at once, but it was Lola that cut over both of them. "Sugar and sweetie are going with you." Her voice rang oddly in the room, like the walls were made of marble instead of fabric. "I know you want to save your friends, and that makes you a good kid. But fate brought all three of you into this, and the only way it's going to let any of you walk away before this thing has played out is by dying. Your mama was never meant to get involved. But those golden threads of fate have you three tied up in a little bow."

"But neither of them can use magic." I paced in front of the table.

"Stop moving and eat a damn biscuit." Lola threw one to me. Its warmth was comforting in my hands. I took a bite and felt the panic raging in my chest back away just a little.

"Have you ever heard the saying fight fire with fire?" Lola asked.

I nodded.

"Well, sometimes that works, but sometimes you need a bucket of water or a fire extinguisher, you get me, love?"

I lifted my chin to nod, then shook my head.

"There are more ways to fight magic than by tossing spells at it." Lola walked over and took the biscuit from my hand, pressing the rest of it into my mouth. "You only have to see the path and take the leap. None of you will survive if you don't go together. I don't even need to look into the shadows to see that, love."

"You're my best friend, Bryant." Devon rose. "Your fight is our fight. I'm not walking away from this."

"Neither am I," Elizabeth said.

"Ah, the nobility of youth," Eric drawled as he walked back through the orange curtain. "Have I ever been that noble?"

"I can tell you you haven't." Lola smirked. "Now darlings," she said, suddenly serious, "the only thing I've got is a strong feeling that this is trouble like you've never seen before." She took Eric's chin in her hand. "I hate wearing black. It depresses me to no end. So, do Lola and favor and come back alive. I don't want to wreak havoc on my wardrobe."

"We'll do our best." Eric kissed Lola on the cheek and squeezed her hand for a moment before striding toward the black curtain. "Let's get this motley army on the march. We have an evil to destroy and a regime to topple. It's going to be a long day."

"You kids take the rest of the biscuits." Lola's voice was thick as she pressed biscuits into each of our hands. "I'll take care of her. You take care of him."

"Yes ma'am." I looked back at the orange curtain. "And thank you."

"Anytime, love," Lola called after us as we walked out into darkness.

21

I didn't mind the walk through the dark on the way back out of Lola's. It didn't feel like I was being trapped forever this time. Instead, I didn't want the blackness to end. Once we got through, I would be leaving my mom behind and leading my best friend and Elizabeth to do something dangerous that could get us all killed. Well, really Eric was doing the leading. But that didn't make me feel any better. Not even a little bit.

The blackness ended, and we were standing at the top of the wall. The sun was high in the sky, and the chaos of the midday bustle echoed under the overpass.

Eric started walking down the wall, keeping his chin tipped up and away. I did the same, trying not to panic as I stepped out onto what should have been a drop but felt like level floor. I looked at the steel trusses high above me, which got farther away as my feet carried me out.

Right when I was getting used to the sensation and my heart had figured out what a normal rhythm should be, I took another step, and the flat smooth ground wasn't there. I waved my arms in the air like an idiot for a second and fell forward, hitting the gravel hard with both knees.

"Watch out," Eric said, completely unfazed, as the rest of the crew marched down the wall, Elizabeth walking normally, Devon looking up like I had been, "the last step is a doozy."

"Thanks," I grunted as I pushed myself to my feet.

"Well, it was already too late for you." Eric shrugged.

"But we appreciate your consideration." Elizabeth all but floated off the wall.

Devon teetered at the edge for a second, feeling the air with his toe, before jumping down to solid ground, muttering, "Weird. This is way too weird."

I agreed.

There was a faint rustle of tarps and cardboard as the homeless emerged from their homes.

"Good morning," Eric said. "We're going to be on our way now."

The big guy stepped forward, lifting his chin and tipping his head to the side.

Elizabeth gasped behind me.

"Take care of Lola for me," Eric said, "and if there are any others sleeping for the warm months, wake them. There could be visitors coming who wish to do Lola harm."

The man glared at Eric through the lower edge of his eyes for a second before he nodded, and all of them retreated into their tents.

Eric started to walk away and Devon followed, but Elizabeth stayed frozen on the spot, staring.

"You all right?" I asked softly.

"Lingering is unwise after we've said our goodbyes," Eric called back, not slowing.

I took Elizabeth's hand and pulled her around the corner and out of sight of the tents, to where Eric was examining the shabby street. The nearest store had windows covered in plywood with the words *Still Open!* spray-painted on in bright blue. Flickering neon signs that had no hope of competing with daylight advertised *lowest price cigarettes* and *best bananas in downtown.*

"This way should be fine." He set off farther into the city, but Elizabeth grabbed his arm with her free hand, still not letting go of me.

"What *were* those things?" she demanded. "They...they looked different last night."

"Sunlight casts away disguises," Eric explained. "It's what it is meant to do. But they are still Lola's loyal guards who now protect Ms. Miller as well. So, perhaps you shouldn't be so concerned with what they are and think more about the good they are doing." He pulled his arm free and strode away.

Devon shrugged and followed Eric. Elizabeth and I took the rear.

"What did you see?" I asked quietly when I had finally gotten her to walk at the same pace as the others.

"Shadows," Elizabeth whispered, her eyes wide like she was still staring at something. "Last night, they looked like dogs. Like dark wolves with big teeth. But this morning"—she took a shuddering breath—"this morning, they were rotting. The big one's hair was torn away so I could see bone. They're all dead."

"It's not uncommon for the dead to serve," Eric said. I hadn't noticed he had fallen in step next to us. "Especially when they owe the living."

I shuddered, trying not to think of what kind of debt could follow a person into the grave.

We walked in silence after that. The street sounds were so normal, which made it doubly weird that I couldn't shake the coldness on the back of my neck as the dead wolf people guarded my mom and we passed dilapidated basketball courts and increasingly upscale bodegas.

In good ole New York fashion, in three blocks, we had left the scary streets behind and were surrounded by Starbucks.

"Where are we going?" Devon asked as he narrowly dodged a Chihuahua hell-bent on peeing on his ankle. "Thanks, lady," Devon grumbled at the owner. "There should be a law about who gets to own a dog in the city."

"We're going to Beville." Eric hadn't slowed his pace during the dog incident, so we all had to run a few steps to catch up.

"Beville, check" Devon said, "but if you haven't noticed, none of us know where or what Beville is."

"Which is why I'm leading the way." Eric pointed forward and kept walking.

"Not good enough." Devon ran two steps and planted himself in front of Eric. "You don't get to lead us blind. Tell us where we're going." He crossed his arms and gave Eric the scowl he usually saved for jerks who catcalled the girls he was busy hitting on.

"To Beville." Eric raised his hands to stop Devon from talking. "The simplest way possible. Well, not simplest, but most expeditious and surreptitious, considering our circumstances."

He moved to step around Devon, but Devon blocked his way again.

"You know, either you are very brave or have very little self-preservation instinct," Eric said. "In either case, get out of my way."

"Not until you tell us where Beville is," Devon growled.

"I thought that would have been obvious." Eric raised a black eyebrow. "Beville—Below the Village."

"You mean SoHo?" Devon asked as Eric sidestepped him and started down the street again.

"I said *below*," Eric corrected. "Not *south of*."

"I hate that guy," Devon whispered. "I really hate that pretentious asshole."

"Most people do," Eric called back. "I consider it to be one of my charms."

"People hating you is not usually considered an attribute," Devon said.

I punched him hard in the arm. "Don't piss off the guy who knows magic!"

Devon rolled his eyes. "I guess if it's the best you've got."

"The best I've got is my patience in not turning you into a sewer rat. But as you don't seem to be appreciative of my kindness..." Eric turned a corner and clapped his hands. "I thought I remembered there being a stop here."

He started down the steps to the subway station. The familiar bouquet of dank, rats, and pee crept into my nose as we jogged after him. There weren't too many people in the station, just some homeless making themselves, well...at home. I glanced back at Elizabeth, but she was looking around the platform like nothing was weird. Maybe the homeless guy eating a sandwich in the corner really was just a homeless guy this time. Part of me wished I could have seen Lola's guards the way Elizabeth had. Part of me was really grateful I couldn't.

Eric walked over and stood behind the yellow line, leaning forward to stare down the tunnel.

"What are we doing down here?" I followed his gaze. "Are we going to wait for no one to be looking and run down the tunnel?"

"You can get to Beville that way if you know the right path," Eric murmured softly as the three of us crowded around him. "But every wizard knows those walking paths. There are a few fake walls in subway stations that hide shortcuts, but those are easily watched. It takes a fine mix of daring, magic, and wisdom to find the...other ways."

"And let me guess." Devon's voice dripped with sarcasm. "You have just the right mixture?"

"Precisely." Eric smiled. "So, I do know of a way in where our arrival will go unnoticed."

Lights appeared in the distance, and a chain of cars roared their approach.

"Whether any of you are brave enough to follow me is another question entirely."

The doors *dinged* open, and we followed Eric onto the train.

"Stand clear of the closing doors," the voice warned.

It should have said *Stand clear of the megalomaniac wizard.* Or *Stand clear of evil mist and shadow dogs.* Or better yet *Stand clear of imminent death and destruction.* But the subway voice only cared about the damn sliding doors. So, I stood clear, and the train lurched forward.

I waited to see if Eric would take a seat or grab the handrail, but he did neither. Instead, he walked to the back of the car, to the door that led out. You know, the one only used by drunk dudes who need to pee or people with a strong death wish.

The train rocked back on forth, twisting around corners as we hurtled through the dark. Eric grabbed the handle and wrenched the door open. And I mean wrenched. They don't make those things easy to open. Mostly because they should never ever be opened.

"Out we go." Eric bowed and held the door open for us.

Devon made a sound halfway between a *tsch* and a growl, which I could barely hear over the noise of the tracks, and went out. Elizabeth followed. But I stayed frozen. Partly because I was terrified of going out onto the forbidden platform while the train raced around in the dark, but mostly because I could feel terribly judgmental eyes on the back on my neck. I turned around.

There was a lone old black lady sitting there, staring at me disapprovingly. Like she was angry I was tossing away all the work she and my other guardian angels had done trying to keep me alive over the years by doing something this stupid.

"We're running short on time," Eric said, snapping me out of it, and I placed one reluctant foot in front of the other. Freakin' peer pressure.

The light reflecting from inside the car cast shadows on the tracks racing below my feet. But around the train was mostly darkness. Every once in a while, a wall flashed right up next to us, but that only made it feel like the tunnel was trying to reach out and grab me from the tenuous safety of the platform.

Eric stood at the right side of the tiny bit of metal we were all crammed onto. "We only have a window of a few seconds," he shouted, his voice immediately swallowed by the rush of wind. "If you don't jump at the right time, there's nothing I can do for you. Get ready. Keep to the very edge. It makes it easier."

Elizabeth stepped to stand next to him.

"We're nearly there."

Devon joined Elizabeth.

"Jump hard, and aim away from the tracks."

"You want us to jump off of the train?" I puffed, when the horror finally registered.

"Yes!" Eric shouted. "In three, two, one!"

He jumped, and Elizabeth and Devon followed. Not thinking, or at least trying really hard not to, I took two giant running steps and leapt out into the blackness.

22

I thought I would meet a wall, but I fell through the air past where a wall would be, then hit the ground with a thud that shook my teeth and sent pain searing through my shoulder.

"Bryant!" Elizabeth screamed.

Coughing, I rolled onto my back, and found a dim streetlight hanging right over my head.

"Are you okay?" Elizabeth helped me sit up. Her face was pale and terrified as I reached up to touch my own with the arm that I could move to make sure everything was in the right place.

Devon appeared in front of me. "That was crazy, dude."

"I said we had a very brief window." Eric stepped next to him.

"Well, maybe you should have been a little clearer on why it was so brief!" Devon spun around, clenching his fists. "We're not some puppets you get to play with. We *break*, asshole!"

"I know how easily humans die, actually," Eric said calmly, rubbing his fingers together.

"Then why the hell did you try to get all of us killed?" Devon shouted.

"If I had wanted you dead, you would be dead," Eric shot back.

"Really, because it's not like you haven't tried to kill us bef—"

"Stop!" Elizabeth shouted. "I think the priority shouldn't be a pissing match of who has the better bad ideas. Can we focus on the fact that Bryant's arm looks dislocated?"

I finally thought to glance down at my own shoulder as my shock ebbed. My arm did look funny. It was drooping down from where it should have been sitting in the socket.

"At least he didn't hit the wall," Eric sighed.

"What wall?" The words weren't even out of my mouth all the way before I turned and looked over my deformed shoulder. A concrete wall rose not three inches from the skid mark where I had landed. A little farther right and having my head dislocated would have been the problem. "Found the wall."

"I can fix the shoulder." Eric knelt next to me.

"Do you need the phone?" I pulled it out of my pocket. It was still shiny, black, and completely unharmed from me nearly getting myself killed.

"No." Eric took the phone and held it in his hand for a few seconds before passing it back to me. "The phone is an accumulation of knowledge, free of the rules of impartment, available at your fingertips. I already have a significant amount of knowledge stored in my brain. *Crantanolous.*" He slipped the word in like it was nothing.

With a terrible *pop* and shooting pain that made me want to vomit, my shoulder went back into its socket.

"*Keeiieeahhwhaaadiidowwww,*" I whined, but Eric was still talking.

"Since you have no magical knowledge except for what's in that phone and it would be easier to stop the Ladies and Thaden"—cold breeze tickled the back of my neck—"if I have an assistant, it is in my best interest to keep you alive and fighting, and the phone will help with that. Do try and keep it safe, though. As far as I know, it is one of a kind."

"And what about Elizabeth and me?" Devon clearly couldn't stop himself from Eric-baiting. "Are we just cannon fodder?"

"Guys!" I raised my now-working arm. "Remember, ya know, threads of fate, Lola, sticking together?"

Devon took a deep breath and tipped his head up, muttering a string of curses the sailors of Fleet Week would have been proud of. "Fine, we follow the twerp and hope he doesn't get us killed." He reached down and helped me to my feet.

My arm felt better, but the rest of me still felt like I had jumped off a speeding train.

"But the next time you ask us to do something that might get us killed," Devon said, stopping Eric mid-stride, "you tell us what the hell it is first. No more jumping blind."

"Fine." Eric nodded and began walking again. "Then it would probably serve you best to know we're taking an illegal entrance into the backside of Beville, which is full of the most desperate kinds of wizards who really don't appreciate uninvited guests and will be perfectly willing to rob and murder us just as quickly as say hello."

"And we chose this way in because?" Elizabeth asked, slipping her hand back into mine like it was routine. I liked it.

"Because it's the only entrance I've ever found that isn't watched by the Ladies or Thaden. And I would rather try to reason with thieves than let either of them know we're here."

Soon, we were out of reach of the one streetlight. Eric muttered something and a light flickered on in his palm, reflecting off the dirty walls. The farther we walked, the weirder it seemed that there had been a random streetlight in the middle of a dark tunnel.

"Why was there a light where we jumped off?" I asked after another minute, more to make a noise that wasn't our footfalls and the distant rattle of the trains than because I needed an answer.

"I put it there," Eric said. "Stole it from a nasty abandoned corner and hauled it on the train. I did receive some very strange looks when I boarded the subway."

I pictured him carrying a full-size lamppost onto a train. My brain said it was impossible, but then, you know, magic...

"I jumped off and planted it there," Eric kept talking, "did a spell to keep the thing lit. It keeps the shadows away. And the last thing you want to jump into is shadows."

"Shadows?" I asked, feeling suddenly like I was back at the summer camp my mom had made me go to where the counselor told us scary stories that made me too afraid of trees to go near Central Park for a year.

"Not literal shadows," Eric said. "I mean things that hide in the shadows. Dark servants created by the magic of wizards who died long ago. Creatures that have crawled up from their own realms and taken refuge in the blackest places of Beville. Not that foul things can't exist in the light—they merely prefer the darkness. And I prefer not to be surprised by things lurking out of sight."

As he spoke, the way his voice echoed in the tunnels slowly changed. The walls weren't eating the sound anymore. And there were noises coming from up ahead.

I listened hard, trying to figure out what I was hearing, but a sickening *crunch* underfoot stopped me. I jumped back, afraid I had broken something. Where my shoe had been was now a small pile of broken white bones. Bile shot up into my throat. I had stepped on a skeleton.

"You okay?" Elizabeth asked.

I nodded, not altogether sure I could open my mouth without spewing.

"Why are there dead things down here?" Devon asked, poking at the shattered bones with his toe.

"Most dead things end up underground," Eric answered, his fast, controlled gait eating up the tunnel.

"Yes, but I thought people lived down here. Wouldn't they want to keep their place corpse-free?"

"In the nice parts of Beville where people build houses and take pride in their surroundings," Eric said as we came to a fork, and he turned left without hesitation, "you would be hard pressed to find anything as unappealing as a dead rodent. But out here where people are outcasts, there's more concern with survival and less worrying about keeping up with the Joneses."

"But why are they outcasts?" I asked. "Did they do something wrong?"

"Not wrong, no." Eric led us down another tunnel, this one barely taller than Devon. "It's more that the people on the outskirts aren't really magical enough to be considered wizards and accepted into our society. But they aren't normal enough to live aboveground with the rest of you. They have enough magic to be noticed, but not enough to be special. It's unfortunate, really."

Eric's voice dropped, and it really did sound like he was sympathetic. "It's not their fault they were born between worlds, yet they're made to suffer for being different. Most resort to crime eventually, but then I suppose if everyone blames you for being born wrong, there must be some relief in doing something wrong. Then at least you have a concrete memory of what you're being condemned for."

"And there's no way to teach them?" Elizabeth asked. "You can't tutor them in magic? Or help them fit in with us in the city?"

"It might be possible if wizards cared to try." Eric's voice darkened as we turned another corner. "But in Beville, being *other* makes you unworthy of help. No matter how desperately you need it."

Suddenly, we stopped short. I had been so busy wondering if I even had enough magic to be considered an outcast to notice the tunnel in front of me until I bumped into Eric.

The tunnel wasn't wide, no bigger than the space between two platforms in a subway tunnel. But both sides had been lined with tents. Made of old Disney bedsheets, filthy canvas, and patchwork t-shirts stitched together, some stretched twenty feet. Others were barely wider than my shoulders. Lights glowed in a few of them, and the noises of life came through the fabric. The tinny *clunk* of a person stirring a pot with a metal spoon, the dull rumbles of people talking and snoring.

Eric headed down the row, and I held my breath, waiting for everyone to emerge from their fabric homes like Lola's guards had. But no one looked out at us. Even the old man lying on the ground barely lifted his head to glance at us. Finally, I let myself breathe, and instantly regretted it.

The air smelled worse than a porter potty at a World Series game. Elizabeth clung to my hand, and if it hadn't been for the fact that I still thought that somewhere in this hell I might actually have a chance with her, I would have thrown up right where I stood.

It took longer for us to march through the row of tents than it did to walk three long city blocks. In front of us was a stretch of dim light, and then nothing but dark. I itched to run into it and away from the stench, but Eric kept a slow, steady pace.

"Funny how you strutted through like that," a voice called from behind as we passed the last tent. "No saying hello to friends, no partaking of the fine commerce Spells End has to offer. It's like you think you're walking down a highway."

I stared at the back of Eric's head, waiting for him to say something. It was a few seconds before he turned.

"Spells End is a lovely place, but we are in a bit of a hurry." Eric's voice was light and friendly, like he knew whoever had stopped us.

I turned to see who he was speaking to. Ten people flanked us. All filthy. All glaring.

"If you're going to use Spells End as a highway," the man at the front said, "you're going to have to pay the toll." The man smiled, baring his blackened, rotting teeth.

23

W e all stood in silence for a moment, waiting to see what Eric would do.

"A toll?" he asked calmly.

Part of me expected lightning bolts to shoot out of his hands, blasting our way to freedom.

"That's right." The man stepped forward, flashing the rot in his teeth.

"And that's a new rule? I mean, I've never been asked to pay a toll before," Eric said, "and I've come and gone from Beville many times."

"New rule." The man gave a gigantic grin. I wanted to look away, but there was something hypnotizing about the way he slowly drew forward. "Times change. Now you pay to cross."

"Right then," Eric said to the man before tossing over his shoulder, "Bryant, call our friend and let him know we'll be a little late as we have to sort out this matter of a toll."

"Phones don't work down here." The leader snorted. "Didn't you say you've crossed our way? Out at Spells End, we don't get to call for help, sorry."

"Well, as you said, times change," Eric said. "As does technology. Call our friend, Bryant."

I reached for my normal phone, realized there was no way a non-magic phone would do anything so far underground, then pulled the black phone out of my pocket instead.

Who am I supposed to call?

My mind raced. I could call Lola, but I didn't know her number. I definitely shouldn't call Thaden. And this phone didn't have a call button anyway.

"And how much am I to pay?" Eric asked.

"Two-Hundred," the man said. "Each."

"You expect me to have eight hundred dollars in my pocket?" Eric laughed.

I opened the *At a Glance* tab.

"Only if you expect us to let you pass," the man said.

Offensive spells. Definitely offensive.

"That's funny, because we've already passed through your little settlement."

My eyes flew down the screen. Why did the words all have to look like nonsense?

"And it's strange to me," Eric said, "that you would wait to demand a toll until we were past your homes. That says quite clearly to me that you have no legal right to do so."

"We're in Spells End." The man edged closer. "Legal don't hold water here. We make our own laws."

Kuraxo. I tapped the spell and scanned the description.

"Well, even if you make your own laws," Eric said, stepping forward so he was close enough to reach out and touch Mr. Tooth Decay, "that means you do, in fact, have laws. Do you understand the concept of a contradiction?"

"Do you understand we'll tear you apart and no one'll find your bodies?" the man smirked.

"Ready for that call, Bryant?" Eric asked.

"Y-yes," I stammered.

"You really want to die on your phone?" the man growled.

"Put in the call to *Erunca!*" Eric shouted. A bright ball of lightning appeared by the ceiling.

Before I realized Eric was doing a spell, the ball had split itself into ten lightning bolts that streaked toward the ten from Spells End.

"*Kuraxo!*" I shouted over the screams. The ground beneath our feet shook.

"Run!" Eric turned and tore down the corridor.

I darted after him, glancing behind my shoulder to make sure Devon and Elizabeth followed. A dull *crack* echoed through the tunnel as the floor gave a fierce jerk.

"Run faster!" Eric shouted as we all sprinted full tilt through the darkness.

The ground was soft dirt, filth made of forgotten rot. The only light was the beam that radiated from Eric's hand. My lungs burned. My legs ached. The tunnel sloped down, but it seemed like whatever depth we were running toward, we would never arrive.

The screams and the ground cracking seemed miles away when Eric finally led us to a dead end. He swept the light from his hand through all the shadows before leaning against the wall.

"Next time"—Eric patted the one hair that had gotten windswept back into place—"when I ask you to do a spell, please choose something that might not get all of us killed. I have very strong preferences on how I die, and a cave-in has never made that particular list."

"You told me," I panted, clutching the stitch in my side, "to make a call. I did."

If it hadn't been for Elizabeth and Devon leaning against the wall next to me just as out of breath, I might have felt bad for feeling like I was going to die. But instead, I glared at Eric.

"Perhaps I should give you credit for not actually collapsing the tunnel on our heads, and, theoretically, you might not have caused severe damage to the subway system or to the street above, so that is something," he said, apparently unfazed by my death glare. "But we should work on unspoken communication for the future. If we survive long enough to have a future. And the odds of that are dwindling every moment."

"Really?" Devon pushed himself away from the wall. "We jumped off a speeding train and made it through the den of thieves you decided was the best path to lead us through. I'd say the plan is going about as well as we could have hoped for."

"While I am willing to admit," Eric said, "the fact that we're alive to have this argument is a feat, the point in my leading us through the *den of thieves* was to be sure we could enter Beville without anyone who wants to exterminate us being the wiser so I could lay our trap. But now everyone in Manhattan will know the ground shook below the Village, and Thaden"—the wind licked my neck—"and the Ladies will both know it was magic that did it, which means not only will they be looking for whatever caused the ground to split between Spells End and Beville, but soon they will be hunting us."

"Look, Bryant didn't mean to—" Elizabeth began, but I cut her off.

"Bryant didn't *mean* to?" I croaked, my throat paper-dry from running. "Of course I didn't mean to! I was told by a sociopath to do magic. I don't know how to do magic. I don't know how to fight! So, don't blame me—"

"I wasn't—" Elizabeth tried to say, but I was on a roll, and the words kept flooding out.

"All I wanted was to return a guy's cellphone. It should have been Devon who picked it up. Then he would be the one trying to figure out what the hell a spell is supposed to do while mole people are threatening to kill him! Devon would be good at it."

"What do you mean *what a spell is supposed to do*?" Eric crossed his arms. "Didn't you tap on the word and check the effect?"

"I tapped on the word, and it said *Causes a split in the ground*," I shouted. "Causes a split in the ground, not an earthquake!"

"How else did you expect the ground to split?" Eric asked, his voice so calm, it made me want to spit.

"I don't know!" I shouted. "A subtle widening of the Earth would have been nice."

"Subtle widening of the earth?" Eric chuckled. "Nothing about magic has ever been subtle."

"How would I know that? I found a phone, you told me I'm a wizard, and my mother is trapped in a cocoon! I don't know how magic works. Because someone"—I pointed a shaking finger at Eric—"only ever tells me things like *I'll kill you*, or *run*, or *make a phone call!*"

"Let me ask you something." Eric pressed his fingers together and planted them under his chin as though he were praying. The light stayed between his palms, making strange shadows dance across his face with every word. "When you were little, did your ice cream ever fall off the cone?"

"What?" I dragged my hands through my hair to keep myself from punching Eric.

"Did your ice cream ever fall from the cone?" he said slowly.

"Yes!" I started pacing. I wanted to run or kick through the walls. Anything that would get me out of the tunnels.

"Well, when your ice cream fell on the ground, what did your mother say?"

"Not to listen to crazy men who never figured out life could be lived in Technicolor," I growled.

"Very funny," Eric said. "I think perhaps a more accurate

representation would be that she told you not to tip the cone or the ice cream would fall down. On this, your first encounter with the terror that is gravity, I believe it's safe to assume she didn't bother with Newton's law of universal gravitation. You were young, and the loss of the ice cream mattered more than what made it fall." Eric grabbed me by the shoulders, keeping me still. His fingers dug into my skin. "This is your first foray into magic, and knowing how the rules work is not nearly as important as staying alive.

"So, I am sorry about your ice cream, but from now on, take the phone literally, do everything I say, and try not to have any more temper tantrums. I already have Sir Moody Pretty Pants pouting because he isn't in charge and there is no one here for him to use his incomparable charm on. I can't try and win this thing if you get angry because you're being asked to play without knowing the rules of the game. I can fill you in this far: win or die." Eric held my gaze with his dark blue eyes. "Are you ready to follow me and do as I say? We don't have time for lessons."

I wanted to scream at him to go to Hell. But without Eric, I couldn't find my way back up to the street, let alone avoid the Ladies.

I nodded.

"Thank God for you, Elizabeth." Eric let go of me. "Leave it to a seer to be the one who can keep her head on straight."

Elizabeth let out a high, strained laugh. "I don't know what being a seer is. I've been creeped out by dark corners and weird things my whole life, and now I'm supposed to believe it's fate that I imagine monsters? I don't understand any of this anymore than Bryant does."

"And yet you're taking it so well." Eric patted her on the shoulder. "And that's the way to do it. Roll with the punches until you get your footing."

"Unless one of those punches kills you," Devon said dryly.

"Well, you have heard of rolling over in your grave, haven't you?" Eric said with a smile that, for a split-second, made me believe he thought he had made a joke. A very bad joke. "Now that we've finished with all this unpleasant worrying about our place in the magical world, we need a plan. A new plan." Eric paced the dead end, his hands still clasped below his chin. "We need to plant the seed. Let Thaden and the Ladies know where we're hiding without letting them actually know we're waiting for them."

"Then, what?" Devon asked.

"Then we watch as they fight each other and take on whoever is left standing when the dust settles," Eric said.

"Doesn't that seem a little shady?" I asked, remembering all the stories of knights and chivalrous armies my mother had read to me. "Isn't it wrong to set our enemies up and wait it out while they do the work for us?"

"You can call it shady." Eric shrugged. "I prefer the term survival savvy. Besides, it's not as though either party is innocent. My conscience is clear."

"Mine, too," Devon said. "How do we leak the information?"

"That's the thorny part." Eric tilted his chin up to stare at the ceiling. "We could send each a message that we want to meet them to discuss turning over the phone and just let them arrive for the same meeting."

"A monkey would see that coming." Devon shook his head. "If you're playing two people, you can't let the play come from you."

"What do you mean?" Elizabeth asked.

"We ask them to meet us, they'll send scouts or set traps," Devon said. "They have to think it's their idea to come and fight us. Then they'll be searching for us, and not our plan."

"I agree with your reasoning." Eric nodded politely. "But how do you propose to get the message of where we are lurking to two parties without actually telling them? Implanting thoughts into someone's mind is magic only the Ladies can accomplish."

I shuddered at the thought of the Ladies playing around inside my head.

"We don't have to plant it in their heads." Devon smiled. "We just have to make sure they hear it from someone who isn't us."

Eric's damn eyebrow shot up again. "And how do we do that? There are very few people in this world I trust, and all of them have been banished from Beville."

"We don't need your shady banished friends," Devon said. "All I need is a cafeteria."

"Cafeteria?" Eric asked.

"Point me to where you people eat." Devon grinned. "And I'll make sure we're surrounded by the big bad wizards in no time."

24

I felt numb as Eric led us back into the tunnels and to the now-familiar crunch of bones under my feet. I didn't ask questions I wouldn't want the answers to. I just walked through the dark, not marking the endless twists or turns. Just walked.

Elizabeth was next to me, not looking at me.

"Hey," I whispered. Devon and Eric both looked at me, but Elizabeth kept her head firmly forward. "Look, I'm sorry I was an asshat who snapped at you."

Eric rolled his eyes, but Devon grinned and gave a tiny thumbs up Elizabeth probably saw.

"I know you were trying to be on my side and I—"

"Bit my head off," Elizabeth said.

"I mean, that really covers a lot of it," I muttered.

"I get that you may not remember," Elizabeth said, "but we've been in class together for a really long time. I've probably sat next to you for a thousand hours of my life, even though you've never noticed."

My heart stopped beating. It seemed impossible that I would still be walking while my heart was stopped.

"And you were special way before you found a cellphone,"

Elizabeth kept talking, apparently unaware of my impending death from heart stoppage. "You're smart. Really smart. And sweet. If you weren't a wizard, you would probably cure cancer or end hunger or something. So don't act all shocked that our lives are depending on you. You were always the type to have lives depending on you. But you were too nice and shy and humble to figure it out. Don't blame me for seeing it or for speaking up. Apparently that's like my thing."

We all walked quietly for a moment. "You're wrong," I said, glad for the darkness as my face burned.

"Wrong that you shouldn't hate me for seeing the truth?" Elizabeth's melodic voice verged on snapping. "Or wrong that you're going to be important whether you like it or not?"

"Wrong that I didn't notice you." My throat was so tight I could hardly breathe. The back of Devon's neck tensed as he pretended not to listen. "I noticed every time I sat near you and every time you walked by. I always notice you."

I always notice you. I wanted to curl up on the floor and die. Forget evil mist Ladies and cellphone programmers. I told the girl of my dreams that I always *notice* her.

Please let the tunnel collapse and put me out of everyone's misery.

"If you've always noticed me," she said finally, "then it should be clear I really am right."

"Is this what high school does aboveground?" Eric asked as a light came into view down the tunnel. "Turn all its victims into blubbering, blushing, hormonal messes who can do math but don't understand love or fate?"

"Pretty much," Devon said.

"Hmm," Eric sighed. "And I thought life in Beville was trying."

"It's nice to see you boys agreeing on something," Elizabeth said as the first house came into sight right behind a sign that read *Center Street.*

I had expected more tents leaning up against the tunnel walls, but the residents of Center Street had built houses. Real, two story houses.

Sort of.

The tunnel had been carved out high above so the ceiling sat at least thirty feet overhead. Lights had been set into the stone, casting the already weird buildings in a warm, eerie glow. Half of them looked like the old brick townhouses from up in the city, complete with wide stoops and fancy front windows. But the other half had given up on the Upper West Side vibe and decided to go rogue in a way no HOA would ever approve.

A giant log cabin had been wedged in next to a house that didn't seem to know quite what shape it was supposed to be. At first glance, it looked like a fancy country home with bright blue shutters. Then I blinked, and the friendly shutters had turned into gaping black windows. Rain pounded and lightning split the air right in front of the house. I glanced at Elizabeth. She was looking at it too, but she didn't seem afraid. So, I checked the house again. This time it looked like a lighthouse with an invisible sun beaming right down on it.

"Are you sure the mist ladies can't see us out their front window?" Devon asked, yanking my attention away from the stone tower the changing house had morphed into.

Devon pointed to a bright white construction made out of some sort of matte metal. The front steps were paper-thin strips of white that floated lazily in the air. The whole thing looked like something out of a sci-fi movie.

"The Ladies don't live down here." Eric waved to a person with shockingly red hair who appeared in the shimmering square that was one of the white house's windows. "They would never live with the masses."

"And the masses all live underground?" Devon murmured. "Fun."

"It allows us the freedom to live a life of magic while having the convenience of a central location like Manhattan." Eric led us down the street.

The curved cobblestones turned to bricks, which turned to sand as the sidewalk changed with each house. "Ideally, I think we would all prefer to live aboveground and have a city of our own," Eric continued, his voice barely loud enough for us to hear, "but with the way the human race has expanded, there is very little habitable room to hide. Modern fiction isn't wrong about the chaos that would ensue if regulars knew magic existed. People seem so determined to hate anything they can define as *other*. Wizards would be no exception. So, down we went, where the people of the city think myths and monsters live."

"Couldn't you go to the rainforest or Antarctica?" Elizabeth whispered as a face stared at us through a stained glass window.

"If you don't mind spiders, snakes, or the constant prospect of freezing to death. Of course, there are wizards who choose to live in such places," Eric said.

"But you're stuck underground?" What I didn't ask was, if *I* would have to pack up a suitcase and move down here. If we lived through the day. Not that I had anything to pack anyway, since I had successfully destroyed both my parents' homes.

"The Consortium came to Manhattan long before it was a buzzing metropolis. We are too ensconced here," Eric said. "This is where our community was built, and this is where it will stay."

"But—" I began.

"I never question why normal people toil endless hours to pay astronomical Manhattan rent they truly can't afford." Eric's dark eyebrows drew together. "The Big Apple is an addictive place. Beville may require sacrifices, but excitement is not one of them."

We had reached the last house on the street, which was a

giant glass edifice Frank Lloyd Wright might have had a hand in. The sounds in front of us changed. Besides the waterfall rumbling through the glass house, there were voices echoing down the tunnel. Lots of very boisterous voices.

We rounded the corner and walked onto Commerce Street. The street name seemed to fit. The tunnel was lined with shops. A normal looking storefront sold electronics, and a low, gross stone building had a rotting sign out front that read *Cheap Herbs.*

In front of the largest, pale stone place was a group with steins in their hands. It looked like something out of a pirate movie. They were all swaggering and talking loudly while slopping their drinks. A lady in the center of the crowd stood on a table, acting out some story that had everyone around her roaring with laughter.

"Damn." Eric spread his arms and pressed us back into the shadows between two buildings.

"Why damn?" I peeked around the corner as the mob cheered and the woman's laugh boomed over the whooping.

"Technically I've been banned from the Witches Brew," Eric said. "Most people have at some point, but Mildred really does seem to dislike me."

"And you didn't think to mention his before?" I whispered.

"It's the middle of the day." Eric huffed. "I figured she would be sleeping."

"So, now what?" Elizabeth asked. "We can't walk into a place that's banned you and casually drop the fact that we're here trying to hide from some murderous maniacs."

"He can't walk in." Devon smiled. "But I can."

"Devon—"

"You know I've charmed my way into far worse places than a magic Ren Faire pub, Bry." Devon checked his hair in the window. "Besides, they'll never suspect a lowly city dweller of planting information."

"He does have a point." Eric looked Devon up and down. "They'll know he's not from Beville right off. We don't get many strangers walking our streets."

"Then he can't go in," I said. "It's too dangerous."

"I'll be fine." Devon waved a hand a little too casually through the air.

"We should find a way for us all to stay together." Elizabeth caught Devon's hand, not to hold it, just to stop its flippant motion. "You don't need to be the hero, Devon."

"But I do it so well." Devon looked away from Elizabeth and toward the pub. "Besides, I'd rather die working on a plan than hiding. Anyone have any cash?"

"I'd rather none of us die," I said, but Devon wasn't listening as he took a handful of bills from Eric.

"We'll meet you in the gray stone house down the next street. Lark Lane." Eric patted Devon on the shoulder. "Stay safe. And just knock on the door."

"See you in a bit, then." And with that, Devon was gone.

I wanted to scream at him to come back. Or to go instead of him. But Eric was right. If anyone was going to charm their way into us not getting killed, it would be Devon. So, I watched my best friend walk helpless into a pack of witches.

"We need to go." Eric slunk into the far side of the shadows. "It will take us a while to cut around out of sight."

"We can't leave him," I said.

Devon had arrived at the edge of the pub crowd.

"I didn't think I would ever find myself saying something nice about that one, but his combination of debonair bravery, charm, and inability to understand that death is lurking around the corner might be what keeps him alive." Eric took both my shoulders and spun me to face him so I couldn't see Devon anymore. "Don't feel like you're throwing him to the wolves. What we've got ahead of us is worse than walking into a pack of angry wizards. For all we know, Devon might outlive us."

I nodded. I didn't know what else to do.

"Then let's go," Eric said, "or we won't beat Devon to the gray house, and then he'll be stranded on the street."

"I should have gone with him," Elizabeth murmured as we cut around the side of the building. "He shouldn't have gone in alone."

"Where we're going we need the best eyes we've got." Eric led us down another alley and out onto the strangest street I'd seen yet.

The buildings here were so black, they looked like shadows leaning out of the tunnel walls. As we rounded the corner, the noise disappeared as quickly as though someone had slammed a door behind us. I looked around for a street sign as whispers from unseen mouths floated through the air. But there were no signs, and the light from above was only bright enough to cast shadows.

"Where are we?" I breathed.

The soup of whispers in the air seemed to hiss in response.

"It doesn't technically have a name," Eric whispered back like he was in a library, "but I've always called it Shady Lane."

"Cute," I said as something brushed past the back of my neck at the same moment that Elizabeth screamed.

"Bryant!"

I spun around, expecting to see someone attacking her, trying to pull her away. But she was swiping her hands around me like she was trying to push away something that wasn't there. Only...there was. Her hands made contact with something I couldn't see. But I heard the *thud* as her punch landed.

"Elizabeth, no!" Eric raced over to pull her from whatever she was pummeling. "Stop! Stop, Elizabeth! They won't hurt him!"

"Then why was that monster touching him?" Elizabeth shrieked.

I spun around, trying to see the monster. But, nada.

Elizabeth's eyes darted around, her fear only growing. "Did you bring us here so they could kill us?" she spat at Eric. "You cowardly piece of shit!"

"I brought you here to ask these fine people for help," Eric said.

Elizabeth tore a hand free and slapped him across the face.

"And they might be a little more willing to help stop the Ladies from killing us if you stopped trying to hit them."

"Unless"—I heard a voice distinctly coming from thin air—"the Ladies are trying to destroy you for a worthy reason." As the voice spoke, a shadow formed next to me. It grew thicker and darker, gaining dimension with each word.

"Charles." Eric smiled and reached out to shake the shadow's hand.

"I didn't think I would see you again," Charles said, "after the last time you set Commerce Street on fire."

"That." Eric waved a hand dismissively. "There were a few underworldlings roaming around, and the pub was the simplest place to corral them."

"You burned Mildred's pub." Charles laughed. The sound came out like a rattling wheeze.

"No one ever remembers you saved their life," Eric sighed. "All they remember is the structural damage."

"You never change, Eric," Charles said. "I'm afraid the only thing that will kill you is death."

"Then let us hope I don't change today." Eric smiled.

He was talking about dying and smiling. I had followed a psychopath onto a street full of shadow people. And the street *was* full of shadow people now. Filling every doorway, more stepping toward us every moment. I reached back and took Elizabeth's hand. Somehow, the fact that I could feel her warmth as her heart raced made the whole thing a little better. We weren't in a mausoleum. Yet.

"And why is it that you would die today?" Charles asked. "If it's the Ladies you're afraid of, surely they have not been so precise. The last time I heard of them deciding upon an execution, it took them three years to carry out the order. The poor man died of fright before they ever bothered coming for him."

"I'm afraid the Ladies have been tracking us since last night." Eric bowed to Charles. "My friends and I have come to beg for your help in escaping their wrath."

Charles gave a crackling laugh, which sounded like it was shaking the ribs I couldn't see. The rest of the shadows cackled, too, filling the darkness. It took a minute for Charles to calm himself down enough to talk.

"You want our help in making sure the Ladies don't kill you?" Charles finally choked out. "You know our solution to avoiding the Ladies, and I doubt you will find it appealing since you have never accepted our path before."

"Nor could I today," Eric said. "The shadow path isn't mine to tread."

"What shadow path?" If these people knew a way to survive, it would be worth it.

"He's fresh, isn't he?" Charles asked Eric.

"You've no idea." Eric smirked, gesturing for Charles to explain.

"The Ladies control all the magic aboveground," Charles said. "Every spell, every potion, every incantation that has ever been written down is in their Library. They dole out pieces of knowledge like every wizard is standing in a bread line. And with their rules of impartment, the magic can't be shared. They may give me *estuna*." A light shone behind Charles, casting his shadow into deeper relief. "You can say the spell, but unless the

Ladies themselves have given you the knowledge, it would only be a word to you."

Like a dog doing tricks under the dark eyes of the crowd, I sounded out, "*Estuna.*" The moment I said the word, I knew nothing would happen. It felt soggy and heavy in my mouth, the texture of it on my tongue making me gag.

The shadows around us laughed.

"Doesn't feel nice, does it? Helluva copyright protection." Charles said when the laughter died down. "They keep us starving for knowledge to maintain their power."

"That's terrible," Elizabeth said.

Charles and the other shadows nodded as one.

"More than you might realize. Having magic pulse through your veins without a way out is painful." Charles' voice lowered as he spoke. "To live to half your potential, not allowed to reach what you were born to become, illiterate to the language that flows through your blood."

"But I never felt any pain," I said. "Does that mean I'm not really meant to be all magical?"

Eric answered this time. "Your magic is undeniable. You wouldn't have felt the pain. You didn't know you were meant for magic."

"It's the atrophy that's painful. Imagine never knowing your fingers should flex," Charles said. "It wouldn't hurt you, wouldn't trouble you at all. But you've lived your life with hands that move. Imagine losing that now."

"That's...I'm sorry," I said lamely.

The Ladies had crippled the wizards they ruled. Suddenly Thaden didn't seem like such a bad guy. Then I remembered that if all went well, he would be trying to murder us in the next few hours.

"But magic didn't begin with the Ladies or The Consortium's Library." The light behind Charles faded as he stepped closer.

"Magic began deep in the bowels of the earth. Below the rocks where the dead lay. We dig into the darkness, finding the magic piece by piece. Filling ourselves with the power the Ladies have stolen from us."

"And the magic turns you into shadows?" Elizabeth's voice shook as she spoke.

"Traveling through the darkness leaves its marks." Charles reached out to her. "Eventually the darkness stops washing off, and we become shadows."

Elizabeth took Charles' hand in her own.

"But with the coating of the darkness, we find the light of knowledge." Charles smiled. "And isn't the spark of illumination worth living in the shadows?"

"No." Eric stepped between Charles and Elizabeth. "Not when the same knowledge can be gained without losing the ability to go aboveground."

"Thaden has granted you so much power?"

"Thaden is a monster, and I was too full of myself to see it." Lines creased Eric's brow, and for a second, he looked lost. Not snarky or brazen, but truly remorseful. It kind of scared me. "I thought Thaden would give us a path to freedom, but his way would only leave magic chained to a different master."

"If the Ladies want you dead and Thaden won't take you, your only choice may be to join us in the shadows."

"The choices we have may look very different come morning." Eric smiled. "Order will soon crumble from above and below."

Charles took a step back.

"The dark one and the light are going to battle today," Eric said as the shadows closed in. "Neither party wants us to survive. The darkened death will draw us all into the blackness forever. The Ladies will never let us walk freely in the light. Would you be content to let wizards live forever in the middle? Buried in a living tomb?"

Whispers flew around the street. Words I couldn't hear or didn't understand. But one syllable rang out clear. *No.*

"Then help us!" Eric's voice pounded through the darkness. "We have an opportunity today that won't come again for a century. And if you help me, my friends, if you stand by my side when the spells shatter our walls, we *will* break free!"

The shadows cheered. And that was the moment I realized Eric was the hero. In a world I didn't understand, following plans I didn't know about, and doing magic I didn't think could be done. Somehow on the way from the Meatpacking District to the Village, I had become the sidekick in my own story.

25

I t took a few minutes for the crowd to stop cheering long enough for anyone to speak. Charles told us to follow him. Eric said something about claiming the day, and the shadows cheered some more. It was like a magical shadow pep rally. Finally, when I was afraid someone would break into a valedictorian speech, the crowd surged down the street.

"It seems you've won the majority, brother." Charles clapped Eric on the shoulder as he led us away. "But be mindful," he added so quietly I could barely hear, "if you lead us to our end, the shadows will follow you forever."

I shuddered even though I didn't know what Charles meant.

"Is he really your brother?" I whispered as we wound deeper down Shady Lane. I know it might seem like a weird thing to be worrying about when you're being escorted by a swarm of silhouettes planning a major battle, but it was the only thing in the conversation that made enough sense for me to try and hold onto.

"Brothers in arms," Eric said.

"Right." I nodded even though Eric wasn't looking at me.

I kept waiting to turn off the street or go into a house, or maybe for the whole parade to turn into a scene from Les Miserables, where we would all stand on tables and sing about freedom.

We reached the end of the tunnel where a solid wall blocked our path, but our companions kept going, melting into the pitch black.

Eric kept walking in front of us like everything was normal. But the closer we got to the shimmering black stone, the more crushing the atmosphere became. My heart picked up speed. The shadow wizards might be able to survive walking through the wall, but not me. I would be smothered into oblivion.

"We can't go in there," I whispered.

"Of course we can," Eric said, all blasé as he stepped into darkness.

I panicked. "Elizabeth." I grabbed her hand, pulling her back the moment before she would have disappeared into the solid stone. "Don't go in there. You'll die."

"You can't see it, can you?" Elizabeth tipped her head to the side like she was studying me.

"There's nothing to see."

A shadow pushed past, jostling me into the crowd.

"Trust me." Elizabeth laced her fingers through mine. "There is a way through." She smiled. And she wasn't afraid or worried. She was perfect, her hair shining against the shadows.

I nodded and closed my eyes, letting her lead me onward. I waited to walk into a wall or for the darkness to crush my lungs till there wasn't enough left of me to breathe. The air got thick for a minute, like I was walking through a storm made solid, but then it became cool and damp. And I took a deep breath. It smelled like a forest after the rain. Not such a bad smell, not the scent of a place where you were going to die any second. I opened my eyes.

I wished I hadn't.

Things moved all around me, but it was like I was catching the movement out of the corner of my eye. Flickers that told me I was surrounded by a hundred things just out of sight.

Charles had faded among the rest of the shadows, his voice just discernible as he shouted orders, but the only people I could see were Elizabeth and Eric.

"What's happening?" I whispered.

"Charles is talking to people," Elizabeth said. "They're putting on armor, but not like any I've ever seen. It's like they're covering themselves in smoke."

"For protection against the Ladies," Eric said.

"Why can both of you see this and I can't?" I grumbled as the largest flicker yet moved past me.

Elizabeth gasped. Whatever had walked in front of us was huge.

"Because I've trained for years to be able to see the things that roam in the darkness." Which, incidentally, grew denser as Eric spoke. "And Elizabeth has a born ability to see what lurks beneath the surface of the world."

"Didn't you mention you've been seeing things creeping around for years?" I asked, trying desperately to keep from squeaking.

"I..." Elizabeth struggled for words as I tightened my hold on her hand, clinging to the one tangible thing in this world of nightmares. "I mean, I've always been afraid of the dark. Like I could see something there, hiding. But I couldn't see it like this. Living people with faces. I chalked it up to being a wimp with an overactive imagination."

"But then why today?" I asked, my voice growing louder as my fear turned into anger. "Why can she suddenly see all this crazy stuff now? What did you do to her?"

"I didn't do anything to her," Eric said. "Elizabeth has always had a special sight. Fate simply chose this time for her to become a true seer."

"Fate?" I half-shouted. "Fate decided I should find a phone and become all magical? Fate decided Elizabeth should be a seer? And what has fate decided for you? That you should go talk to shadow Charles and start a magical war under Manhattan?"

"Fate builds on what is already there." A shadow moved out of the corner of my eye, and there was Charles. "We have wanted the same things Eric has been working for for years. When Thaden appeared"—a *whoosh* like a terrified whisper shot around the room—"we thought he would be the answer. A way to knowledge without a life in the darkness. We are not shadows, but students of the oldest magic. Thaden promised us a way out, but his way is filled with more death and despair than we are willing to bring into the world. Thaden wants control. Not freedom. Living under his rule would be no better than living under the Ladies."

"Right, okay." I clenched my head in my hands. "None of this makes any sense. Am I just supposed to go along with the fight between the black pieces and the white pieces like this is a game of chess? I'm getting dragged through this crazy shit, and I'm only seeing the surface. I don't even know which side I should be on."

"On this side." Elizabeth took my face in her hands. I stared hard into her sparkly eyes, and for a moment, the world stopped spinning.

But I couldn't stay still. Things were still out of control, still uncertain.

"How can you even trust Eric," I directed my words at a shadow I thought might be Charles, "if Thaden is your enemy and you know Eric worked with him? He's only fighting Thaden because he messed up and now Thaden wants to kill him."

"Don't question why allies are allies," Eric cautioned.

"None of us are innocent," Charles's voice came from a different shadow than the one I had been speaking to. "When you're trapped between two different evils, one can begin to look like a savior. We've been fighting for a freedom away from the shadows and the Ladies for a long time. Eric isn't the first to have seen false promise in darkness."

"Thank you, brother," Eric said.

"And I'm just supposed to trust that this is a great idea?"

The shadow of Charles's head bobbled like he was nodding.

"You have to, Bryant," Elizabeth said.

"Because Lola has my mom, and if I don't do what Eric says, I may never get past the decaying dogs to stage a rescue?" My voice sounded dry to my ears, like I had just aged ten years.

"Because the Ladies are out for blood. *Our* blood," Elizabeth said. "They didn't speak to us or try to make things right. They went right for the kill."

"Eric tried to kill us at my dad's."

"And he failed," Elizabeth said. "Which means if he doesn't turn out to be the one we want to support, we'll kill him."

"I suppose that's as good a vote of confidence any leader of a rebellion can hope for." Eric laughed.

"If you're going to call yourself the leader, you should probably get to the leading." Charles' voice came from right behind my left shoulder. "Coat the girl first."

"Do what?" Elizabeth said.

I spun to face the voice, pushing Elizabeth behind me.

"You need to be able to see," Eric said, his voice so calm I wanted to deck him.

"She can see," I growled. "She can see all your friends surrounding us."

"If she were coated, she would be able to see without being seen," Charles said.

"But then I would never be able to go home." Elizabeth's voice shook. "You said the shadows can't go aboveground."

"If they coat you in shadow, it will wear off in time," Eric said. "The effects outside the tunnel would be minimal and temporary. If we want to be able to see the battle as it happens, we need you to be able to get close."

"It won't hurt," Charles said. He was close now. He had crept around my back between me and Elizabeth.

"Don't!" I shouted, but I couldn't move my arms. They were pinned to my sides by hands I couldn't see.

"It will feel like a cold fall rain," the shadow said.

Elizabeth looked terrified as the shadows closed in.

"Stop!" I screamed as drops of black appeared on the top of Elizabeth's head. It was like someone was pouring a bucket of ink over her, the black dripping down her head, covering her face, her arms, hands. "No!" I roared, but the blackness didn't stop. It was swallowing Elizabeth, changing her into something I couldn't see. "*Aarantha!*"

I reached for the tips of Elizabeth's fingers and pulled her close to my chest as the wind whipped around us, howling into a twister.

Screaming cut through the wind. It sounded like the people on the outside were as scared as I was. But I couldn't see them. Only shadows dancing in and out of the wind.

"Bryant, stop!" Elizabeth screamed. "Stop it!" Her warm cheek pressed into mine. "I'm okay. He didn't hurt me."

Slowly, I let go of the spell. And when I say I let go, I really mean I stopped wanting to destroy everything in sight for killing Elizabeth, and the funnel cloud sort of went away. But *letting go of the spell* sounds way cooler and much more like I was in control, so we're going with that.

Part of me expected the shadows to attack as soon as the wind died. I think Elizabeth thought the same thing since she kept close, her back pressed to me. Her arms reached back and she grabbed my hands. Her breathing resonated through my chest. But all I could see was a wisp of smoke where Elizabeth's bright blond hair should have been.

"*Aarantha*," a voice whispered from somewhere deep in the darkness.

"How did he find *Aarantha*?" another voice hissed.

"The Ladies have that magic!" a third voice cried. "He has come from the Ladies."

"No!" I shouted as the rumble of anger surged through the crowd. "I found the spell on Thaden's phone. It's on a list of defensive spells. That's why I've used it."

But the rumbling didn't stop. It worsened, the voices encircling us. Eric backed up so he was only a foot from me. There was barely enough room to fit Elizabeth.

"There is no way the boy should have that magic!"

"He's in concert with The Consortium!"

"The phone is Thaden's!" I shouted, but no one was listening.

"The spell did not come from the Ladies." Eric's voice rang out clear over the crowd. "Look at him. Does the boy look like he's seen the magic of Beville? He's a city dweller. Thaden himself found a way into the great Library and stole the magic from the Ladies." The crowd quieted. They were listening to Eric like he was giving a speech in the state house. "Thaden made a device that could carry all the knowledge of our books out into the world. A device that is untouched by the Ladies' rules of impartment and allows magic to move freely into the learner. The boy found it. The magic opened itself to him. He used magic, massive magic without any knowledge of how it works, and he survived. He continues to use it and survive."

A hiss of *impossible* floated through the crowd.

"It is not impossible if fate has chosen him to be a part of this great day," Eric said. "The golden threads have drawn him here as they have drawn each of us. Do not fear this boy because his strand of fate has pulled him to this battle in days instead of the years it has taken the rest of us. He is here for a purpose. We are all here for a purpose. Our purpose is to clear a path to a better tomorrow. To a future where the choice is not between prison or darkness. This is a battle a century in the making. And the strings of fate pulled this boy here to stand at the point of it all! Who will stand with him?"

I was shouting, cheering with the crowd. We were going to change the magical world I didn't know anything about but had already ruined my life. And then I realized Eric was talking about me. That *I* was special. That I was somehow destined to be a part of a battle that would unfold in the next few hours. A battle that might get me killed.

But the cheering didn't stop, and hands I couldn't see patted me on the back and dragged me forward. I felt a hand close around mine and knew it was Elizabeth without whispering her name. Eric led us to the end of the shadowy tomb room.

I barely heard Eric shout *"Portunda!"* before the black wall shook, and a door appeared. The door wasn't bright or shining, but after the blinding darkness, even that little bit of color overwhelmed my eyes and I had to blink before I could clearly make it out. It was wood painted gray, but even through the thick coat, the wood looked heavy and old.

"Charles, will you come through with us?" Eric said.

"As you wish," Charles said.

My brain registered Charles giving commands, but the words floated right by me.

Then Eric opened the gray door, and I tightened my grip on Elizabeth's hand and followed him into the house.

But forward isn't always safer than back, even if back wasn't all that nice to begin with.

26

I spun around as the door shut behind me. There was a shadow next to the door. It didn't look frightening or thick. It looked more like the person making the shadow had forgotten to show up. Like Peter Pan's shadow had finally won his bid for freedom.

I took a breath and looked down to where I still held Elizabeth's hand. She didn't look like someone had dumped ink over her head anymore. It was more like she'd become a charcoal sketch of herself, drawn in gray scale with soft edges all around. The only white left was her eyes.

Elizabeth sighed. "Well, choices were made. Some choices were bad."

My laugh caught in my throat.

"I find the choice with the best chance of leading to my survival is usually the right choice," Eric said from across the room.

"And I don't have to be"—my voice faltered on the word—"*coated* to survive?"

"You won't need it for your work in the battle," Eric said,

"and I have no intention of hiding my whereabouts. Alas, Elizabeth is the only one in need."

I wanted to say something witty or brave about work in the battle or even make fun of Eric for saying *alas*, but nothing came to mind, so I studied the room instead. I wish I could tell you that looking around this room didn't surprise me because I had already been in a vault of shadows and in a sub-overpass lair of a seer. But I don't know if I could ever achieve the level of cool required to not be shocked when I walked from a place of blackness into a Victorian Row House, complete with lace curtains and plush window seats with fancy-looking green fabric covering the cushions.

There was a sofa near the table and a settee, at least I think it was a settee, near the fireplace where flames crackled merrily away. A fancy lace cloth covered the table in the middle of the room. And a silver tea tray with five china teacups rested on top. Like someone had been expecting the four of us to arrive. With a cup saved for Devon.

The walls were covered in bookshelves. Old books, new books, titles I recognized, some with titles in languages I had never heard of before.

"You know, if the Ladies came to tea, they would banish you from Beville for hoarding magical knowledge from The Consortium." Charles poured himself a cup of tea. Watching a shadow pour tea into a cup is freaky. It didn't seem like his hands should be substantial enough to lift the cup, let alone his intestines to process the tea.

I tried not to think about shadow digestion as Eric chortled, "Well, most of the forbidden books were given to me by you." He poured himself a cup and sat down. "Besides, I have the house well trained to hide all the less innocuous items should I have guests who might not appreciate my collection."

Without him saying a spell or clapping his hands or

anything, the bookshelves trembled for a second before the bottom half disappeared. Now from the ground to my waist was normal wall with pale blue and white wallpaper.

"Handy." Charles took another sip of his tea.

"This old place has been in the family so long," Eric sighed, "I hate to bring the fight to her, but she's a tough old broad. I've taught her to mend herself, so she has as good a chance of making it through the night as the rest of us."

Elizabeth's hand started to shake in mine.

"Do you want some tea?" I asked lamely.

I think there was a whole conversation about tea being comforting in a play my mom had directed. Devon had been obsessed with it ever since. I'm hardly a fan myself, but in the moment, it seemed like the best thing to do.

Elizabeth nodded, and the movement of her head left smudges of black in the air that lingered briefly, before fading away.

I poured us two cups, adding cream and sugar carefully before stirring. It felt so bizarre. To be sipping our tea out of fancy, gold-decorated china while we waited to find out if Devon had managed to set us up to be at the eye of a battle.

Armed with cups, Elizabeth and I took the sofa. It was large enough that there could have been space for another person between us, but Elizabeth sat right next to me, her hip pressing into mine. My stomach jumped up and down like I had swallowed a hyperactive poodle.

"Devon should be arriving soon." Eric pulled the curtain back an inch and peeked outside.

"And he's told them to come to your house?" Charles said. "I suppose I should give you points for bravery."

"It would be terribly rude of me if I arranged for a battle on someone else's front steps." Eric's lips quirked. "Besides, all things being equal, I prefer to fight on ground that will fight with me."

"Fight with you?" I asked.

"I did say my house is very well trained."

"How do you train—" But I never finished my question as Elizabeth asked her own, and well, her topic took precedence.

"Won't they still be able to see me?" Her voice never wavered as she looked down at our hands that had somehow found their way back together. "I mean, I can see me."

"Thaden, yes," Charles said. The house groaned at his words. "But not the Ladies, and they're the ones whose tricks we may not be able to see until it's too late."

"Thaden," Eric said, "draws his magic from the same place as Charles and the other shadows. Think of it as being able to read the same language. If—"

"When," Charles interrupted.

"When," Eric conceded, "Thaden brings a few of his shadow beasties with him, Charles and his friends will be able to hold them back while Thaden is distracted by the Ladies."

"But whatever the Ladies bring along"—Charles' outline shifted like he might have been shrugging—"maybe we'll be able to catch a glimmer of them."

"And where I might be able to get a healthy gist of what's going on," Eric said, pointing to Elizabeth, "she can see the Ladies' magic for what it is."

"And now that we've coated her," Charles finished, "she'll also be able to see what Thaden is doing without being seen."

"So you're going to put me someplace high up where I can be safe while I watch my friends risk their lives?" Elizabeth's voice was hollow.

"They're going to put you someplace high up where you can try and help us win," I said. "We can't do this without you."

I don't know if I can do this at all. I wanted to shout at Eric that I was done. That I was in way over my head.

When this whole thing started, it was like I was snorkeling in shallow water. Maybe I couldn't touch everything at the bottom, but I could see the fish and the sand swirling. That was plenty, but now I had swum too far. Out over the deep where all I could see was dark water.

Before I could try and put all of that into words that didn't sound like they belonged in a creative writing competition, there was a knock at the door.

Eric's neck tensed, but as I moved to stand, he held up a hand to keep me in place.

"That could be Devon," I whispered. I don't know why I whispered, it just seemed like the thing to do.

"The house knows who it should let in," Eric said.

The distant *creak* of a door opening carried up the hall. A few footsteps, and then a door slammed. I held my breath, waiting for Devon to call out, but instead there was another *slam*. Then another and another. Footsteps pounded toward us along with a string of curses.

"Devon!" I shouted, and a second later, he sprinted into the parlor. His shirt torn, his face panicked, but it was Devon, very much alive. Something inside me unclenched.

"Is this place trying to kill me?" Devon panted, glaring at Eric. "The house *chased* me."

"Don't think of it as chasing. Think of it as escorting without words," Eric said.

I think Devon would have seriously blown up, but then his eyes found Elizabeth. "What did they do to you?" he breathed.

"My own personal camouflage and night vision," Elizabeth said. "I'm told it's temporary."

"Right." Devon nodded and looked to me. "Bryant?"

"I'm good," I said. "What happened to you?"

"*Pft.*" Devon shrugged. "It all went according to plan. Well, at least the important life or death bits. Everyone at the bar knows Eric is hiding in the gray stone house, the Ladies are after him, and he has something Thaden wants."

"And then they attacked you to stop you from warning us they're going to tip off Thaden and the Ladies?" Eric asked, pointing to Devon's ripped shirt. A trickle of blood marked his skin where it looked like he'd been scratched.

"What?" Devon looked down at his chest. "Ah. I mean, maybe a few of the guys who looked really tough wanted a piece of me for saying a few nasty things about our two sets of baddies. But Mildred wasn't having any of it. She pulled me into her backroom. And well, the scratches are from *her* when she got a little too intense about protecting me. It's okay though. I told her I had to defend my friends, and I think she swooned a little as I split."

"Only you"—Elizabeth shook her head, leaving smudges in the air again. Devon was smart enough not to say anything if he noticed—"would be able to walk into a group that wanted you dead and walk out with a woman swooning over you."

"And that's what makes him useful," Eric said. "How long ago did the minions scatter to their masters?"

"I would say about forty-five minutes since Mildred pulled me into a closet." Devon walked over and poured himself a cup of tea, chugging it before pouring himself another.

"Then they should be here at any moment." Eric stood, clapping his hands together. "Devon, you go with Elizabeth up to the lookout."

"I should stay down here to fight!" Devon's perfectly shaped brows pinched together.

"Fists and good looks won't be of use when the spells start to fly. Go with Elizabeth. Your job is to tell us everything she sees." Eric tossed Devon a mirror. "Stay low and out of sight, speak into this, and we'll hear you. Go through that door, and the house will lead you up the stairs." As good as Eric's word, a door appeared in the bookcase on the back wall.

"What about Bryant?" Elizabeth asked. "Where is he going?"

"He'll be far from the fighting," Eric said.

"Far from the fighting," I repeated. "What does that mean?"

"It means you'll be with the phone. I don't need you collapsing the tunnel on us while we fight," Eric said.

"So, I'm going to stand there with a deadly object and hope no one notices?"

"More or less," Eric said.

"It's a good plan," added Charles.

Devon's eyes whipped to the shadow at the same second he spat out his tea. "What the—"

But before he could ask why a shadow was talking, the house rumbled. It felt like we were in the belly of a growling beast.

"Showtime." Eric fixed his hair in the mirror. "Lady and gentleman, if you will." He took Devon and Elizabeth by their arms and led them to the new door.

"But Bryant—" Devon said.

"I'll be fine," I said, not feeling at all confident in that fact. "Take care of Elizabeth."

"Yes, that's all very sweet." Eric gave them a shove as the house rumbled again.

"Be careful, Bryant!" Elizabeth shouted as Eric slammed the door behind her, and it disappeared.

"You, too," I whispered to the books.

"Now you come with me." Eric walked me over to the fireplace. "Step through the flames and stay put." He pressed a mirror into my hand. "This will allow me to let you know if the plan changes."

"But I should be out there fighting with you," I tried, but Charles spoke gently over me.

"My apologies, but we don't have time for this." His shadowy hand pulled back the lace curtain.

"Listen to me, Bryant." Eric stared at me fiercely. "For some reason, fate has chosen you to survive. You played with fire and didn't get burned. You escaped me twice, and the Ladies. I was half-sure the shadow wizards would kill you for being a city dweller with the audacity to go to them asking for help."

"That wasn't my—"

"But you've survived," Eric said, his eyes dazzling. "Elizabeth is right. Fate has great plans for your life, and I won't risk those plans on my very own lawn. Part of living an extraordinary life is knowing when the game is up. A hero doesn't live forever." Eric gave me a shove, and I tumbled backward into the fire.

"Make your adventure great." Eric's words echoed as I fell through the dancing orange flames and into the darkness.

27

I was flat on a cold floor. The fire was gone, and I hadn't been burned.

I pushed myself to my feet and felt around. As far as I could tell, I was in a stone room the size of a walk-in closet.

Fumbling in my pocket, I pulled out the black phone. I pressed my thumb to the button, and the screen flicked on.

"All this for a phone," I muttered.

But then I heard Eric's voice in my head. *This isn't about a phone. It's about freedom of knowledge. It's about living outside the darkness.*

I scrolled across the screen to a button that looked like a ball of light. I tapped it with my thumb and instantly found the glowing sphere in my free hand, 3-D and working.

I had guessed right, the room was top to bottom stone. The same stone as the fireplace. There was a meeting of two—make that three—deadly forces a hundred yards away, and I was locked in a fireplace. I wasn't even a sidekick anymore. I'd been demoted to helpless bystander.

I sat down on the ground and leaned back against the wall. My blood pumped hard through my veins, my body telling me to run or fight. But I couldn't do either. I was trapped. And it didn't sound like Eric was planning on coming back for me.

A hero doesn't live forever.

I gripped my head with my hands, feeling my hair singe where I pressed the light to it. I couldn't even hold a magical flashlight without messing it up.

I screamed in rage and frustration. I roared and cursed. But when I stopped, the screaming didn't. The shouts came from my pocket, from the mirror Eric had given me before shoving me into this damn safe room.

I pulled out the mirror. Devon's face appeared.

"I don't know if this is working right." His voice cut clearly through the distant screams. It sounded like banshees wailing in anger.

"Just keep talking to it," Elizabeth said. "There's nothing else we can do."

"Fine, what do you see?" Devon asked.

"Flying at the end of the tunnel," Elizabeth's voice carried to the mirror like Devon was holding a phone on speaker near her face. "It looks like women. Shadowy women with big bat wings. Charles' people, too. They're running toward the flying women. I think they can see them. At the low entrance in the middle. Shit...."

Her pause made my heart leap to my throat.

"Devon, stay down, don't let them see you. It's the Ladies, but there's more of them. Thirteen I can see," Elizabeth said. "Eric, watch out! Behind the ladies. There are things."

"What things?" Devon asked.

"I don't know. I don't know what they are. They look like clouds, but clearer, cats maybe. Oh God, they're fast. Eric, in front of you!" Elizabeth shrieked, and I jumped to my feet.

Why was Eric out there fighting already? He was going to let them destroy each other, and then we would take on the losers.

Unless that hadn't really been the plan. Only what he had told me to keep me from trying to break out of the chimney.

"Sorry for the scare, Elizabeth," Eric said. "I think I've got them following me now."

"You thought right!" Elizabeth shouted. "Run faster. Eric, the flying shadows, there're more. They're penning you in."

I pounded my fist on the wall. Pain shot through my hand, and no, it didn't really help matters, as bangs, howls, and screeches came through the mirror.

"Keep going, keep going, you're almost clear," Elizabeth chanted. "The Ladies are still by the low entrance. They're watching the fight. Wait, there's something at the far end. I can't make it out. It looks like a shadow."

Everything went silent. I stared at the mirror, terrified the connection had been broken. Or, a hundred times worse, Elizabeth and Devon weren't there to talk anymore.

"He's here." Eric's voice broke the silence.

"Eric, get out of there," Elizabeth whispered, as though terrified to be overheard. But an instant later, screams of hatred like I had never heard before burst forth so viscerally, they shook the walls of my prison. It was like Hell had just let all its demons pour out onto the street.

"Elizabeth!" I shouted. "Devon! Get off the roof."

"Thaden." Elizabeth's voice was strong and clear. "He's got crawling things with him. And more women flying above. Eric, climb up on something, now. Spiders, I think they're spiders. Eric, the Ladies. They're aiming for Thaden. Eric, they aren't looking at you, run. The cats are leaving the shadows behind. They're coming toward you. Eric, run left, now!"

I listened as she gave him directions. It was like she was choreographing him as he fought.

"Good!" she shouted triumphantly.

A thunder blast echoed through the mirror. "Eric, one of the

Ladies. She's turned away from Thaden. She's coming for you. The shadows are heading your way. Another Lady is leaving Thaden. Oh God! She sees me. Eric, she's coming toward me. Eric, what do we do? Eric!"

But I could hear Eric shouting spells, caught up in his own battle. Besides, he was on the street far below Elizabeth and Devon. They were trapped on the roof, helpless.

"Let me out!" I screamed at the chimney. "I said let me out!"

I waited stupidly for a moment like the walls would listen to me and realize that I had to get out. Of course, the dark stone stayed in place.

"Fine!" I shouted. "*Portunda!*" The word felt heavy in my mouth and the wall didn't move. Muttering curses under my breath that would have made Devon proud, I whipped the phone out of my pocket and started searching as soon as the screen flickered on.

"Eric, they're coming!" Elizabeth's voice echoed through the mirror.

I tried to scroll through the spells, but my fingers shook too badly.

"Get down!" Devon shouted a second before Elizabeth screamed.

"They're dying!" I bellowed. "My friends are dying. *Please* let me out."

Yes, screaming at a solid wall never did anything for anyone, but Elizabeth was in danger, and I didn't know what else to do. "Please, I have to save them."

With a *crack*, the stone in front of me split, leaving a gap barely large enough for me to fit through.

"Thank you." I squeezed through the opening. I wasn't back in the parlor. I was at the bottom of a wooden staircase lined with doors. They were spaced along the walls every few feet, not high enough up to be on the second floor, some at odd angles, and none where doors should have been.

The crack behind me shuddered closed, and I started running up the stairs. Except, if none of the doors made sense, how was I supposed to know which one led to the roof? As I raced up, the doors in front of me opened, slamming as I passed as though I was being chased—or maybe led to where I was supposed to go. I ran up and up, screams still coming from the mirror. It wasn't only Elizabeth and Devon I was hearing now, but also inhuman, high-pitched wails.

I ran as fast as I could, but the stairs still wound up. Maybe this was the house's way of keeping me safe, making me run and run while the others fought, never getting close enough to help them.

Just when I thought I would never reach the top, a door opened to my left. It was slanted toward me, like an attic hatch. All the doors in front of me and behind me slammed at once with a *bang* that pounded in my ears, but the hatch stayed open. As I neared it, I heard Elizabeth again. Screaming and terrified, but alive. I jumped from the steps to the trap door, pulling myself up and through without breaking my stride.

And then I was on a roof like any normal roof in Manhattan, covered in tar paper with a foot-high brick edge. For a horrible second, I thought I had run too far. That I was aboveground in the Manhattan skyline. But the sounds in the air weren't from traffic, and the lights above didn't come from the skyscrapers.

White things swooped over my head. Birds with raptor beaks, bat wings, and reptilian tails.

"Leave him *alone*," Elizabeth growled.

I spun to face her.

Devon was on the ground. He was unconscious, bleeding hard from his head, and Elizabeth stood over him, swinging her bloody fists at the birds as they dove at her, clawing and pecking.

"Elizabeth!" I screamed. Everything froze.

Then she looked at me. As her lips curved around my name, her voice was drowned out by the wailing screeches of the birds streaking straight at me.

And then it was like everything slowed down. I saw the birds, their feathers and their scales. Their red hateful eyes. Instinct told me to raise my arms and protect my face. But there was another, calmer voice, and somehow I spoke, "*Aarantha!*" The vortex formed around me, and I ran toward Elizabeth, ducking low as the birds tried to hit me.

"Bryant!" she screamed as I held her close, shielding her head with my arms as the winds fought to pull the birds away. But these birds weren't like the fire, mist, or shadows. They had wings to fight the wind. Their wings pummeled the air as they struggled to break free, screeching and howling. And something in their cawing made sense.

You will die, usurper of magic. You will die below the earth.

It was like I was understanding words I didn't know existed. And as the first bird broke free from the vortex, I wished I hadn't understood.

"*Abalata!*" I screamed, and the thick black unspooled from my palm, pummeling the bird and knocking it through the twister and far out of sight.

But there were still more birds calling for my blood. I gripped the phone in my hand and flipped to the fire tab, hoping I knew what I was doing. Tapping the fire button, I tilted the scale all the way to the burning edge.

Instantly, the flames filled the vortex, and the birds screamed. Terrible screams, almost human. Their feathers twisted and blackened, their scales charred, and one by one, they dropped out of the air. I clutched Elizabeth to me, waiting for the smoke to smother us or for something larger to catapult down to kill us.

But the last bird vanished into the flames. Still, I waited for a moment, the heat from the fire roasting my face, before I dropped the scale to the other end, extinguishing the inferno. I let the spell go, and the vortex faded away.

I took a breath. And then another. But nothing flew at us or crept over the edge of the roof. Elizabeth clung to me, not talking, just staring around. The only sounds were our shaky panting and the echoes of the fight far below.

"Devon," I said after a minute, kneeling next to him. Bruises peppered his face, and a gash on top of his head sluggishly bled, painting his skin and hair a bright, kitschy shade of crimson.

Elizabeth tore off her sleeve and pressed it to his scalp. "He was trying to protect me." Her voice was thick with tears as she bound his head. I think she had learned that in last year's spring play. "I was watching the battle, and then those things came."

The screams and bangs bellowing up were nightmarish. Noises that weren't even human. But I suppose the things I had killed weren't human either.

I laid a hand on Devon's chest. Once I made sure it still rose and fell, I crept toward the edge of the roof, keeping my head low until I was close enough to peer over the bricks.

I had never thought I would need to describe something like that. The roof was higher than it should have been. Six stories up at least, but even from here, the blood that coated the ground by the left tunnel shone red in the dim light, where wisps of shadow still battled shimmers of brightness.

By the low cavern, only two Ladies had been left standing. One of them was familiar from our run-in back at my mom's apartment. The other looked twice as old, bent over at the waist, hair hanging limp and spider-web-thin around bony features.

In front of the house was another Lady—the other one who had tried to off me at my mom's. She hovered between Eric and Thaden, her head twitching back and forth like a snake's as they all fought each other in a horrible three-way battle, trading spells and trying to shield themselves as the dark winged women flew overhead, casting spells on the Lady and Eric, and the shimmering things and spiders indiscriminately attacked everything that wasn't their master.

I wanted to watch, maybe find Charles. But even if I had been able to tell the shadows apart, I couldn't have pulled my eyes from Thaden. Tall and broad, like some hero from a story-book, with jet black hair that curled up at the ends.

He looked for all the world like my dad. My breath caught in my throat, and the cacophony of the battle disappeared.

My dad was Thaden.

He was going to turn around and make eye contact with me. Then we would have the big moment—*Bryant, it's true. I am your father.*—and the whole battle would stop. Every time he had missed my birthday, he was digging under the city tunnels, creating evil minions. Every overseas trip had been a sham. My father wasn't a workaholic businessman. He was a homicidal wizard.

But there was something much bigger than Thaden/Dad pushing out of the tunnel. Something dark and as large as a house that made me forget about shadowy family reunions. Eric was the first to see the monster. He froze, immediately forgetting the Lady and Thaden, and sprinted away, casting a green, shimmering spell in his wake.

The Lady aimed another spell at him, and waves of shaking red shot toward Eric, but before they even met their mark, the Lady turned and saw the ink-black monster. I didn't think it was possible for a Lady to turn any paler, but as the monster bore down on her, she turned white as a full moon. Her screams echoed up to the roof as the beast reached down and picked her up in its hands, squeezing her until the screaming stopped.

I wanted to throw up, but didn't have the time. Thaden was

giving his creature orders, and the thing was turning toward Eric, who ran straight for the fighting shimmers and shadows.

"Stay with Devon," I said to Elizabeth, feeling like someone else was forming the words. "Get him back inside."

"Where are you going?" She grabbed my hand, looking terrified. "You can't go down there. There's a giant minotaur, in case you hadn't noticed!"

Part of me wanted to scream, *I have to stop my dad from murdering people*, but the other part knew it didn't matter if Thaden really was my absentee millionaire father. It was like fate was whispering in my ear that it was my turn to be a hero, no matter what waited for me on the bloody floor.

I looked down, trying to make out that mythic shape Elizabeth saw so clearly. But for me, it was just darkness on Eric's heels. "I have to help him," I said. "If he dies, we all die." And it was true. Even if Eric had meant to go out in a blaze of glory and leave me alive for whatever dumb thing he thought fate had planned after this, he was wrong.

"Bryant—"

"I have to," I said, trying to find the words to explain. But Elizabeth took my face in her hands and kissed me. My heart raced, and my head spun.

"Don't die," she whispered before stepping back to Devon.

I nodded and turned to the edge of the roof.

28

I stared dumbly for a few seconds, wanting to do something heroic like leap from the edge and to the battle below. But then I would be dead as soon as I hit the ground, and what good would I be to Eric then?

I took a deep breath and pulled out the phone, tapping my way to the *Quick Escape Spells at a Glance. Aarantha* was at the top of the list, but I wanted a way down, not a tornado to do even more damage to the top of Eric's poor, sentient house.

So, I scrolled down, hoping a spell would look right. *Escata.* The word jumped out at me like I had known I was looking for it. Like I knew the description was *a speedy decent with relative assurance of survival* before I read it.

I climbed up onto the brick parapet. The giant shadow was gaining on Eric. It was now or never. I wanted to look back at Elizabeth and Devon to make sure they were still safe. But I knew if I did, I wouldn't be able to step off of the roof and into thin air.

I took a deep breath and jumped, shouting, *"Escata!"* My speed didn't slow when I said the word. I was still falling, fast. I was going to hit the ground and break my legs. At best. And just as I closed my eyes so I wouldn't have to watch my own bones shatter, I hit something. Not something hard or bouncy. It was more like I had jumped off a high dive and into a pool of pudding.

I opened my eyes, and my feet were still a foot aboveground, and I was sinking slowly, too slowly. Charles' shadows at the far end of the tunnel were screaming as the monster closed in. I picked one foot up, and the air made a horrible sucking noise before my spell vanished and I fell forward onto the street, landing flat on my face.

Pushing myself off my stomach, I raced toward the monster. The black shadow looked taller and broader from down here. It was at least twenty feet high with shoulders as wide as I was tall, and giving off a terrible, angry roar as it waded into the shadows. A few charged him, a suicide run.

A high scream and a terrible crunch sounded from high in the air. I didn't need Elizabeth's breathless, "He ate that woman!" to come through the mirror to know the result.

And while the shouts of anger and fear carried through Charles' men, and the shrieks of the women flying above mixed with the growls of the shimmering white cats and the bellows of the minotaur, one sound carried above the rest. A low laugh that shook the walls and was more frightening than all the shadows and mist combined.

I spun toward the sound. Thaden walked slowly in the minotaur's wake, drinking in the panic. Veiled in inky black, his face was darker than the minotaur's shadow, but somehow, I could still make out the details. His mouth cocked in a triumphant grin. His eyes locked on mine.

I searched his features for something familiar. Something that would tell me my dad had a good reason for becoming the evil Thaden.

"Dad!" I shouted above the screams. "You have to stop this!"

For a moment the blackened face shimmered, transmuting into a mocking grin.

But the lips were wrong. The top one was so narrow, I could barely see it. And his eyes were set too far apart, and his chin too chiseled.

"You're not my dad." A laugh tumbled out of me, shaking my ribs, before another scream and crunch told me the shadow monster had eaten another one of Charles' people.

"I am the father of a whole new world, a world where magic will reign." Thaden's voice shook the air.

"Still way better than I thought." I ran a hand over my face. "Not that this isn't awful but—"

"I am glad death amuses you."

"Amused isn't really what I'm feeling."

"You might have a place in the world yet." Thaden smiled. "You have something that belongs to me." He was still a hundred feet away, but it might as well have been inches. My skin prickled.

For a second, I thought about lying, or running. But the phone was in my hand, and there was nowhere to go.

"Yep!" I finally answered, as loudly as I could muster.

"If you give me what is mine," Thaden said, "I may let you leave with your life."

"Really?" The tone of mock belief that came out of my mouth shocked me. I sounded badass. And knowing I sounded like I wasn't afraid kind of made me feel a little less like I had jumped helpless into a battle I couldn't even see properly, thinking my dad might be a mass murderer and finding out, no, a stranger was going to kill me instead. "Because I was under the impression you were the kind of guy who kills everyone who gets in his way."

"I am not unreasonable." Thaden stepped closer, his voice shifting to what in some version of reality might have been considered kind. "You did not know what you were doing. You were led astray by Eric Deldridge. But it was Deldridge that failed me. Deldridge that betrayed me. He was to sit at my right hand, and now he must die. But you could escape his fate. You could take the destiny he so carelessly threw away."

The minotaur roared behind me, but Thaden didn't even look up.

"Being able to use the spells on the phone without any proper training is remarkable." Thaden's voice was so low, it was just above a whisper, but I could still hear every word.

I hated it. That whole *whispering deathly things into your ear* thing is seriously creepy.

"Such natural ability is rare these days," Thaden continued. "Imagine how powerful you could become if you let me teach you."

"Teach me what?" I asked. The ground shook beneath my feet, and only my years of riding the New York subway kept me standing.

"To be a real wizard. A powerful wizard who will see the darkness and the light that control our world." Thaden was close, only a few feet away now. "Fate has pulled you here, boy. Fate has drawn you to greatness. Don't let this chance slip through your grasp. Give me what is mine, and I will show you a new world you cannot even imagine."

"You don't even know his name." Eric's voice came from over my shoulder. "Nor care to, Thaden. He may be very new to magic, but he isn't stupid enough to think you'll let any of us live. I thought you were the sort to allow new magic to thrive, but I was wrong. The only magic you want to survive is what you can control. You are no better than the Ladies. Trapped between a prison and a tomb, and I was fool enough to follow you."

"You stole from me." Thaden rounded on Eric.

"Stealing is such a dark term for losing something you lent

me," Eric said. "But I suppose semantics aren't important now that we're trying to kill each other."

"Do you think you stand a chance against me?" Thaden tipped his head to the side, examining Eric. "How strange that I never realized the extent of your delusions of grandeur."

"I did learn from the best." Eric bowed, not taking his eyes off his opponent. "*Bryant*," he emphasized my name like he was trying to rub in that Thaden didn't know it, "do me a favor and keep that minotaur from eating me while Thaden and I continue our little chat."

"O-Okay," I stammered, taking a few steps back.

As soon as I was behind Eric, he launched into a long stream of words. The air in front of him glowed a reddish-purple before morphing into a glistening wall.

Thaden screamed something, his words strange and muffled. The ground at his feet cracked and more of the horrible spiders scurried out as he shouted something else and green balls of light streaked out of his palms. I ducked, covering my head, but instead of being burned to death, there was sizzling *smack* after sizzling *smack* as they hit Eric's purple wall and petered out.

"Bryant, the minotaur, please," Eric said as Thaden drew a deep breath.

"Right." I turned away from Eric and toward the sea of shadows.

Everything was darkness now. The thin, white glimmers the Ladies had left were gone. I glanced over to the short entrance where the two Ladies had been before I jumped off the roof, but there was no sign of them now. I hurried toward the shadows, trying not to think of the Ladies rallying troops to come in and kill us all.

I stared up at the minotaur as I ran. For a moment, I thought I could see him properly. The head of a bull with great deadly horns as thick as my torso, on top of the body of a man. But the next step, he was just a shadow again. My foot slid under me, and I tripped over something I couldn't see. But I could feel it. The thing I landed on. It was a person. A person long past moving.

I swallowed the bile that had flown up into my throat and pushed myself to my feet.

The minotaur had reversed course and was rambling back toward Eric and Thaden. He was going to get Eric from behind. Kill him before he could stop Thaden.

"*Abalata!*" I shouted. The black taffy mist pulled from my hand and shot out. For a split second, I was afraid the spell would go right through the shadow. But then the beast roared in anger and turned toward me.

I couldn't make him out, but if you ever have the misfortune of having a giant, angry minotaur staring down at you, you'll know what I mean when I say I felt his eyes ripping me to shreds.

This is how I die. Not a mugging or a fire or old and in bed surrounded by grandchildren. I'm going to be eaten by a minotaur, and there is nothing I can do about it.

The ground shook as he bore down on me, and I wondered if it would take the minotaur long enough to eat me that Eric might be able to beat Thaden. My eyes shot over to their battle. Eric was crouched on the ground with his arms over his head as Thaden floated above, showering him with spells that sizzled the air as they streaked toward Eric.

I'm going to be eaten by a minotaur, and it won't even have helped anyone.

"Bryant!" Elizabeth's voice came out of my pocket. "Bryant, there's black blood coming out of the minotaur's left side!"

"What do I do?" I shouted into the mirror as I pulled it out of my pocket.

"I don't know, but aim for there!" There was something in the way Elizabeth said it—like she actually thought I could fight a giant shadow minotaur—that made my mind race and not because I wondered how much being eaten alive would hurt, but because I was searching for a plan.

"*Abalata!*" I shouted again, not aiming for the minotaur's knee this time but for his left side. There was a howl of pain and fury as my spell hit its mark.

"*Erunca!*" I screamed as the minotaur lurched forward. Lightning streaked down from the ceiling. It was like watching a cloud being lit up during a storm. I could see the minotaur's teeth as he howled and his long, broken fingernails as he tried to bat the lightning away. But he kept up his progress, one shuddering step at a time.

"*Kuraxo!*" I shouted, and the ground shook. I turned and ran from the spell, hoping Eric and Charles' shadows wouldn't be caught in it, and the ceiling wouldn't cave in and bring down half of Manhattan on our heads. A *boom* scrambled my brains, and the earth rolled so hard, I fell forward.

"Bryant, he's on the ground!" Elizabeth screamed.

"*Parapus!*" I roared at the shadow spread-eagled on the cracked street.

Lines flew from me and hung in the air, outlining the figure I couldn't see. The minotaur bellowed in rage, but the lines held.

"What now?" I asked Elizabeth.

"Kill it," she said, her voice filled with horrible certainty. "He's tearing the lines apart."

The binding spell wasn't permanent on wizards. How long could it last on a minotaur? Hell, all I knew about minotaurs was my mom made me paint a foam sword for one of her educational shows in school so the hero could slay one.

A sword. You kill minotaurs with swords.

I looked down at the phone. But there was no icon for a

sword. I scrolled down the list of *Last Resort at a Glance spells*, but nothing screamed medieval cutting weapons.

"I need a damn sword!" I shouted at the phone as the minotaur howled and the ground shook.

"Make one," Elizabeth said.

"There isn't an app for that!"

"You can do magic, Bryant. Magic a sword."

"Swords don't grow on..."

My words faded away as the minotaur shook in his binding, cracking the ground under my feet into razor-sharp shrapnel.

I grabbed a pointy-looking piece and ran toward the minotaur. "*Milkawa.*"

I didn't watch to see if it would work, I didn't have time. The rock grew heavier in my hand as I started climbing the thin bands that bound the monster like a jungle gym. There was nothing solid below my feet, but I could feel the minotaur's squishy flesh as I clamored to his chest and raised the rock high over my head. But it wasn't a dinky rock anymore. It was three feet long now and growing, with a vicious point at the end.

"You're too far left," Elizabeth warned from my clenched fist where the mirror cut into my palm as it pressed into the end of the rock sword. "You're not over his heart."

I shuffled right a little. "Here?"

"Up a bit," Elizabeth said.

I took a step forward, and the minotaur's chest shook as he growled.

"There!"

I plunged my sword down with all my might. The tip met something hard, but I pushed down with all my weight, not stopping until the back end squelched out of sight.

A whimpering scream shook the tunnel before the monster under my feet went still.

"You did it!" Elizabeth shrieked. "You did it. You did it!"

"I did," I panted.

You would have thought that killing the minotaur would have made the fight go quiet. That everyone would have recognized I had done something epic. But the battle hadn't stopped. Eric was standing now, and a dozen bright white whips surrounded him, shooting out at Thaden in turn.

I had to get to him. I started pulling at the sword, trying to free it from the minotaur's chest. The sound of blood and who knows what else squelching as I yanked the sword free was quite possibly the worst thing I had ever heard.

"Elizabeth, say something," I said as I slid down the dead minotaur's side.

"Why?"

"Because if I die, I don't want dead minotaur gurgle to be the last thing I remember." I leapt the cracks in the ground toward Eric, ignoring the spiders that clicked at my feet.

"Bryant Jameson Adams, you had better not die. I decided yesterday that I really like you, and I don't want you to die before we get to have our first date."

My heart jumped so high in my chest, I swear I flew the last twenty feet to Eric's side.

Eric was bleeding from a gash across his cheek. It looked worse on his bright white skin than it would have on a normal person. Well, possibly. What did I know about bloody battles?

"Took care of him?" Eric smiled. "I knew fate had something wonderful planned for you."

"There is nothing more wonderful than a glorious death," Thaden growled. "Let the shadows sing songs of your passing. The songs will last far longer than your lives ever could."

"You know"—Eric pulled himself to stand up straight, wiping the blood from his face with his sleeve—"I thought perhaps this battle was going to be my last blaze of glory. A chance to pass the torch on to a new wizard. But Bryant killed your minotaur, and the last of the Ladies have fled. So perhaps Bryant and I can both live to fight another night, and he won't be a new wizard alone in the world with only a phone and a dream to see him through. What say you, Bryant?" Eric raised a dark eyebrow. "You and me wreaking havoc. Running amok in Manhattan."

"Sounds pretty good." I smiled.

"Then how about we finish this for good?" Eric said. "Whichever spell you fancy."

"I will destroy you!" Thaden cried, "*Talisma—*"

"*Milkawa!*" I shouted, without anger or fear, my eyes trained on the rock at Thaden's feet. It was like I had always known the spell was supposed to be important. Like fate had made sure the word felt familiar on my lips.

The street underneath Thaden's feet swelled, rising and pulsing like a living thing.

"*Ilmatiot!*" Thaden shot back, and a vice closed around my chest, squeezing out every last ounce of air.

The stone from the street began to grow, wrapping itself around Thaden's legs.

Blood pounded in my ears as my vision grayed.

Thaden was wound to his chest in stone, and the column rose.

Pain shot through my knees as they hit the ground.

This is how I die. Far below the streets, lost in the blood of shadows.

Thaden's arms were pinned by the stone.

Maybe Eric will win. Maybe my fate was to make sure he lived. Not such a bad way to go.

A spell made my bones buzz as it shot through the air. Thaden's face twisted in terror, then everything went black. And it was a relief.

29

"Bryant," a voice pleaded.

Maybe it's my mom. Maybe she's dead, too. Oh God. She's gonna be pissed I got us both killed.

But the voice was lighter than my mom's. Shakier, too. Scared instead of mad.

"Bryant!" another voice chimed in. This one did sound angry. "Come on, man, you can't be dead."

Devon. Devon was mad at me for being dead. Warm prickles filtered down into my chest.

Clearly I'm not dead if fire ants are eating my lungs. Then, the pain worsened.

Someone was crying next to me.

Elizabeth.

"Bryant, you promised."

The pain in my chest morphed into an uneven throbbing.

"What are you doing?" It was Eric. He sounded tired but alive. If he was alive, Thaden must be dead. I wanted to scream at Eric to take Devon and Elizabeth and run before more monsters could come after them, but I still had no air.

"Saving my best friend, you asshole," Devon growled and the pressure on my chest grew.

Lips clamped over mine. Someone tried to blow air into my lungs, but they were solid metal now. Unable to be moved by air.

"Get out of the way," Eric said.

"We aren't giving up on him." Elizabeth's hair fluttered around my face as she tried to push her breath into my chest.

I wanted to thank her for trying, but the pain had taken over, lighting my veins on fire.

Maybe if they let me die, it won't hurt quite so much.

"I don't believe I mentioned giving up," Eric said. "*Palmuntra!*"

Agony like nothing I had ever imagined shot into my lungs.

Eric's going to torture me before he lets me die. Probably because I didn't stay in the chimney.

"*Palmuntra!*" Eric shouted again, and again the pain struck.

And didn't stop. It flooded my leaden lungs with air. I hacked it out, but more took its place. Things in my head, in my chest, spun out of control, while the voices around me cried, "Bryant!"

But then the pain in my veins ebbed away as wonderful oxygen raced through my body. I took a normal, though shuddering, breath and opened my eyes.

Elizabeth knelt over me. Tears had left wide, pale tracks through the charcoal that covered her face. Devon crouched next to her, the blood-covered bandage still on his head. Eric stood behind them, all traces of the battle gone.

"And he lives." Eric grinned.

I pushed myself to sit up, and the cavern swayed. Elizabeth wrapped an arm around me, holding me steady.

"Careful," she whispered over the moans of pain and cries of grief lingering after the battle.

In front of me was a pillar of stone. It was like Big Blue in the park, growing like a sped up video on crack.

"Thaden?"

"Eric chopped his head off," Devon said.

"So, he's dead?" I asked as the pillar of stone pierced the ceiling, pushing up like a new flower bursting through the earth. With a shuddering crack, the ceiling split, sending a shower of dirt and debris tumbling down.

"*Primurgo,*" Eric cried, and a shimmering dome enclosed us.

The dirt fell around it like filthy, polluted snow, glancing off the surface as though we were trapped in a perverted snow globe.

I waited for the ceiling to split in two. But after the dust settled, the ceiling stayed up, and the stone column continued to grow.

"I think Thaden is very dead," Eric said as the shimmering bubble disappeared.

"What about the Ladies?" I tried to push myself to my feet. Nope. My legs shook too badly.

"The Ladies will remain a problem for another day," Eric said. "But with so many of them gone, I would say it's safe for you to collect your mother and go home. I think you can officially be declared a hero. For today at least. One battle does not a true fighter make."

"Some hero I am," I muttered as Devon half-dragged me up.

"You are." Elizabeth stepped in front of me. "You kept your promise. You didn't die." She wrapped her arms around me and kissed me. Not fast, like she had before. But slow and deep. Holding me close like she didn't want to let go.

"Not dying is a very good beginning," Eric said after a moment. Or a century. I was never good at keeping track of time when Elizabeth kissed me. "And we did destroy Thaden and his minotaur, so I don't think today can be considered a waste."

Elizabeth took a step back, and I looked into her sparkly

eyes. They were smiling at me. I wiped the tears from her face and the black washed away.

"Not a waste," Elizabeth said.

She took Devon's place with her arm around me, helping me over the cracked ground.

"Do you think Charles is okay?" I asked as we crossed the blood-slicked ground.

"He is." Elizabeth pointed toward the far end of the tunnel. "I can see him with his people." Her voice caught in her throat. "They lost a lot."

"They did," Eric said. "And not just today. Thaden had been picking them off for years. They are finally free to explore the dark without fearing him and his monsters."

"Why did you get involved with Thaden again?" Devon asked as Eric led us over to the low tunnel where the two Ladies had disappeared.

"Choices were made." Eric shrugged. "When you've spent your life stranded between two types of evil, one of the evils can begin to look like hope. But perhaps all you need is a catalyst to shake the rocks apart."

"Look, Bryant," Devon said. "You're a catalyst." Devon swayed little, and Eric caught him.

"I've forgotten how badly non-wizards do after battles," Eric said. "*Concursornio.*"

Devon breathed in sharply through his teeth. "Please don't magic my insides without asking me first." He shook his head hard and then stood up straight.

"You're welcome."

"You know," I said, scrunching up my nose against the words, "for a second there, I thought Thaden was my dad. Like he had lived a creepy double life and was trying to kill us all."

"I think your issues with your father are more a matter for a therapist than magical in nature," Eric said.

Devon and Elizabeth both started laughing, and in a second, I was laughing with them. It was weird, laughing as we walked away from battle, but it felt right. Like it was somehow an affirmation that the four of us had survived.

"This way please," Eric said.

I didn't want to leave the scene with the street cracked and the dead shadows to be buried, but Eric led us through the tunnel. It started sweeping up toward the surface. I didn't even want to begin to imagine how long it would take us to climb to the streets.

But soon there were lights hanging from the ceiling, casting our shadows across the ground.

Elizabeth gasped and took a step back, knocking me off-balance as she pulled her arm from around me.

"What?" I spun around, trying to find what had scared her.

"Don't you see it?" she whispered, before looking up to me. "No, I suppose you can't."

"What do you see?" Eric asked.

"We're all there, like a picture in a storybook." Elizabeth pointed to our dark shapes on the ground that looked like nothing to me. "The hero, the adventurer, the apprentice, the seer. All tied together by golden thread." Elizabeth smiled. "It makes one whole picture. The four of us. And it was always going to be that way."

"Fate pulls the threads as it sees fit." Eric stepped through the shadow.

"Just for the record," Devon asked, "who was the hero?"

Elizabeth laughed and wrapped her arm around my waist, not to hold me up, just because.

We walked a little farther until tiles began popping up, scattered in with the stone. A roar sounded right over our heads, but I wasn't afraid. It was only a subway car carrying people home.

A solid wall rose in front of us. Without stopping, Eric said,

"*Portunda*," and a metal door with peeling-off white paint appeared.

Eric opened it, bowing for us to walk through.

The bright, industrial light made me blink for a moment before I saw that we were in the Columbus Circle subway station.

"*Portundo*," Eric muttered, and the door disappeared.

"Columbus Circle has an entrance to the magical underworld?" Devon shook his head. "Really, this is the best you could come up with?"

"It's a nice central location." Eric headed toward the stairs that led aboveground.

I looked at Elizabeth, but she was staring at her reflection in a poster.

The shadows had worn off her skin, but her hair was still jet black. "My mom's gonna kill me."

"It'll wear off eventually." Eric waved a dismissive hand as he walked back to us. "You've only been coated once."

Elizabeth looked at me, her sparkly eyes shining with tears.

"You still look beautiful." Blood rushed to my face.

She leaned over and kissed me quickly. An old woman next to me scoffed her disapproval, and Elizabeth pulled away, smiling.

"Well, I suppose it's only fitting for you two to be kissing after he slew a monster." Eric shrugged, leading the way up the stairs and to the street. I was starting to get used to him shrugging at me. There was something in his exasperation that felt comforting. Like I was destined to frustrate him.

"*Wooh*," Devon whistled as soon as we reached the street, and I didn't need to ask what he was talking about. A giant stone spire had split the skyline. Big Blue's rocky twin was peeking out above Times Square.

"I wonder what the reporters will say about that," I said,

trying not to think of Thaden's body sans head locked in the stone.

"I suspect they'll call it installation art." Eric wove south through the awed crowd.

"And if they try to follow it to its root?" Elizabeth asked.

"Charles and his people will take care of it." Eric stepped out onto Broadway, gazing up at the stone tower.

"If Charles will take care of that," I asked, "what do we do?"

"We go collect your mother," Eric said, "let Lola know we haven't died, and after that, it's up to you."

"What do you mean?" I watched a helicopter fly overhead, circling the new addition to Times Square.

"Well"—Eric turned his gaze toward me—"you can collect your mother and return to being a normal high schooler. Apply to colleges. Work in an office. Try to find a way to give life meaning..."

"Or?" I asked.

"Or you can join me in a world beyond your imagination and dare to face adventures most can never even dream of."

A guitar began playing in the night. Cabs rushed past. Sirens echoed in the distance. All the sounds of New York I had known my whole life. But I was in a different New York now. One deeper and greater than I had ever imagined.

"One question," I said as an elderly black lady knocked my toe with her cane. "When my parents get new apartments, are you going to destroy those, too?

"I never try to predict destruction. It ruins the surprise." Eric grinned. "Just think of it as a nice fall cleaning. And I'm sure Devon and your charming girlfriend will be pleased to help you sort through the rubble."

Elizabeth laughed but didn't argue. I held her hand tight as we began the long walk to Lola's, strolling peacefully through the chaos of Manhattan.

In less than four days I had become a wizard, stopped a bad guy, toppled a regime, and gotten a girlfriend.

"I wonder what we'll be up to next weekend," Devon said as we passed by a stand of reporters all babbling about Big Blue and the stone tower.

"In my experience, it's best not to ask," Eric said. "The path fate has chosen for you will find you. And we'll meet the next adventure when it comes."

We walked through Times Square past Thaden's tomb. I ignored the chill tickle of wind on my neck and shoved down the feeling that someone was watching me.

I'm glad I did. If I'd known what waited in the shadows, I might not have been brave enough to stay in Manhattan.

Eric was right. Fate would lead us to whatever journey came next, whether we were ready or not.

Bryant's journey continues in Seven Things Not to Do When Everyone's Trying to Kill You. *Read on for a sneak preview.*

BRYANT'S ADVENTURES CONTINUE IN...

Continue reading for a sneak peek of *Seven Things Not to Do When Everyone's Trying to Kill You.*

1

The monster dodged around the people of New York, daring to run within inches of the unsuspecting humans before darting down another path. But the tourists of Central Park were oblivious to the imminent danger charging toward them. Unaware that at any moment a magical creature could attack. Only one wizard was brave enough to hunt the beast. Only one wizard had the heart to defend the good people of New York.

"There!" Devon shouted, yanking me out of my inner monologue. "He's over there."

I bent double, squinting between the legs of the horde of tourists who crowded the Central Park paths. A streak of brown fur skidded across the frozen ground and off through the trees.

"Dammit." I pushed my way through the crowd. "Why is it still running?"

"Just come on!" Devon sprinted ahead of me, chasing the beast.

My lungs ached as I dodged people and trees, barely keeping the thing's tail in view. Buildings cut through the grass, blocking the creature's path. Soon we would have it pinned.

"Where does it think it's going?" Devon puffed. It was nice to know the last hour of running through the park had actually winded him.

A guttural roar split the air, and my heart sank as I recognized the brick buildings in front of us.

Of course the thing was running straight for the Central Park Zoo.

"We can't let it get in there!" I ran as fast as my exhausted, scrawny legs could muster. If that thing got into the zoo, there would be too many places for it to hide. Too many cages for us to search. If a zookeeper found it, it would make their career and headline news. And really ruin my week.

The creature dashed through a clearing in the trees as he made his final sprint for the zoo buildings.

"*Stasio!*" I shouted, my eyes fixed on the blur of brown fur. The air surrounding the thing shimmered for a moment before the creature smacked into the brand new solid box my spell had formed around it.

"Nice one, Bry," Devon panted, his hands on his knees as he stopped next to the creature.

"Thanks." I don't mean to sound like a prick, but I really was pretty proud of myself. A perfect, crystal-clear square, like Snow White's glass casket, sealed in the angry critter. "For a little guy, he's freakin' fast."

The fur ball squeaked and clawed against the spell like he had heard my words and found the term *little* to be insulting.

"He really doesn't look so bad." I knelt, letting the chill of the frozen ground drain the heat of the run from me.

"Doesn't look so bad?" Devon rubbed his gloved hands over his face. "How often do you see a two-headed squirrel the size of a house cat with a bright green lizard tail running through Central Park?"

Devon's description was on the whole completely accurate.

Though the squirrel was a little smaller than my mom's cat, it did have two heads, both of which swiveled to glare at me. One had black eyes, the other creepy red. I shuddered as they simultaneously started chirping at me. The forked lizard tail curled up over its head like a scorpion ready to strike.

"Okay, so it's a little creepy. *Conorvo*." The squirrel's makeshift cage shrank, stopping just short of squishing the little guy.

"What I want to know is how no one noticed him," Devon said as I shrugged out of my bright red backpack. "A weird little nut-hunting baby dragon running around New York for two months and no one said anything? How is that even possible?"

Nutty McDragon, because the little dude deserved a name, squealed as I slid him into my backpack and closed the zipper.

"Really?" I hoisted myself to my feet, legs shaky after having run so far. "After everything that's happened, you think people pretending not to notice a weird squirrel in Central Park is strange?" I pointed to the sky west of us where a giant blue flower cut through the trees of Central Park, and then to the south where a stone tower loomed over Times Square.

"Okay, okay"—Devon raised his hands in surrender—"but still, people, man."

"People." I sighed and followed Devon back toward the path.

Nutty McDragon squealed like a mutant demon in my backpack, but other than a few people looking nervously at their phones, no one seemed to care as we made our way west.

Part of me wanted to be disappointed in humanity for not caring about weird squirrels, giant flowers, and stone towers of doom appearing in Manhattan, but since I was the one who had caused all three of them, I couldn't be too mad.

See, I'm a wizard. A super new wizard. Once upon a time, about two months ago, I had four really bad days. I found a phone that holds an illegal magical library, destroyed both my parents' homes, defeated an evil wizard, pissed off some other crazy powerful people, and almost died a couple of times. Not to mention the, you know, obvious magical damage to Manhattan. But I came out on the other side alive, a wizard, and with a girl-friend who embodies all things wonderful in the world, so really the hell days were worth it in the end.

We walked past the chain-link fence that surrounded the base of Big Blue, protecting the giant flower from protestors and wannabe flower killers. Scientists were researching the flower as a genetic anomaly. On the other side of the crisscrosses in the fence, they circled Big Blue's base like they did every day. Doing all sorts of sciencey things. I could make someone's career by giving them Nutty McDragon, but I didn't need another disaster on my head.

"Winter is here!" a protestor screamed as we passed. "It's time for the plant to die!"

"Wow," Devon muttered. "Do they have nothing else to do with their time?"

There were at least twenty people protesting around this side of Big Blue. And I had to give it to them—it was a little weird that, while the rest of the park had succumbed to the December freeze, Big Blue had stayed just as...blue. But the sign that read *The Aliens are breeding, destroy their nest now!* was way off. Aliens didn't make the giant bloom. I did. I blushed and ducked my head as we passed the alien protestor, like he might be able to read my mind or something.

I'd seen news stories about protestors surrounding the Times Square spire, too—some claiming demons from the underworld, others angry about sinking real estate prices with the new massive mineral neighbor. I had been upholding my New Yorker obligation and avoiding Times Square lately, so I didn't really know how weird those protestors were. Only that they were there every day and really pissed about my accidental architectural addition.

"Let Eric know we're on our way," Devon said when we reached the far west side of the park.

I pulled my phone from my pocket, checking to make sure I had the right, non-magical phone before pressing my finger to the scanner and dialing Eric.

"Did you finally manage it?" Eric drawled in a bored tone.

"Hello to you, too," I said. "And yes I—"

"We," Devon cut in.

"—*we* got it. I'm taking him to my mom's."

"Delightful." I could almost hear Eric's eye roll through the phone. "I'll meet you there."

I hung up and slid the phone back into my pocket.

"Is your mom going to be okay with Eric and Nutty being at the apartment?" Devon's eyebrows scrunched together. A pack of girls in chic winter coats passed, and his face immediately smoothed into racially ambiguous perfection. The girls giggled and waved as they passed. Nutty McDragon squealed his displeasure at the noise.

"Mom'll be fine with it." It wasn't true. I knew it wasn't true. Even Nutty, who was squirming around in my backpack more than any magically-contained creature should be able to, knew it wasn't true. But I didn't really have another choice, so we kept walking to my mom's, Devon winking at every remotely attractive woman, me trying to look inconspicuous with my shrieking backpack.

"You got a sewer rat in there?" An old black lady eyed my bag as we waited for a crosswalk.

"No ma'am, just trying to get his cat back from the vet," Devon said calmly as I opened my mouth to say...I don't know what. "The carrier broke, and it was the best we could do."

"It doesn't sound like any cat I've ever heard." The woman

shook her head. "You better be careful playing with angry animals. Some bites don't heal too well."

"We'll be careful."

The woman *tshed* her disbelief at our promise and waddled down the street, shaking her head.

Devon grabbed my elbow and steered me away. My feet wanted to carry me south to my mom's old house, but seeing as that one had been mostly destroyed, we turned north instead.

The doorman didn't look up from the dinging video game in his hands as we walked to the elevator.

"What service," Devon whispered sarcastically.

We lived on the twelfth floor of this building, and the elevator protested the whole way up. It wasn't a great place, but it was what my mom could afford. My dad offered to buy us an apartment—he was already looking for a new place himself, so he had a real estate dude and everything—but my mom wanted nothing to do with it. The concept of taking help, let alone money, from my dad was enough to turn even Mom's best moods sour. So we ended up in a place with chipped linoleum floors that smelled vaguely of nursing home.

Voices carried through the door before we reached it.

"I don't even want to know what you're bringing in here," Mom growled as I slipped the key into the lock. "What are you bringing into my home?"

"Seeing as you've just contradicted yourself," Eric said, "I'm not really sure how to answer you, Ms. Miller."

"Hey, Mom," I said, cutting her off as I opened the door. "How are you?"

"It depends on why Mr. Deldridge"—Mom growled his name—"is here."

On cue, Nutty McDragon started squealing. The squirrel knew just how to get me in trouble.

"Oh good God." Mom sank into a chair as Mrs. Mops, our

shaggy, gray, obese cat, leapt up onto the table by the door to bat at my bag.

"We found the squirrel," I said lamely, smiling to soften the blow.

"It only took you a week." Eric held out his hands for my backpack.

"But we found it." Devon flopped down onto the couch. "Had to run all over Central Park, mind you."

"One down, two to go." Eric pulled the shimmering cage that held Nutty McDragon from my bag. "At least we hope only two."

"Just try for optimism." Devon sighed and closed his eyes.

"I'm sorry," I said for the millionth time. You see, the same day I accidentally made Big Blue, I did another spell. One I thought hadn't worked at all. Only it had. Little bits of magic drifted off into Central Park and did a minuscule amount of damage to a few of the resident animals. And by damage, I mean an extra head and lizard tail. At least for Nutty. We hadn't actually seen the other two animals.

"What in the hell are you going to do with it?" Mom leaned in to examine Nutty, her eyes narrowing as he chittered at her. "I will not have an animal exterminated in my home."

My mom would never kill a mouse or rat or anything in our apartment. I never pointed out the irony of letting Mrs. Mops do the killing for her. I just wanted the rodents dead, and if Mrs. Mops wanted to be a vermin serial killer, so be it.

"Can you make him a normal squirrel again?" I sank onto the couch next to Devon.

"It might be possible." Eric held Nutty up to the light. "But it would be difficult to remove the right head. I'm not entirely sure which holds most of the poor thing's brain."

"So, what are you going to do?" I asked over Mrs. Mop's growling as her paws slid uselessly down Nutty's cage.

"Rehome it." Eric shrugged. "I can take it to Beville. The

thing seems to have a reasonable temperament. There might be someone in need of a new pet."

"Would Lola want him?" I asked, thinking of her colorful home with lots of drapes to climb.

"Lola doesn't approve of rodents." Eric placed Nutty back into my backpack. "And I don't think Lola's guard would like him hanging around either. Don't worry, I'll find a home for him somewhere. You should concentrate on finding whatever other disasters you created."

"Any tips on how to start?" My feet throbbed at the very thought of tracking down the other two creatures I'd inadvertently created.

"The same I've given before. Track the magic in Central Park. If it's an animal that doesn't look right, catch it before we have any more magic making headline news." Eric strode to the door. "Call me when you've found something else."

And with that, Eric, Nutty, and my backpack were all gone.

"I really don't like that man." Mom got out the vacuum and started cleaning where Eric had stood. "I really, really don't like that man."

"I can meet him somewhere else." I spoke over the *whir* of the vacuum, hope rising a centimeter in my chest at the suggestion.

"You are not meeting him unsupervised," Mom half-shouted. "I may not be able to keep my son from being a wizard, but I will not have him fraternizing with criminals without supervision."

"Right." I didn't dare look at Devon. "You're totally right."

"Ms. Miller, is it okay if Bryant comes out with me tonight? I want to walk around, but it wouldn't be safe to go alone." Devon sounded disgustingly sincere, young, and hopeful.

"Of course, Devon." Mom nodded. "I think Bryant spending time with his *normal* friends is a great idea."

"Thanks, Ms. Miller." Devon and I both leapt to our feet.

My legs twinged in protest at being asked to move again. But sitting wasn't an option. We had places to be, and we still had our coats on and everything.

"Be back soon," I said as we walked into the corridor.

"You should invite Elizabeth," Mom called after us.

"Only your mother would worry more about you spending time with your mentor than your girlfriend," Eric said in a thoroughly bored and disdainful tone as he leaned next to our door, holding my red backpack.

My stomach did an Olympic gymnastics floor routine at the word *girlfriend.*

"Well, Elizabeth has never almost gotten all of us killed," Devon said as we headed down the hall.

Eric smiled. "Touché."

To continue reading, get your copy of Seven Things Not to Do
When Everyone's Trying to Kill You *now!*

ESCAPE INTO ADVENTURE

Thank you for reading How I Magically Messed Up My Life in Four Freakin' Days. If you enjoyed the book, please consider leaving a review to help other readers find Bryant's story.

As always, thanks for reading,

Megan O'Russell

Never miss a moment of the danger or hilarity.

Join the Megan O'Russell mailing list to stay up to date on all the action by visiting https://www.meganorussell.com/book-signup.

ABOUT THE AUTHOR

 Megan O'Russell is the author of several Young Adult series that invite readers to escape into worlds of adventure. From *Girl of Glass*, which blends dystopian darkness with the heart-pounding danger of vampires, to *Ena of Ilbrea*, which draws readers into an epic world of magic and assassins.

With the *Girl of Glass* series, *The Tethering* series, *The Chronicles of Maggie Trent*, *The Tale of Bryant Adams*, the *Ena of Ilbrea* series, and several more projects planned, there are always exciting new books on the horizon. To be the first to hear about new releases, free short stories, and giveaways, sign up for Megan's newsletter by visiting the following:

https://www.meganorussell.com/book-signup.

Originally from Upstate New York, Megan is a professional musical theatre performer whose work has taken her across North America. Her chronic wanderlust has led her from Alaska to Thailand and many places in between. Wanting to travel has fostered Megan's love of books that allow her to visit countless new worlds from her favorite reading nook. Megan is also a lyricist and playwright. Information on her theatrical works can be found at RussellCompositions.com.

She would be thrilled to chat with you on Facebook or Twitter @MeganORussell, elated if you'd visit her website MeganORussell.com, and over the moon if you'd like the pictures of her adventures on Instagram @ORussellMegan.

ALSO BY MEGAN O'RUSSELL

Ember and Stone

Mountain and Ash

Ice and Sky

Feather and Flame

Guilds of Ilbrea

Inker and Crown

Myth and Storm

Heart of Smoke

Heart of Smoke

Soul of Glass

Eye of Stone

Ash of Ages